# TO LOVE A MONSTER

Marina Simcoe

To My Hunter

Marina Simcoe

Marina.Simcoe@Yahoo.com

Facebook/Marina Simcoe Author

This is a work of fiction. Names, characters, places and incidents are a product of the author's imagination. Locales and public names are used for atmospheric purposes. Any resemblance to actual people, living or dead, or to businesses, companies, events, institutions or locales is completely coincidental.

Cover Design by Naomi Lucas and Cameron Kamenicky

New Cover Edition

Spelling: Canadian

Editing by Two Horses Swift

Proofreading by Nikki Groom, The Indie Hub

To Love A Monster is a paranormal fantasy romance with graphic descriptions of intimacy, coarse language, and potential triggers. Intended for mature readers.

# Chapter 1

## Monster

Intruders!

He leaped out of the icy water onto the rocky riverbank and shook his hide.

Rising on his hind legs, he stretched to his full height, sniffing the air. The breeze was in the wrong direction—he didn't smell them yet. But he *felt* the trespassing. He was all the way by the river bordering his property at the east. The intruders must have entered from the road to the west.

He had no idea what date it was, but judging by the leaves falling from the trees and the frost on the ground in the morning, it must have been around October, maybe November. Either way, the hunting season would be in full swing, which could mean that the intruders were hunters.

There were plenty of *Private Property, No Trespassing,* and even *Violators Will Be Prosecuted* signs placed all along the barbed wire marking the boundaries of the estate. However, this didn't seem to deter the occasional hunter from crossing over in a pursuit of a deer or an elk.

As long as it was the deer that they were after, he had nothing to worry about, except that people in general were a nuisance.

Maybe the cougar will get them.

The sneaky cat had been stalking him for years. Of course when he wished him to show up and chase the intruders away, the cougar wouldn't be around.

He drew in another lungful of air, searching for any foreign scent on the breeze.

Nothing.

Still, the nagging feeling of the intrusion wouldn't leave him, forcing him to move west, towards the house. It couldn't hurt to make sure the hunters stayed away from it.

He sped up until he broke into a full-on sprint, his paws hitting the leaf-covered ground soundlessly. Hot blood pounded through his veins along with the satisfaction of being alive.

Further west, an inhale of air finally brought in the scent of the strangers, bringing him to an abrupt stop so fast, he almost tumbled over his head like a clumsy puppy.

The scent wasn't what he expected.

None of the usual smell of oil and gunpowder of a hunter. Instead, the faint scent of fancy cologne and delicate, flowery perfume reached his sensitive nose. And it was the subtle, delicate scent of female bodies underneath the perfume that hit him like a punch in a gut.

His blood boiled, his vision clouded, and his cock hardened so painfully fast, it slapped his underbelly with force.

Primal need forced him up onto his hind legs again. He threw his head back, his long horns pressed against the shoulder blades. Flexing his fingers, he released razor-sharp claws, and roared into the cold air around him.

The mating call of a beast reverberated through the woods, bouncing off the tree trunks in cascading echoes.

# Chapter 2

## Sophie

"What was that?" Ashley froze in her tracks. Following closely behind her, I bumped into her.

"What the fuck?" Jason, my boyfriend of over two months, tightened his grip on the axe in his hand, his knuckles white.

I was pretty sure my face was just as pale. The deafening, blood-curdling howl had made my insides turn to chilly slush.

"No clue," I replied. "But it certainly sounds vicious."

"We should go back, guys," Ashley muttered.

"It's just some wild animal. Probably a wolf." Jason seemed to have recovered quickly. "There are three of us. It won't attack in broad daylight. Come on." He moved ahead, lifting the axe he had brought to cut through the bush in his right hand and cradling his precious camera to his chest with the other.

"There was too much roar in that howl for a wolf." Ashley pointed out, not moving from her spot. "And it sounded way too loud. If it really was a wolf, it must be the size of a bull."

"I'm with Ashley on this one." I nodded, not moving either. I'd known Ashley for three days and in that time we hadn't agreed on everything, but right now we were definitely on the same page. I shivered. Our fun afternoon outing didn't feel that harmless anymore.

Last night, after a long conversation with a drunk at the bar of the hunting lodge where the three of us were staying with a group of

Jason's hunter friends, he decided to go on a search of an abandoned cabin in the woods.

The drunk had described it as *the most fucking beautiful hunting' 'cabin that you'd ever see*, which spiked Jason's interest as a photographer.

"I think we should go back," Ashley sounded more adamant by the moment, glancing around nervously, her hands twisting the cord of her backpack.

Unlike her boyfriend, Ashley didn't hunt, and neither did I. Bored out of our minds from waiting at the lodge for the hunting party to return every night, we tagged along with Jason for something to do.

"We're almost there, Ash," Jason insisted. "Look, if you really want, you can go back and wait in the truck."

"Uh-uh." Ashley appeared resolute. "I've watched way too many horror movies to be the one waiting in the car. If we go, we all go together." She moved ahead muttering under her breath, "At least this way I'd have a chance to get away if that thing attacks *you* first."

I hesitated for a second. The blood still ran cold in my veins, and the terrifying sound of the howling roar continued to ring in my ears.

From my limited knowledge about wild animals though, they rarely attacked unless provoked, and I had no intention of provoking anything.

Jason and Ashley started walking away so I hurried after them not wanting to be left behind.

"Aha!" I heard Jason exclaim triumphantly. "This must be the driveway the guy was talking about." He pointed at the dense, seemingly impenetrable wall of wild rose bushes to our right.

"A driveway?" I stared at the prickly shrubs, confused.

"He said the old driveway is overgrown with rose bushes, and the cabin itself is surrounded by them."

"It makes no sense. Why would the driveway be more overgrown than the woods around it? Shouldn't it be the other way around?"

"Fuck if I know." Jason shrugged. "Isn't the Wild Rose the provincial flower of Alberta? You're from Alberta, Sophie. I'm from BC. If you don't know why it grows the way it does, how am I supposed to know?"

The bushes in front of us might have been Alberta Wild Rose, but I'd never heard of them growing like this, high and dense, forming an impassable hedge.

I rolled my eyes at Jason's logic, but kept silent. Lately, I'd noticed it was best not to reply in cases like this. Jason would never miss a chance to argue simply for the sake of having an argument—just another opportunity to hear himself talk.

"Anyway," he continued. "All we have to do now is follow the rose bushes all the way to the cabin."

"Easy-peasy," chimed in Ashley, marching ahead with much more bounce in her step than could have been expected after her earlier hesitation. And I followed, trying to keep up.

It didn't take long before we ran into another wall of rose bushes. This one grew perpendicular to the one we had been following. This time of the year, the delicate pink flowers of the wild rose, had already been replaced by red, glossy fruit.

"And there it is," Jason grunted with satisfaction then started swinging his axe left and right to crush the thorny branches in our way in order to make a passage through the hedge.

Ashley squeezed by him as soon as he stopped. "Holy cow!" I heard her whistle. "Is this *the cabin*?"

"Yesss," Jason hissed triumphantly and thrust the axe back in my direction then lifted his camera as soon as I took the axe from him. "This is something else! Totally worth the trip."

I stepped around him and into the clearing. The rose bushes circled the yard of the cabin in a neat shape, like a live fence, with a spectacular building in the centre.

"I wouldn't call it a cabin." I took in the enormous structure in front of me.

Two stories high, with a third-floor glass observatory on top, the sprawling log-and-stone building looked more like a high-end estate home or a movie star's retreat.

"Who would build something like this here?" I asked in shock.

"Some rich folks who didn't know what else to do with their money." Jason already snapped busily away with his camera.

"How did they get all these rocks and logs in here?"

"Hey guys," Ashley called from the front porch. "Wanna go in? The door is open."

The circular gravel driveway that led to the four-car garage on one side of the house and the wide carport on the other was surprisingly clear of rose bushes. Instead, the forest undergrowth had sprouted through the gravel here and there.

"Sure," Jason jogged ahead, holding the camera in front of him like an army standard.

The solid, wooden front door must have been half-open for at least a few seasons now. Leaves, dead grass, and dirt piled up high on both sides of it, firmly holding it in place. The gap was big enough to walk through.

"They just left everything behind, eh?" The echo of Ashley's excited voice bounced off the solid timber walls inside when I entered the huge open space of the main floor.

An enormous stone fireplace, big enough to drive a truck through, was the main focal point of the living space. Half a dozen French doors behind it let in the afternoon sun. The broken glass in one of the doors had fallen out, and the cold November air blew freely through the house piling dead leaves and pine needles in every nook and cranny.

Faded area rugs littered the oiled-wood floors. Couches, side tables, and armchairs stood around at random, some lying on their sides.

Ashley was right, the house seemed to be fully furnished, even if everything was buried under a layer of dirt.

"Sophie! You've got to see this kitchen!" she called from around the corner.

I followed her voice in that direction.

"They at least should have taken the appliances. This fridge alone must have cost thousands of dollars," she lamented, stroking the double-door of a built-in fridge. "Maybe they figured it was too expensive to haul it all the way from this far up North?"

"They don't seem like the type of people who would worry about anything being too expensive," Jason scoffed.

Through the arched opening behind the massive kitchen island, I could see him choosing the best angle to shoot the fireplace.

Whoever had decorated the place was obviously going for expensive rustic chic with a mix between a hunting cabin on steroids and a medieval castle—timber, wrought iron, and natural stone. There were even a few animal hides and antlers on the walls.

I headed to one of the two sets of staircases that led to the second floor balcony overlooking the main floor. Several second-floor doors visible from below must have led to more rooms upstairs.

"The coffee maker is still plugged in," Ashley observed from the kitchen, then I heard the sound of cabinet doors opening and closing. "Guys, they even have booze in here!"

"I'm going upstairs." I traced my finger along the dusty surface of the ornately carved railing.

To me, the place felt like a museum with a mystery of an abandoned house mixed in. Suddenly, I wanted to know more about the people who'd occupied it, wondering what compelled them to build this monstrosity in the middle of nowhere and then leave it all behind.

I had no idea how long the house had been sitting abandoned, but there was not a creak in any of the stairs as I ascended.

Built to last.

At the top of the landing a massive set of double doors greeted me, imposing in their size and ornateness.

This must be the master bedroom.

With a loud screeching noise, the rusted hinges turned, letting me into the spacious room with a stone fireplace in the middle and a massive four-poster bed far behind it.

The expensive, over-the-top décor of the downstairs was carried over to this bedroom as well.

The extravagance of it reminded me of the many residences of Henri, my father, even as the style of the rustic wilderness here was a direct opposite to Henri's taste in opulent French elegance.

I leant the axe against the wall and took a step towards the bed when the same blood-curling roar suddenly reverberated through the house, making me jump up in horror as my heart all but stopped.

This time, the howling sound didn't break into pieces of echo in the woods. Instead, it appeared to be trapped inside the house, shaking it to its foundation.

Whatever made the terrifying noise was in here. *With us.*

"Jesus fucking Christ!" Jason's voice held so much terror it made the hair on the back of my neck stand up.

"Run, Sophie!" Ashley's piercing shriek full of horror cut through the air.

Run!

Panic shot through my veins, propelling me downstairs. From the window on the landing, I glimpsed Jason's back as he sprinted towards the passage in the rose bushes.

Jumping over the two bottom stairs, I almost crashed into Ashley dashing past me to the main door, chanting "Run, run, run . . ." under her breath.

Then I saw *it*.

Standing on the other side of the fireplace was the hulking figure of a beast.

Bigger than any wolf, it balanced on its hind legs.

Horns. Massive head on wide shoulders. Scruffy, dark fur all over. . .

I didn't pause long enough to notice any more details, as the monster bared his teeth and produced another booming roar.

Without wasting another second, I turned on my heels and dashed to the front exit. Ashley's back had just disappeared through the gap in the rose bushes, and I headed that way too, afraid to turn around to see if the thing was chasing me.

But the very moment I reached the hedge, something slammed in my back and I heard the thick fabric of my khaki jacket rip.

The impact knocked me off my feet, and I crashed into the bushes—my outstretched arms in front of me.

Another roar came right from above me.

I scrambled to all fours and crawled towards the gap in the hedge, in desperate denial of reality refusing to believe that there was no escape.

A powerful blow from a heavy paw threw me away from my path to freedom. I flew through the air a few feet and landed on my butt, painfully hitting the ground.

The monster leaped after me, and I crab-walked backwards in a hopeless attempt to flee.

My breath came in harsh pants. I couldn't even yell for help—every ounce of my energy was directed towards getting away.

The animal slammed a hind paw on my leg, pinning me in place.

Frozen in horror, I expected it to lunge forward and rip my throat out.

The beast rose over me, and I had to crane my neck to be able to see its face.

Long snout, eyes glistening deep under a heavy brow. What was this thing? It was like no animal I'd seen before.

The glimpse of his erection in the thick, long fur of his crotch struck me with another stab of terror.

*It* was certainly a *he*.

I whimpered, and made another pathetic attempt to crab-walk away.

With a low roar, he pounced after me and clawed at the front of my sweater, slashing it all the way down. The two halves fell open, exposing my cotton bra underneath.

A growl rumbled out of his throat, and he buried his snout between my breasts. Feeling his cold nose against my skin, I stiffened in horror, expecting his sharp teeth to tear into me next, but he only sniffed and snorted his way up to my neck.

With his huge body now flush with mine, the stench of something like a wet dog assaulted my nostrils. A clawed hand pawed at my inner thigh, slicing through my jeans with a flash of searing pain up my leg.

The weight of his bulk pressed me into the ground, forcing all air out of my lungs. With my feet and hands scraping uselessly against the ground, I couldn't breathe to let out the scream building in my chest.

I was pinned to the ground, completely incapacitated.

Just like then!

I had the same feeling of helplessness once before. And just like then debilitating panic overtook me. The scream that had painfully stuck in my dry throat finally escaped in a sharp high-pitched shrill.

The sound must have been enough to stun the animal on top of me. He stopped his wet sniffing and lifted his head enough to meet my eyes.

After a gasping exhale, I screamed, "No!" in his maw hovering over my face, putting everything I had into that one word.

Dark and wild, his eyes were almost completely glossed over by animalistic lust.

Almost.

A faint spark of . . . something—a light, an awareness, some clarity—flickered in his gaze. Then a low growl rumbled deep inside his chest in response, but the glimmer of understanding was undeniable now.

His lips drew back, baring long sharp-looking teeth, and he roared into my face, washing it with his hot, humid breath.

The next moment, he shoved back from me and disappeared around the corner of the garage, running on all fours, the animal that he was.

I lay there for another second, trying to process what had just happened. The ringing in my ears replaced any outside noise, and white spots danced in front of my eyes.

The need to get out of there in case he returned finally registered with me, urging me to stumble to my feet and lunge for the opening in the bushes.

With the rose hedge behind me, I didn't stop running.

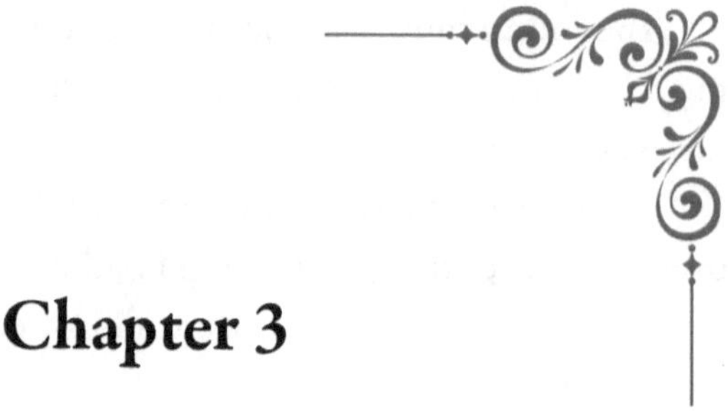

# Chapter 3

## Sophie

Dodging shrubs and tree trunks, my lungs on fire and my heart pounding high in my throat, I didn't pay any attention to the direction I was running, as long as it was away from the house and the raging, nightmarish creature.

However, after running until I was breathless with a painful stitch in my side, I realized that there was nothing but deep forest around me, and I had no idea in which direction the road lay. There was no sign of the chain-link fence, either.

Panting and pressing an arm to my side, I turned slowly, scanning my surroundings.

Trees, undergrowth, dead leaves and pine needles. Nothing else.

The good news was, I saw no monster chasing me, either. But how was I supposed to get out of here?

The sun had moved low behind the trees. With the evening fast approaching, frost was setting in. I felt it even more through the rips in my clothing. A biting chill seeped through the fabric of my jeans too, quickly stealing the heat I'd worked up while running.

My teeth began to chatter, and I attempted to close my jacket over the torn pieces of my sweater. It didn't help much—the holes on the back from the animal's claws only opened wider as soon as I closed the jacket in the front.

My knitted hat was long gone, lost during my struggle with the monster. I belatedly remembered my leather gloves, tucked in my pocket, and quickly put them on. I was dressed appropriately for a daytime walk through a forest in autumn, not a night out without shelter. And now, I feared the very real threat of hypothermia.

If I didn't get out of here soon enough, I was screwed.

I inhaled deeply, trying to stop from diving head first into panic.

It was obviously a large property, but not infinite. If I walked in one direction, eventually I would most likely hit the chain-link fence that surrounded it. Then I could follow it back to the road.

Would Ashley and Jason still be waiting for me? I didn't expect them to go into the woods searching for me—they had no guns to face off that monster, even Jason's axe I'd left in the bedroom. But hopefully, they'd be honking the horn or flashing the headlights, waiting for me in the truck. So, I had a chance to hear or see them maybe even before I saw the road.

In any case, I couldn't remain still for long and risk freezing. I needed to find the fence.

Wrapping my arms around my middle, I kept moving. Hunger began to gnaw at me, and I took out one of the granola bars I had lying in my pocket next to my Swiss Army knife.

Trudging along, hopefully, in a straight line, I had no idea how long I walked, but the shadows thickened and it soon became too dark to see where I was going. The air turned even colder, and I was too scared to stop.

Hugging myself, with my head down, watching the uneven ground under my feet, I would have missed the fence if my shoulder hadn't hit the post.

There was no chain-link here, the property line seemed to be marked by log posts placed at even intervals and connected by a string of barbed wire stretched at the top, high enough for me to pass under without noticing it in the dark.

What was the purpose of a fence if it didn't prevent anyone from entering?

Maybe keeping visitors out wasn't the point? Obviously, the thing that lived here didn't have to worry about trespassers—people or animals. He must be the largest predator around here.

A chill, unrelated to the cold of the night, ran down my spine when I thought that he was still out there somewhere, roaming through the same woods I was trying to escape.

Nearly frozen inside the thin leather gloves, my fingers shook as I opened my pocket knife. Not much of a weapon, but I felt safer with it in my hand.

I kept following the property line, from one pole to the next, keeping an eye on the wire, which glimmered in the faint light of the moon between the dark clouds shrouding the sky.

The hair on the back of my neck rose every time I heard a cracking noise in the distance. Was it the monster coming back for me?

Even if he were stalking me right now, I couldn't see him behind the dark tree trunks. I curled my fingers tighter around the pocketknife and focused my attention on counting the steps between the posts. Eight. I had to make eight steps before the next post would hit the palm of my outstretched hand.

My prospects were grim. I had no map, no water and no way of knowing where I was in this wilderness. If I allowed myself to consider in earnest my bleak situation I would quite possibly lose it and break down. If I wanted to give myself the best chance of survival, though, I should just focus on each step I made instead.

The moon fought to break through the clouds, leaving me in almost complete darkness under the tall pine trees of the forest.

My foot slipped off something, a moss-covered rock or a fallen tree, my ankle twisted at an odd angle. A scream ripped out of me as sharp pain shot through my leg and I crashed to the ground dropping the knife.

Whimpering, I grabbed my leg just above the ankle and carefully straightened it. The pain was agonizing, making me afraid that a bone might be broken. I prodded around it gently through the jeans and wiggled my toes inside the boot. It still hurt like hell, but there didn't appear to be any fractures.

Carefully, holding on to the nearest fence post, I hauled myself up, and tried putting some weight on the injured foot. Gritting my teeth against the searing pain, I let go of the post and even managed to hobble a couple of paces, before collapsing to the ground again.

"No, please," I groaned.

I could no longer ignore the hopelessness of my situation. Shivering from the freezing cold, with a busted ankle, getting hungry again, and, by now, very thirsty too—whatever composure I had mustered crumbled. Tears pricked at my eyes, and I stifled a sob.

Not caring if anyone or anything heard me, I threw my head back and screamed on the top of my lungs in anger, fear, and frustration.

Oddly enough, it helped—as the sounds of my meltdown quieted, rational thinking returned. My body shook from the cold. Adrenaline coursed through my veins, pushing me to do something.

I was still alive. Jason and Ashley were out there somewhere. I just needed to keep going, lest I freeze to the ground sitting here. I could find a stick, thick enough to use as a crutch and keep walking.

In search of my dropped pocket knife, I rummaged through the dead leaves and pine needles around me as far as I could reach until I felt the cold press of metal. Snatching the blade up, I clutched it to my chest with relief.

Now I needed to find a stick. Propping myself up with my arms, I attempted to crawl forward, searching for one. Pain speared through my ankle again, making me grind my teeth.

The only choice I had right now, I reminded myself, was either to keep going or lie down and freeze to death.

Sucking in a deep breath I crawled ahead.

# Chapter 4

## Monster

He remained on the west part of his estate, giving the intruders a chance to leave. After a while though, the foreign presence in his brain drove him to skirt the property along the southern fence, all the way back to the road.

There were no cars visible anywhere. However, the annoying presence of a stranger remained like a splinter inside his head.

Back, deeper in the forest, he caught a whiff of her scent.

Did they leave her behind?

Once again, he fled to the river, circling the area with her scent, hoping the others would come back for her soon. They would take her back to the life he no longer wished to have any part of and would leave him in peace.

The wind in his ears, the blood rushing through his veins made him feel alive. Running, swimming, chasing prey, falling asleep with his belly full—those were the things that made him content.

Not happy—content.

Happiness was a human emotion—the highest of high. And for him it came at the price of excruciating emotional pain—the lowest of low.

For years he had fought the uphill battle for his humanity only to lose it to the animal inside him at the end. Instead of a complete despair, however, he got an unexpected consolation prize for his defeat—the oblivion of a simpler mind.

When he was hungry, he hunted. When he was tired, he slept. Hunger and cold became his biggest problems, his only worries. All the complexities and tortures of the emotions experienced by a human heart faded into the background.

That was what kept him alive all these years. Embracing the animal within instead of fighting it was what had helped him survive for so long.

The girl ruined it all today. One look into her autumn-sky grey eyes opened the door into the human world with all its torturous emotions.

Hope, longing, loneliness . . . anger. So much anger.

Why was she still here? This was his property, the only place on earth where he could exist. She was free to be anywhere else. Why did she come here? Why of all the people in his life, did *she* have to be the one to show up?

The nagging sense of her presence added to his headache, which always increased at night. His horns felt ten times their usual weight, crushing his skull. He collapsed to the ground at the water edge and pressed his forehead to the cold rocks beneath him. The frost on the rocks felt calming through the fur.

Why was she still here?

He seethed with anger while the headache pounded against his skull.

Even if he had to roar in her ear again to chase her away, the stupid girl needed to get out of here.

No, not just *the girl*.

A painful exhale rushed through his tightened throat.

He never thought it would be possible, but the moment their eyes connected and the animalistic lust evaporated, blown away by recognition, he remembered her name.

Sophie Morel.

She wasn't stupid, either.

Long ago, in what felt like a different lifetime, she was a math tutor and an A-student in high school.

# Chapter 5

## Monster

Impatience and something akin to anxiety—he could no longer accurately name the long-forgotten emotions—made him break into a run through the forest again, searching the frosty air for her scent.

This time, the warm perfume of her skin was laced with the coppery smell of blood when it reached his nostrils.

The blood from the wounds *he* had inflicted on her, he realized the same moment another emotion rose from the dark grave deep inside him. This one could not be mistaken for anything else—*guilt* weighed heavily on his shriveled soul.

He'd done more than simply roar in her ear, hadn't he?

Acting like a feral animal—a true predator that no one would want to be near—he'd hurt her.

He'd done enough to scare any sane person into running for the hills.

Yet she was still here. The only explanation that made sense was that she couldn't physically leave for whatever reason.

The moment her scent was strong enough to indicate she was very close, he slowed down and halted his breath. He didn't need a delicious lungful of Sophie Morel in his chest, lest he run berserk with lust again.

The wind had picked up, but the sky was still overcast, with the moon peeking through now and then.

He could see well enough, even without any moonlight—one of the few benefits of his condition.

Regular humans couldn't see well in the dark, though. Maybe that was Sophie's problem. Had she somehow got lost on her way off the estate? In that case, all he would have to do was to spook her again and make her run in the right direction.

He realized that was not going to happen the moment he saw her. The way her right leg was carefully extended in front of her indicated she was hurt beyond the wounds of his doing.

She obviously couldn't walk. With her friends gone, she had no other option but to spend the night out in the open. *On his property.*

Fuck!

The old familiar anger rolled over him, along with nervous anxiety. She couldn't stay here. He couldn't allow it. Nothing good could come for either of them if she was anywhere near someone like him.

Not wanting to betray his presence to her was the only thing that kept him from howling in frustration.

Instead, he paced under the cover of nearby trees, trying to consider what best to do when Sophie's muffled groan captured his attention. She was attempting to crawl along the ground, dragging her right leg behind her, confirming what he had suspected—she could no longer walk.

Her prospects weren't just grim—they were dire. The temperatures would reach below freezing as the night progressed. If she remained where she was, hypothermia would claim her before morning. That was, of course, if other predators didn't find her first.

Wolves ventured onto his property every now and then, mostly for the same reason human hunters did, chasing prey. Bears were frequent visitors. And he noted a cougar following him on quite a few occasions in the past three years.

The cat was huge, much bigger than the average size. He seemed to wander in and out of the estate, sometimes disappearing for weeks or even months. But he always returned.

The wind had finally ripped through the clouds, and the moon peered out. The eerie, pale light pierced through the dark branches of the forest.

A wisp of an ominous scent reached his sensitive nostrils—just a small tendril of it before the wind changed direction again—the cat was out hunting.

Now, he was faced with the very real possibility of finding Sophie's half-eaten remains in the morning . . .

He cursed under his breath and turned towards her again, searching for a pair of glowing eyes or a flash of sandy-brown fur of the cougar in the surrounding trees.

Her cowardly boyfriend would most likely be back tomorrow, probably with the Royal Canadian Mounted Police in tow.

The cat might be the one to get her, but *he* would be the one hunted if her dead body was discovered anywhere on this property.

Sophie sat a few feet away from the place he saw her last and held a thick tree branch. She was busily trimming off smaller branches and twigs with a pocketknife.

He realized, with mild surprise at her resourcefulness, that she was fashioning a crutch for herself.

Not stupid at all.

The cougar's scent tickled his nose again, much stronger now. He scanned the area and this time quickly found what he was searching for—a pair of eyes, glowing in the moonlight, as the cougar stalked easy prey.

He had met his share of predators since he became one himself. Some he fought, some he stayed away from. He learned all he needed to know about their behaviour to stay alive in the woods. Most of the predators he encountered would give him a warning and run away if he challenged them back. Not the cougar. The cat stalked his prey from behind, invisible and deadly. There was no warning of his attack until it was too late.

And right now, the glowing eyes were glued to the unsuspecting Sophie.

Monster lowered his head to the ground, aiming the horns straight ahead, and shifted to the side to stay clear of the tree trunks.

He leaped through the air the same moment the cougar pounced.

# Chapter 6

## Sophie

I could no longer feel my fingers inside my gloves. My whole body shook violently, rendering any attempt at coordinated movement useless. Still, I kept trying. My crutch didn't need to be perfect. It just needed to be functional.

A sudden growl behind me made me raise both the knife and the branch as I twisted around towards the source of the noise.

Two large shapes collided in the air.

With a yelp I lurched backwards, fiery spears of pain from my twisted ankle shooting up my leg.

Massive bodies rolled on the ground, growling and clawing at each other. The moonlight bounced off the pale fur of a huge cougar that had its teeth sunk into the shoulder of the wild animal I recognized as the beast that had attacked me earlier.

The cougar's powerful hind paws, with their razor-sharp claws were tearing the monster's side to shreds, ripping out chunks of dark fur and slicing into the flesh underneath.

With a deafening roar, the monster rose to his feet—his own claws deep in the cougar's front paws at his neck—he threw himself to the ground, crushing the cougar under the mass of his enormous body.

The two wrestled on the frozen earth. The cougar growled and hissed every time the monster's massive frame ended up on top. Finally, the feline used the moment when the beast rolled to the side to let go of his shoulder. It sprang up and melted into the darkness of the surrounding trees.

I glanced around nervously, half expecting the cougar to come back.

Then turned my full attention to the monster, who heaved himself up with a low grunt. He met my gaze a moment later. His eyes glistened menacingly in the moonlight.

"Don't . . ." *even think about it* was what I was going to say, but my teeth chattered and my voice got caught in my dry throat.

I tightened my hold on the makeshift weapons, willing my hands not to shake.

"Go away!" I yelled as fiercely as I could muster, waving the stick in front of me in what I hoped was an intimidating manner.

The monster sat on his haunches and tilted his head to the side. I swore I could see amusement glinting in his gaze now.

"You'll die if I go."

I dropped the branch, my head spinning in shock and disbelief.

It spoke?

Or did I start to hallucinate from hypothermia just like people did from high fever?

The way he spoke—mocking me calmly—also stunned me.

"I would prefer to avoid dealing with the mess of your decomposing body in my woods." His voice was low and raspy. The words sounded a little distorted, requiring an effort to understand him at first, although the sarcasm dripping from his mouth was unmistakable.

"You talk." I blinked, still trying to come to terms with the existence of a talking animal in this world. Afraid I'd drop my pocket knife again if I continued to brandish it at him, I wrapped my arms around me in a futile attempt to control my shivering.

He sucked in an exasperated breath. "So very observant of you."

"T-that's c-crazy!"

"Isn't it?" he scoffed then added slowly, "Listen. If I leave you here now, you'll be dead before morning—"

"We'll s-see ab-bout that," I interrupted.

Sitting on the ground, hugging my ripped clothes to my shivering body, I must have looked pathetic, but I lifted my chin in defiance. Something in his sneering tone pricked at my temper.

"It isn't f-finished until it's finished. I'm not d-dead yet."

"Even if the cat doesn't come back," he continued evenly, as if I hadn't spoken at all. "Exposure will finish you. It wouldn't take long, since you're not even dressed for the weather. Jeans are hardly suitable attire for this time of the year around here."

Ripped jeans.

I didn't say it out loud, not wanting to remind him about the lustful frenzy in which he ruined my clothes. As insane as it felt to have a conversation with a talking monster, at least he was calm and seemed reasonable at the moment.

"I'll find my f-friends—"

"You're friends are gone!" he bit out with undisguised disdain and added under his breath, "fucking cowards."

"Gone?" I gasped. "As in 'left'? Or did you . . . do something to them?"

"Like what? Swallowed them whole, camera and all?" he smirked. "They ran out of here so fast, I never got a chance to do anything."

"They'll be back," I whispered, even as my resolve wavered, along with the faith in my own words. "They just went to get help . . ."

"When they come back—*if* they come back—it will be too late for you. And as for help, the closest police office—RCMP—is almost a two-hour drive south from Rocky River, which would be almost three hundred kilometres from here. I do believe the RCMP officer comes to town once a week. Not sure what day of the week that would be, though. Chances are six to one that it's not tomorrow." The thick sarcasm in his voice ground on my nerves, even as the chilling realization of having to spend the night in the dark freezing woods settled in my brain. "In any case, no one will come for you at least until tomorrow morning." His gaze weighed heavy on me. "So I'm stuck with you."

"What d-do you want?" I tightened the grip on my knife.

He heaved out a sigh.

"I'll take you back to the house." He rose to his hind paws, and I thrust my pocket knife in his direction again.

"No!"

He tilted his head at me, definitely more amused than intimidated by the knife in my hand.

"You don't have a choice."

"There is always a choice," I retorted. "Even if it's just between freezing in the woods or being raped and eaten."

He flinched as if I punched him in the face, and it took him a moment to reply.

"I'm offering you the chance to survive the night." His voice was grave and absolutely serious this time, with not a hint of mocking.

"In exchange for what?" I held his stare.

"Your silence. You're not going to tell anyone about me. And if your *friends* come back for you in the morning, you'll lead them off the property and back to wherever the hell you all came from."

Anger and undisguised dislike coloured his words.

I could argue with him all I wanted. Deep inside I knew he was right. If Ashley and Jason were indeed gone, my chances for survival here were slim to none.

But how could I trust him not to attack me again?

I craned my neck, carefully regarding his impressive figure in front of me.

The moonlight brought out pale highlights in his thick mane and in the fur on his wide shoulders. Streaks of light glistened along the polished horns spiraling out of his head. Cold hostility glimmered in his deep-set eyes as he gazed at me. With his hands relaxed at his side, the set of sharp-looking claws I had seen earlier was hidden from sight. Retracted.

I shot a tentative glance at his crotch. His fur was darker and thicker on his lower stomach and inner thighs, completely hiding his genitals from view. Not finding an erection there this time, I exhaled in relief.

The monster must have noticed the direction of my gaze and seemed to sense the tone of my thoughts for he shook his head.

"I'm not going to pounce on you again. All I want is for you to walk out of here in one piece." He gave me another heavy look and added with force. "And never come back again."

"There's nothing I want more," I assured him quietly. "It's a deal then."

"There'll be no police report, no investigation. Understood?" he added in a steely tone.

I nodded, perfectly aware that I was not in a position to argue. All I wanted was to get out of these damn woods and then put this whole thing behind me, bury it as if it had never happened.

"I p-promise. No police."

He rolled his injured shoulder in a surprisingly human gesture then walked on two legs towards me. I shrank back involuntarily, wishing to keep as much distance as possible between us.

He paused for a second, towering over me. "I'd rather you walked on your own, too, but you can't. So—" He grabbed me and heaved me up in his arms with a grunt.

I wrapped my arms tighter around myself, trying not to touch him.

His fur was spiked with frost where it brushed against my skin. The faint smell of a wet dog hit my senses again, and I turned my face away from him, straining my muscles to minimize any contact with his body.

My injured ankle dangled in the air, sending sharp pain up my leg with his every step, and I bit my lip to stop any cry of pain.

Being this close to him was not just unpleasant, it was also foreign and alarmingly unsettling. His arms around me felt confining, like a set of restraints, and I had to force myself to remain calm and not freak out and demand that he release me.

He expended no visible effort in carrying me as he moved swiftly between the trees, seemingly finding his way with no trouble.

Despite the fast pace he maintained, it still took us quite a while to reach the house. By the time the dark mass of the building appeared behind the dense rose bush hedge, I was frozen from head to toe. The only part of me that still retained any kind of warmth was the side pressed to him.

Inside, the house was dark and cold when he carried me over the threshold. The wind had dropped, but without any heating, being inside offered little comfort.

The monster unceremoniously deposited me on one of the couches in the main room then shoved it closer to the fireplace.

"I'll fetch some wood," he informed me before moving to the kitchen area. A moment later I heard him exit through a door.

I shifted in my seat, carefully adjusting the position of my injured leg, then prodded it with my fingers in an attempt to assess the damage.

"And?" His voice came from right behind my shoulder.

"What?" I jerked in surprise.

"How bad is your leg?" He stomped to the fireplace, carrying an armload of firewood topped with a handful of kindling, and a pack of matches.

"I'm pretty sure it's just sprained."

"Pretty sure?"

"As far as anyone can tell without an x-ray. I went to medical school for a year . . ." I stopped myself, wondering why I had volunteered this information. It wasn't like he'd asked.

He didn't comment as he skillfully arranged the wood and the kindling, and soon bright flames cheerfully danced inside the fireplace.

I was yet to feel any real warmth from the fire, but the mere sight of it lifted my mood and I reached towards it.

The monster disappeared again for a moment then returned with two heavy blankets. He tossed one of them over my legs.

"Thank you," I gratefully pulled the blanket over me, noticing that my shivering had already subsided as a result of his efforts.

"I'm simply making sure you survive the night," he threw curtly over his shoulder. "That was the deal."

Fine. Be that way. I huffed in frustration. I'm not thanking you again.

His behaviour was far from friendly, but he wasn't nearly as aggressive and threatening as he'd been at our first encounter. Rude and outright hostile, he still caused icy needles of unease prickle inside my chest, but he no longer made me feel like I was in any immediate danger.

Good enough. At this point, I'd settle for rudeness if that meant my survival.

Huddling under the blanket, I contemplated my situation.

I must have wandered in the woods for hours. Jason and Ashley had likely left before the night came. They would have a hard time finding their way back to the lodge in the dark, otherwise.

I hoped they would come back for me once the sun is up in the morning, either with the RCMP or with people from the hunting lodge where we all stayed. Then I would get out of here and wouldn't have to see the monster ever again.

As I warmed up, I observed him in the flickering light of the fire.

The sentient being who talked like a man but had the appearance of some mythical beast.

What was he?

It was obvious that he must be closer to a man than an animal—he walked on two legs, had opposable thumbs, and could speak. His intelligence appeared normal, if the sarcasm and general knowledge he exhibited was anything to go by.

Though I couldn't catch any regional accent in his speech, he talked using modern terms and intonations. His voice didn't sound completely human. Rough and deep, it was close to an animal growling.

In the glowing light of the fireplace, I was able to discern more details of his appearance.

There was nothing human about his face at all. The long snout reminded me of a wolf, as did the pointy white teeth that were visible every time he spoke. His eyes were all but hidden under a heavy brow, glaring at me every now and then as he attached the second blanket over the broken backdoor using a hammer and nails.

The thick fur that covered his head and shoulders brought to mind a lion's mane. I also noted the long bushy tail that flickered at his ankles.

And then there were his horns.

The horns were actually spectacular. They must have been close to two feet long. Thicker at the base, they wound up in ribbed spirals that tapered to sharp, glossy points high above his head.

He finished arranging the blanket over the back door, meanwhile, and came to tower over me. Unable to stand the heavy silence rolling off him I blurted out the thought, which occupied me at that moment. "What are you?"

His fingers twitched before his hands balled into fists, and his chest expanded.

"*What* do you think I am, princess?" His voice was clipped, mocking again, but I sensed a shadow of hurt deep underneath and kept quiet. "Isn't it obvious?" His voice rose, a derisive note cutting sharp through it.

"Watch and tell me." He rolled his shoulders back, raised his head, and a blood-curdling howl escaped his lungs, turning the frozen needles in my chest into a solid block of ice.

The howl thickened in his throat, joined by a low rumble that grew into a full-on deafening roar within seconds. He leaned over me, his burning gaze fixed on me.

"*What* am I?" He bellowed in my face. "What does *this* look like to you?"

What about my question would have offended him this much? Was it my choice of word *what* instead of *who*?

I closed my eyes in fear and pressed my back into the couch, wishing I could just fall right through it to hide. Terrified, I couldn't move a muscle or form any reply.

"What do you think I am?" he demanded and grabbed the couch on each side of me, his claws piercing through the upholstery with a sharp sound, then gave it a rough shake. My leg jolted painfully, and I cried out in pain.

"Monster!" I squeezed past my tight throat and whispered with my eyes shut, "You are a monster."

He shoved away from the couch immediately, releasing me from his confining presence and letting me breathe once again.

Only then I ventured to open my eyes a little.

"That's exactly right, princess. I am a monster. Inside and out." His tone was surprisingly calm, as if he found my insult oddly satisfying.

I blinked, still shocked by his outburst, and more than a little confused by his sudden composure.

He turned away from me, revealing his injuries. The blood from the wounds inflicted by the cougar had crusted in rusty streaks, blending with the russet brown of his fur. I noted the furrow of his snout—the movement must have pulled on the cuts, causing him discomfort.

Compassion warred with resentment in me, and the empathy won out.

"You're hurt." I cleared my throat. Hoping not to cause another fit of rage in him, I continued carefully. "You'll need stitches. I could do it if—"

"I'll be fine," he barked.

And I thought it wise not to insist. Despite some theoretical knowledge on how to stitch a wound, I never went far enough in my medical studies to treat injuries with confidence, even if he let me touch him. Besides, I strongly doubted the house boasted much in the way of medical supplies for me to do the job anyway.

"Why did you fight the cougar?" I asked instead.

He leaned against the fireplace, giving me a measuring stare.

"I told you. I want you to leave here in one piece. There'd be a lot of bloody pieces littering my woods, had the cougar got to you."

"He was after *me*?" I sat up, my back rod-straight from shock. The image of the cougar's claws embedded in the monster's flesh churned my stomach—those were meant for me. "You saved my life."

He shrugged and looked away, acting uncomfortable for the first time since I met him.

"You should at least get them clean," I suggested, tipping my chin at his mangled side. He saved my life—I didn't want him to die from infection because of it.

"Don't you have your own wounds to worry about?" he snarled, reminding me of the cuts on my legs and back. The ones that *he* had inflicted.

I pressed my hand to the blanket over my injured thigh and kept my mouth shut.

"That's right, Sophie, think of yourself," he muttered, turning to leave. "Don't you worry about me." The mocking derisiveness in his tone was once again off-putting.

Fine. Rot in hell for all I care.

Wait a minute. Did he just say *Sophie*?

"How do you know my name?" I called at his back.

He stopped on his way to the kitchen and turned around slowly.

"The redhead yelled it as you were all running for your lives."

"Ashley?" I remembered her screaming a warning to me.

"What kind of friends would leave you alone with the likes of me, anyway?" he scoffed.

I felt the need to defend Ashley. She wasn't obligated to put her own safety at risk for me.

"Ashley and I are hardly friends. We just met three days ago. She's the girlfriend of a distant friend of my boyfriend."

"And your boyfriend is that moron with the camera?"

"Jason," I corrected. "He's a photographer. Among other things."

"What's his excuse for leaving you behind?" There was unmistakable contempt in his voice. "He ran so fast, he never even got to scream a warning your way. Just hurled the camera at me and took off."

"No," I sighed, suddenly acutely aware of my boyfriend's shortcomings. "No excuses. Except for the fact that you'd make anyone run for the hills."

"Never have to try too hard, either," he muttered under his breath, continuing on his way to the kitchen.

"Hey, what's your name? Now that you know mine."

Without stopping or even glancing my way, he threw over his shoulder, "*Monster* is fine," and disappeared in the kitchen area.

Was he mocking me again? I couldn't tell whether he was serious, because even when he seemed to speak in earnest, there was often a streak of thinly veiled sarcasm, making me feel like he was laughing at me.

I fingered the last granola bar I had in my pocket. My stomach growled, and I took the bar out.

The monster seemed to take seriously his promise to keep me alive until a search party came for me. It seemed I would be back in civilization again soon so there was no need to hoard the bar.

A sudden noise by the open front door made me jump up in fright. A spike of adrenaline shot through me then settled down again when I saw it was the monster clearing the dead leaves and debris away from the door with a snow shovel.

"God. You scared me." I exhaled, clutching my chest with one hand and using the other to pick up my granola bar from where it had fallen on the blanket.

He shrugged a shoulder, continuing with his work.

Finishing the bar made my thirst come raging back.

"Um . . . Monster," I winced. Was he or was he not truly okay with me calling him that? I would prefer not to continue insulting him further. "Would you happen to have any water anywhere here? Please? I'm really thirsty."

He had finished shoveling the dirt away and pushed the massive door closed then opened it again, testing the hinges. The door protested with a loud screeching noise but moved under the power of his shove.

"How long can a human survive without water, Sophie?" he asked matter-of-factly, inspecting his work.

"Um . . . about three-four days, I believe."

"When was the last time you had a drink?" he continued, without sparing me a glance.

"At lunch time, today," I replied, remembering my water bottle left in Ashley's backpack.

"So, you have at least two more days, right?" He glowered my way. "I promised to keep you alive until tomorrow, not to provide you with a high level of comfort, princess."

Without saying another word, he left through the front door, shutting it behind loudly.

Well. Monster it is then.

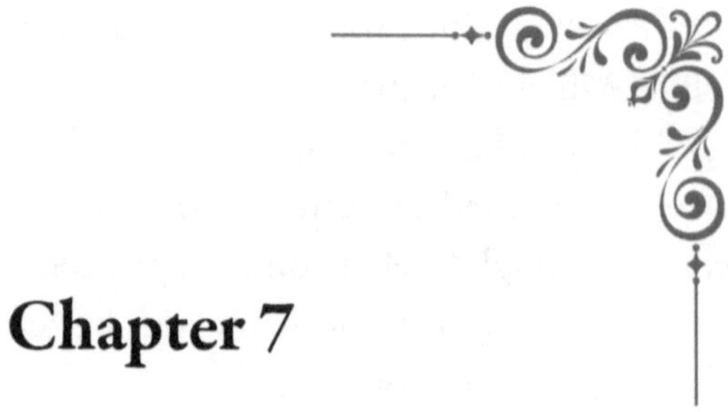

# Chapter 7

## Sophie

My mouth felt lined with sandpaper when I woke up to the chill of early morning. At least I was reasonably warm under the thick blanket.

The flames in the fireplace were high when I opened my eyes. Enough warmth radiated from the fire to keep me asleep through the remainder of the night, it seemed—the sky outside the glass doors was already light grey.

All my senses zoomed in on what woke me up in the first place—the appetizing smell of roasted meat.

I sat up on the couch, noticing the monster reclining on the floor in front of the fireplace, with his back leaning against the couch at my feet. He held a long stick in his hands, roasting a strip of meat in the fire. Several more sticks with seasoned meat on them lay in a tray on the floor next to him.

"Morning," he barked out, without looking at me.

"Good morning." I rubbed the remnants of the sleep out of my eyes.

Still staring into the flames, he reached to his side then pressed a mug of water in my hands.

"Oh my God! Thank you so much," I croaked out, forgetting all about my resolution not to thank him anymore.

"It's from the river. Drink at your own risk," he warned me.

The water seemed clean and felt icy-cold. I reasoned that most of the bacteria in it must have frozen to death already. If not, I was ready to deal with it as I gulped the water up.

"Oh, that was so good." I put the empty mug down on the floor, and he shoved the stick with the meat he had roasted in my hands as soon as they were empty.

The meat smelled amazing. Ravenously hungry, I tore into it immediately.

"This is delicious! What is it?"

"Rabbit."

I paused my chewing but only for a moment. This was the first time I ever had to eat a rabbit. It tasted excellent though, with the texture of very tender dark chicken meat.

"It's good," I complimented around a mouthful of the deliciousness. "The seasoning is so yummy, too."

"Montreal Steak Spice. Found a jar of it in the cupboard." His voice was void of emotion. And I fought the urge to ask if he was okay. Chances were I'd get another one of his rude replies, so I just ate quietly for a few moments, watching him furtively.

In the pale light of the graying sunrise, his brown fur was spotted with silver highlights. With one of his hind legs bent on the floor in front of him, he rested the elbow on the raised knee of the other. The pose was very human, even as his legs still reminded me of a wolf.

"Ashley mentioned there was some alcohol in the kitchen," I blurted out the first random thing that came into my head at that moment.

It wasn't like I hoped for a real conversation here, but despite his gloomy mood, he hadn't roared or snarled at me. As far as I was concerned, for him, it was an improvement.

"There is. Whiskey. Why?" He turned to face me. "Do you want some?"

"No." I exhaled a short laugh. "It's way too early for that."

"Suit yourself." He shrugged. "It should be a good one if you change your mind—the bottle has been sitting there for at least six years."

"I guess you don't drink?"

"No. Not anymore. Alcohol has devastating effects on me." His somber expression darkened when he clarified, "Devastating for others."

'Not anymore.'

What other human things did he use to do? Did many of them prove to be *devastating for others*? Could that be one of the reasons why he was alone now?

I held back the barrage of questions his answer had evoked, not wishing to be rebuked once again.

He handed me another meat skewer.

I bit my lip, forbearing to thank him yet again as I accepted it, and struggled to come up with an innocuous question. One that would be less likely to flare up his temper.

"Have you been living here long?"

"I don't live here."

This was easy to believe—the house appeared deserted.

"Did you ever live here? Whose house is it?"

"You want to ask *what* I am again next?" he rebuked, effectively stopping my questions.

He twisted to the side to pick up another stick with raw meat from the tray, and I noticed a slight wince on his face.

The wounds on his back and shoulder appeared better than they had last night, definitely cleaner.

He had said the water for me was from a river. It seemed he had cleaned his wounds in the river, too—the blood that had caked his fur was gone.

He must have felt my curious gaze because he glanced my way, his deep-set eyes clouded under the heavy eyelids.

The way he held his head, moving it with extra caution, told me he might have pain not only in his injured side. He lifted his hand to rub his forehead then, and my suspicions grew stronger.

"You have a headache. Don't you?"

He turned away again.

"It should get better in an hour or so. It usually gets better by midday." He handed me the last stick of meat and made a move to get up.

"Wait." I stopped him. "I could try to help you . . . If you let me." I put the stick down on the tray and folded my hands in my lap. "I know several massage techniques to relieve different types of headaches."

He lifted an eyebrow at me skeptically but remained sitting.

"Does it actually help?" A corner of his upper lip curled up again, only this time it came out more like teasing than mocking.

The faint hope in his voice encouraged me to continue.

"Most patients report a significant improvement." I nodded with confidence.

"Even patients with horns?" A faint spark of amusement broke through the clouds in his eyes.

"No. Never had a client with horns." I was unable to hold my own smile back.

His gaze stayed on mine for a few moments, as he seemed to consider my offer before nodding.

"Couldn't be any worse, I guess."

I slid to the other end of the couch, positioning myself behind him. Massage was something I enjoyed doing, and it tied perfectly with my innate desire to help people. Of course, it was not always as effective as a strong dose of painkillers.

In his case, hopefully, it would at least ease the tension hanging around him like a dark shroud.

Reaching around his horns carefully, I pressed the tips of my fingers to his temples. The solid bone underneath was a striking contrast to the softness of the short fur covering it, and I wondered if his biology was similar enough to a human's for this to work.

I continued to move my fingers in small circles up to the top of his forehead, applying even pressure as I went.

He sat completely still, giving me no indication if any of it was working for him. On the other hand, he made no attempt to stop me either, so I kept going.

I moved my fingers along his forehead, tracing around the place where people would have a hairline, except that he had none—the short fur on his face gradually turned into the long wavy mane on his head.

Then I encountered a problem—the horns were in my way.

I hovered my hands above his forehead for a second, considering the best way to proceed, then gently pushed at the base of the horns, making the same even circles all the way around each one.

He shifted slightly under my touch, and a low rumble vibrated deep inside his chest. Unsure of what it meant, I paused for a moment.

"Are you okay?"

"I'm fine," he bit out sharply and rose to his feet abruptly.

I think I made him mad again.

So much for relieving the tension.

I watched him move to the front door.

With a huff, he went down on all fours, looking even more like an animal this way. His long tail flicked the hocks on the back of his legs like that of an angry cat when he opened the door and left without saying a word.

# Chapter 8

## Sophie

Left alone after the monster's sudden departure, I finished my breakfast then inspected my injuries.

My ankle had swollen overnight, and it throbbed like crazy when I lowered it off the couch. Pain still prevented me from putting any weight on it.

I couldn't see the scratches on my back, but the ones on my legs were angry-red and definitely in need of medical attention.

All I could do at the moment, though, was to hope that Jason had already let someone know I was here and that help was on the way.

The monster appeared in the front door.

"They're here, princess. Your search party has arrived."

Relief flooded through me.

"Did you see them? Is it Jason?"

"No, I didn't *see* them, but I *know* someone is on the property, on their way here. I'll carry you out towards the road." Monster stomped to the couch where I sat. "I don't want them to come anywhere near here."

He scooped me up and carried me out of the house.

The morning frost in the air outside made me lean into him, seeking the warmth of his fur. It had fully dried, with not a hint of the wet dog smell anymore. Instead, the fresh, rather pleasant scent of frosty pinewood filled my nose.

On the other side of the rose hedge, he cleared his throat. "I'll take you about halfway to the road. Remember our deal, get them off the property."

The forest around us was calm and silent. Apart from the odd bird call or rustle in the dry leaves, I couldn't hear much.

"How do you know anyone is here?"

"I always feel if someone crosses over the property line. I get this thing in my head. It's like something is poking me all the time the person is here." He rolled his head. "Not a very pleasant feeling, to tell you the truth."

"Have you been having this unpleasant feeling from my being here, too?"

He glanced my way.

"Among a million other feelings," he muttered under his breath then stopped and lowered me to the ground. "They're moving this way. It won't be long."

"Wait," I called when he turned around to leave.

What else could I possibly want from him? He had delivered on his promise—he kept me alive. During the night I spent in his presence, he was rude, even mean at times. At this point, I wanted more than anything to get away from here, but I couldn't just leave him like this.

"Thank you for keeping your promise," I started when he glared expectantly at me over his shoulder.

He shrugged. "Make sure you keep yours."

"Listen, I'll be in the area for a few more days," I continued hurriedly, afraid that he'd leave without letting me finish. "If there's anything you need from the town, I could get it for you . . ."

My offer might have been somewhat unexpected even for me, but it came from the heart. As happy as I was to return to civilization myself, I had mixed feelings about leaving him here alone.

Regardless of what or who he was, whatever human was in him made it hard for me to just leave him behind. After all, he was injured while saving my life and seemed to be completely on his own.

At first, it appeared he wouldn't respond. Silent, he turned around and moved into the trees surrounding us.

After a couple of steps, though, he threw another glance my way then stopped suddenly.

"Painkillers. Leave them on this side of the fence, I'll find them."

"Painkillers?" I didn't know what, if anything, I had expected him to ask from me, but there was something so heart-wrenching about his request that I felt sudden tears prickling my eyes.

"Leave them by the fence. Don't come into the woods again, Sophie."

He went down on all fours and with a bound disappeared between the trees.

I watched him leave until the last glimpse of his russet fur blended completely with the undergrowth, and a heavy feeling of sadness sank deeper into my heart.

# Chapter 9

## Monster

As soon as he was confident that the underbrush concealed him from view, he stopped and peeked through the branches back to where he'd left Sophie.

He convinced himself he needed to make sure she didn't lead her rescuers to the house. The fact was, he didn't want to let her out of his sight.

The nagging feeling of intrusion intensified with the search party approaching. He caught their scent, long before they came into view.

There were just two of them—her wimp of a boyfriend accompanied by a female RCMP officer. There were no dogs, he noted with relief, no hunters with guns either, although the officer held a handgun, pointed at the ground ready to fire.

"Sophie!" the boyfriend exclaimed a little too dramatically to Monster's ear and rushed to her side. "Thank God, you're alive!" He looked around nervously. "Where is that thing? Is it gone?"

"Miss Morel?" The officer knelt next to Sophie and holstered her gun. "Are you injured?"

"Officer, the house is that way." Jason pointed east.

The officer squinted at him in a mixture of amazement and disgust. "I think our priority right now should be Miss Morel's physical condition."

Jason had the decency to appear ashamed even if just for a moment.

"I'll be fine, I don't think anything's broken." Sophie glanced towards the bushes where Monster was hiding, even though he was positive she couldn't see him and had no way of knowing that he was still here. Her gaze flickered to Jason, then back to the officer. "Just cold, tired, and anxious to get out of these woods."

"We're going to get you out of here," the officer promised. "It's lucky we found you this fast—mere hours since you were reported missing." She frowned Jason's way.

"I reported as soon as I could, Sophie." He avoided the officer's glare. "It's not my fault that it took us forever to find the way back to the lodge in the dark. It's not like there's any cell phone reception in these damn woods. And half of these roads aren't even on Google maps."

"We should go." Sophie sounded tired.

"Did that thing attack you?" Jason pawed at her back, tugging at the ripped fabric of her jacket. "Is it still at the house? We should search it." He turned to the RCMP officer again. Apparently, the presence of her gun made him much braver than he was yesterday.

"Miss Morel needs medical attention," the officer pointed out and reached for Sophie to help her up. "Can you walk?"

"I'll try." Sophie nodded. "I twisted my ankle, Jason." The steely note in her voice felt like music to Monster's ears. "I should see a doctor, the sooner the better."

She took the officer's arm and staggered to her feet, obviously well prepared to leave, making good on her promise to keep them off his property.

"We can always search the place later," the officer added in a flat tone, signaling to Jason to follow them back to the road.

"Wouldn't you need a warrant to do a search?" Sophie pointed out. "It's a private property, isn't it?"

"Yes, it's private land. I'd need a statement to obtain the warrant."

"Why would anyone need any statements or warrants if there is an alien beast on the loose?" Jason, The Prick, was becoming increasingly more annoying.

"An *alien beast*?" Sophie tilted her head, gazing at Jason as though he'd gone mad. Monster had to silently applaud her acting skills. "Jason, it was a bear."

"A bear? Are you saying a bear did this to you?" He poked at her back and Monster had to stifle the low, threatening rumble building in his chest.

Touch her one more time, you fucker!

"Yes, a bear. I played dead like in that movie, remember? The bear lost interest and left. I spent the night in the house, but then I thought I should move closer to the road today to make it easier for any search party. It took me a while, hopping on one leg, but I made it this far."

"A bear? How could it be a bear? That thing had horns, Sophie!"

"Are you sure, Jason? I don't see how you had a chance to take a good look at him. Unless you have eyes in the back of your head."

That shut the coward up.

Sophie turned to the officer.

"Can we go please? I'm really cold."

"Absolutely."

Monster watched with an odd sense of satisfaction as Sophie ignored Jason's belated attempt to help. Instead, she leaned heavily into the officer, who wrapped her arm around Sophie's waist, helping her to hop along in the direction of the road.

He fought the impulse to follow them. Instead, he forced himself to face east and move towards the river.

His jog soon turned into a full run as he dashed between the trees faster and faster, ready to jump out of his own hide.

This morning, he didn't need the icy waters of the river to cool the burning headache. Sophie's touch had done more than the river ever could.

The pain had become an inseparable part of him over the years. Under the slight pressure of her fingers, it had moved into the background, dissolving into a faint echo of its usual intensity.

With the pain but a distant hum now, emotions took over, bombarding him with a completely different type of hurt.

Confusion, loneliness.

Longing.

Everything he had forbidden himself to feel, rushed him at once, threatening to drown him like a tsunami. The faster he ran to get away from it, the more it consumed him.

His chest tightened and his eyes burned. He stopped in his tracks, stood up on his hind legs, just like the man he'd once been, and leaned his back against a nearby tree.

He *sensed* her leave the estate the moment she drove away. He didn't need to see her get into the truck or to hear the engine start. The sweet ache of her presence in his head simply disappeared, and he knew she was gone.

He missed the intrusion.

She was the first person he'd talked to in almost three years, the first woman he'd held in twice as long. Why did she also need to be the one who haunted his memories with guilt and regret?

He fought the urge to howl in desperation, out of fear that the sound would reach the road, but his whole body vibrated with tension as he battled the onslaught of all emotions at once.

Bitter remorse.

Anger, so much of it burnt his insides.

And pain. The pain of failure and loss.

Alcohol was his way of coping with pain back then, and his hands shook itching for that unopened bottle of Crown Royal in the kitchen cabinet in the house.

Instead, balling his hands into fists, he closed his eyes and let the maddening lust take over.

The feral desire that hit him the moment he drew her intoxicating scent into his nostrils. The savage need that he held in an iron grip of self-control through the night while she was near, reining in the raging beast within—he set it free now.

With a wild growl, he took a hold of his steel-hard erection, allowing himself to feel everything.

The faint sting of his claws didn't make him ease his grip—the physical pain alleviated some of the tension in his chest when he recalled images of her.

Gone was the flat-chested awkward high-school student he remembered. Whatever Sophie had been doing all these years, her body had used this time to fill in and blossom.

But it wasn't the glimpses of her skin, not even the temptation of her curves primly concealed by the simple white bra that pumped the heat of desire through his veins.

It was the memories of the warm weight of her body in his arms, the mouth-watering scent of her hair at his shoulder, the light touches of her fingers on his face.

He closed his eyes, fisting his painfully swollen length. The growl in his chest grew into a roar as the speed of his hand increased.

Her big, grey eyes—the colour of autumn sky—and the warmth of compassion in them when she offered to treat his headache.

The one and only smile she ever gave him.

All the things that he was incapable of appreciating about her when he was a man. Things that were forever lost to him now that he was a beast.

Tears from the onslaught of yearning and regret burned his eyes at the same moment the hot spurts of his release shot onto the fallen leaves and dead pine needles.

Spent, he slid down the trunk to the ground.

The anxious, incapacitating tension had eased somewhat. However, no amount of self-pleasuring would ever make the pain of his past go away.

He knew from experience the only thing that would help was to give up on his humanity and go back to being an animal.

It took him years to get there the first time. And it might take him just as long again now. But all he had was time.

Lots of it.

Unless the cat, hunger or illness got him, he faced many long, lonely years ahead.

# Chapter 10

## Sophie

After I made a big deal about my injuries to get her and Jason out of the forest and away from the monster, Officer O'Neil drove me to the nursing station in Rocky River, the closest town south from the hunting lodge.

Upon leaving me in the care of the local nurse, she went to recall the search and rescue efforts already underway, including a small airplane about to take off to scout the area of my disappearance.

There had been instances of people getting lost and even perishing in the woods around these parts, just like in many other remote places in The North. Everyone I'd met since my return seemed to be extremely glad that I'd been found alive within hours.

"I strongly advise you to rest."

The nurse was about my age, with kind blue eyes and light brown hair. Over the course of small talk during her assessment of my injuries, Joanna and I discovered many similarities between us.

The glaring difference between us was that she had actually completed her degree and was now gainfully employed as a nurse in Rocky River. She was the only staff member at the nursing station that serviced the people living in town as well as in the sparsely populated surrounding area, which encompassed hundreds of miles. A doctor visited Rocky River once a week, so it was Joanna's responsibility to assess and treat all ills and injuries between his visits.

"The doctor flies in on Thursday. It would be better if you stayed in town until then, so he could take a look at your leg before you go back home." Joanna finished inspecting my foot as she spoke.

"Thank you, Joanna."

"Oh, please, call me Jo. That's what everyone else does. Do you need anything? Let me know if I can get you some groceries. You shouldn't put any weight on your leg for now."

"Thanks. I should be fine." I shifted in the chair where I sat with my leg up in Jo's neat examination room.

Officer O'Neil assured me on the way here that one of her close relatives, owners of the only restaurant in town, would be more than happy to rent their upstairs apartment to me until I was fit enough to travel home to Calgary. Apparently, the place came with room and board, and I had immediately agreed, grateful she was happy to complete the arrangements on my behalf.

I had no desire to return to the lodge with Jason, and he didn't ask me to come with him, either. Instead, he promised to bring all my things over before he went back to Calgary.

Remaining a couple would have been awkward for both of us after what had happened. The decision to separate was mutual, as parting our ways seemed more natural and easier at this point.

It would've been surprising how little the breakup affected me emotionally, if it wasn't actually the norm for all of my relationships with men. As few as I had of them, all my relationships tended to be brief and superficial, and the one with Jason wasn't an exception.

I cherished the escape from loneliness that having a boyfriend provided, but the physical and the emotional intimacy that came with a committed relationship terrified me. I avoided it by settling for self-absorbed men who wouldn't demand much commitment from me because they were incapable of offering any themselves.

"I'm planning to rent the apartment from Bob and Melanie, the owners of Bob's Place," I said to Jo. "I was told it comes with meals provided."

"Oh, you're in good hands then. Melanie's cooking is phenomenal." Jo beamed. "I'm busy here at the station tomorrow morning. And I'm giving a healthy eating class in the school in the afternoon. But I'll come check on you once you've settled."

"Thank you."

"Baby your leg until then. That's a nasty thing to deal with on a hunting trip."

I kept the account of what happened to me vague. True to my promise to Monster, I refused to file a police report, brushing all concerns off.

"Well, yeah. I shouldn't have gone out there at all. So, it's my own fault in a way. Serves me right for trespassing. Would you happen to know who owns that property?"

"No idea. I've never been out that way." She shook her head. "I've worked here for a year now, but I rarely leave the town. If I have any time off at all, I use it to fly back home to Edmonton, to see my family. You should ask Melanie. She was born and raised in Rocky River. I swear she knows everything and everyone around here."

I mentally added a note to talk to Melanie or anyone else who could shed any light on the origins of the sprawling property deep in the woods and its grumpy, mysterious resident.

# Chapter 11

## Sophie

Bob's Place was a mix between a diner, a family restaurant, and a sports bar. As the only place in town that served hot food and had a liquor license, it functioned as everything for everyone, depending on the time of the day and circumstances.

Despite Jo's instructions to look after my leg, a day after I moved in, I got bored sitting in my upstairs apartment alone. Besides, I could hardly wait to find out more about Monster and the property he occupied. With more keenness than skill, I managed to hop downstairs not long after breakfast.

"I have no idea who the real owner of that place is, honey." Melanie was busying herself in the huge open kitchen downstairs, prepping for lunch and dinner, as I sat on the barstool at the counter nursing a cup of tea she'd made for me. "But I believe he is dead now."

"Dead?" Obviously, it wasn't Monster she was talking about.

"No one around here knows how he died. I'm afraid no one even knows for sure who he was or even if it was a *he*. One thing is true, it must be someone who had more money than they knew what to do with, I'd say, if they ended up building that mansion out there." Melanie drained a huge pot of macaroni into a colander in the sink before continuing. "A lot of tradespeople were flown in from places like Calgary and Edmonton, but a few local guys ended up being hired to help with the construction, too. My Bob did some catering for the workers out there. And my cousin, Stan O'Neil, who runs the general store here, was contracted to maintain the grounds and some equipment on the property a while back. No one got to meet the owner, though."

I twisted the earring in my ear, considering her words.

"Wouldn't it be in public records? The land ownership?"

"I've heard it's owned by some trust, but the beneficiary's name has not been made public. Easy enough to check if you want." Her dark eyes flickered my way. "Why do you want to know? Do you have a beef with the owners over the bear attack?"

"No. Of course not." I nearly choked on my tea. "That was all my own fault. If anything, the owners probably have a case against *me* for trespassing. I'm just curious. Who would build something like that in the middle of nowhere, only to abandon it?"

"I tell you, some people really know how to waste their money." She blew a stray strand of glossy black hair away from her forehead and started arranging the macaroni into a casserole dish. "Places like that need a lot of maintenance, you know. One can't just let it sit empty for years."

"So, no one has ever lived there?"

"Nope. Not for any length of time, that is. I've heard of some loud parties being held there for a few years right after the construction was complete. People flew in from the cities for a few days here and there I guess. None of them came into town that I know. They just drove to the property straight from the airport." She paused her work for a second as if needing all her focus to recall. "The parties have quieted down for some time now. A guy still came to look after the house for a few years afterwards. I've heard the place is overrun with wild animals now—dead deer carcasses have been found all around there. Guides from the hunting lodge say they've seen a cougar nearby."

The back door in the kitchen opened, letting in Bob, Melanie's husband, as he carried a flat crate filled with groceries.

"Hey, hon," Melanie greeted him. "What was the name of that guy who came to check on the house in the woods?"

She turned my way again. "Bob gave him a lift from the airport on his way to the hunting lodge a few times. Didn't you, hon?"

"I sure did," Bob nodded to me in a greeting, "Morning," then sat the crate on the counter next to the large fridge. "His name was David. He told me the owner passed away, leaving him in charge of maintenance of the property. Apparently, the owner was from Calgary."

"David stopped coming, too?" I prompted.

"Yep. Guides at the lodge said he passed away as well. Someone made a call about a payment for equipment David had rented for that house. They were told he died from a heart attack. It's been about three years now, I think."

He walked back outside.

"It's best to stay away from there, honey." Melanie's eyes glistened with concern. "Not that one would ever want to go back to that place after what happened to you there." A small shudder shook her plump shoulders. "I tell you, thank goodness, your ordeal ended well. Could've gone all kinds of horrible. God knows plenty of folks get lost without a trace in the wilderness."

After sharing another cup of tea with Melanie and then helping her peel a couple of dozen boiled eggs, I hopped back upstairs where I went over my conversation with her and Bob.

I wondered if I might have known the person who built the house. With over a million people living in Calgary, there still weren't that many who had the means to build a house of that size all the way out here.

As a student in the most prestigious high school in the city, I had spent years surrounded by the city's elite and their children.

Henri, my father, had insisted I get my education in the most exclusive private school in Calgary. I personally knew many who would have had the finances to build that type of house so far up North.

Some of the people I used to know, however, would likely be delighted to hunt Monster down if only for the bragging rights of having the trophy of his head to hang over their fireplace rather than allowing him to roam freely on their property.

The more I thought about him the more his origins puzzled me. Where did he come from? And how did he end up all alone?

# Chapter 12

## Sophie

The doctor inspected my ankle on Thursday and confirmed I had a sprain. Since no bones seemed to be broken and the swelling had gone down, I was given instruction to stretch my leg daily and was allowed to move around with care.

Jo came to visit me almost every day after work. She claimed there was not much for her to do in the small, isolated town like Rocky River and she enjoyed having someone new to talk to.

We would watch old movies and play board games at night. She'd tell me about the people in town and her parents back in Edmonton.

Jo wasn't planning on extending her contract with the government to stay in Rocky River after the current one ended.

"As much as I'd love to leave already, I know I'll be sad when the day comes," she said one evening. "I like the people I've met here, and I'll miss the children the most."

Jo did more than just healthy eating classes at the local school. In her spare time, she ran several after-school programs for kids of all ages.

"What else am I supposed to do with my two days off every week? Sit by the window and watch the snow fall? Nothing makes the time pass faster than spending it with kids." She laughed. "I like being busy. Makes me feel useful."

I understood the feeling. Ever since I'd dropped out of medical school, I'd been doing volunteer work with every charity I could find. Soup Kitchen, Meals on Wheels, women's charities, animal shelters—I did them all.

I started it still in high school, but with time charity work had become my job, my hobby, and pretty much my only social life. Some days, I'd schedule my shifts back to back and work around the clock, sleeping right there at the shelter.

As long as I worked, I felt useful to somebody. Even if I failed to become a doctor and treat the sick, I was still helping someone by feeding them at the shelter, cleaning after them, or listening to their problems when they needed to talk.

If I worked every single minute, there was less time for guilt or the feeling of failure that plagued me ever since I dropped out of medical school for poor academic performance.

Also, my nightmares seemed to be occurring less when other people were around. So, if I didn't have a boyfriend to sleep at his place, I made an extra effort to pick up as many night shifts at the shelter as I could.

With my incomplete degree, without a job that would pay me instead of the other way around, I lived on the money from the trust fund set up for me by Henri, who never wanted much to do with me. The last conversation I had with him had taken just over ten minutes and consisted mostly of him yelling at me for failing in school. It was also the longest conversation I ever had with my father.

Yet I kept allowing his trust fund to support me, even as I donated almost all of the five-figure amount deposited into my account monthly to support the many charities on my list.

Listening to Jo's complaints about the lack of healthy food for children made me think about possibly rearranging some of that money around this month to see if I could buy some healthy snacks for school.

I wasn't staying in Rocky River long enough to start any long-term projects, but I could still find a way to help out a little.

AS SOON AS I COULD move around with the assistance of a walking stick, I made my way to the general store in Rocky River.

There, I stood in front of a pharmacy shelf, feeling rather at a loss as to what sort of medicine to get for Monster. Would human medicine work on him at all? Or did he mean for me to get it from a vet? What animal could I even tell the vet I needed the pills for?

With a sigh, I grabbed two family-size bottles of painkillers from the shelf and limped towards the cashier. According to the expiry date on the bottles, the pills were good for two years. They should last him for a while before he needed a refill.

How *would* he get a refill? Did someone use to get him pills before me? Was it the same person who taught him how to speak English?

Somehow the monster knew of painkillers in the first place. In fact, judging by the manner of his speech, he seemed to be very well acquainted with the modern human world. As if he had been a part of it once.

If he had, would there possibly be other things he'd miss?

I passed by a display of fruit. Fresh fruit was not cheap around here, and the selection was rather small.

Oranges would be definitely one of the many things I'd miss if I lived alone in Boreal forest.

On impulse, I picked up one of the three oranges on display and placed it on the cashier's counter along with the bottles of painkillers.

# Chapter 13

## Sophie

The forest looked very different from the previous week. Since I'd been here last, close to two feet of snow had fallen, weighing down the branches of the tall pine trees and covering the ground with pristine white.

The snowfall stopped two days ago, and by now most of the roads had been cleared. Even the private forestry road that led to Monster's property was passable.

Bob's old pickup, which I had borrowed for the trip, held its own, going through the icy patches of frozen mud and taking me to the chain-link fence in just over two hours.

It was barely noon when I pulled over and trudged through the snow on the side of the road.

I was much better dressed this time—snow pants, hooded parka, and winter boots, not to mention a warm hat, scarf, and gloves. My leg hardly hurt anymore, but I still walked with a slight limp and used a walking stick to help me make my way through snow and ice.

Monster told me to leave the bag by the fence, and I stopped hesitantly. How long would it take him to find the bag? It wasn't like he came here looking for it every day, was it? What if it took him a few days to pick it up?

The damn orange would definitely freeze by then or some forest critter would find it. My impulse purchase quickly turned from a goodwill gesture into an inconvenience, and I felt stupid for making it.

He probably doesn't even eat oranges. He hunts rabbits, for goodness sake!

I shuffled through the snow to the opening that Jason had cut in the fence and crawled through it to the other side. Walking along the fence for a little while, I was still thinking what to do about the stupid orange. What if I tied the bag to a tree branch? Would it be any safer than leaving it on the ground?

I didn't hear him approach. Somehow the snow didn't crunch or squeak under his paws. I knew he was there only when I was spun around and thrust against the fence, the air was knocked out of my chest, and the plastic bag fell out of my hand.

"What are you doing here?" His breath misted the air between us, his gaze fierce. "I told you not to come back."

"Monster . . ." I croaked, trying to calm my racing heart, which wasn't easy as the bulk of him still hovered uncomfortably close to me.

With his hands on each side of my head, he hooked the claws through the links of the fence. His body came flush with mine, and his snout dipped to my face.

"You shouldn't have come," he rasped against the skin on my cheek and rubbed the side of his face against mine.

I felt his cold nose travel along my cheekbone then down the side of my neck.

The initial fright of his sudden appearance eased, but the tiny icy needles of trepidation were still there. His voice, his touch, even his words felt both unnerving and intimate at the same time.

"I—I brought your medicine." I winced, wishing he would let me go.

We weren't on the ground. He was not lying on top of me. But the heavy weight of him and the cage of his arms were beginning to feel too restrictive.

My complete inability to move triggered the old feeling of helplessness, sending my heart into overdrive. I fought the familiar panic already tightening my throat and desperately tried to stall the imminent meltdown.

"The painkillers . . . Remember?"

"Of course you did. Wouldn't that be just like you? Cute, little Sophie shows up in the dark, desolate place, bringing in light and medicine." His voice sounded coarse, and his words delirious. "Did you bring your asshole photographer, too? To document your act of kindness?"

What was he saying? And why?

He pushed further into me, rocking his hips into my lower stomach. The fence groaned under the pressure.

"Let me go." It came out more like a warning than a plea while I clung to the shreds of my control.

My breathing turned shallow and fast, and my sight dimmed and narrowed to a black, cloudy tunnel.

"What if I don't? What if I hold on to you this time and never let go, keeping you all to myself?" His breath was hot against my neck. His words made no sense.

The suffocating helplessness of being trapped—unable to move—closed in on me.

Choked with horror, I could barely hear him.

The next moment, the incoming wave of full-on panic attack hit all my senses.

"No! Please. Let me go!" A terrified shrill cut through me as I thrashed against him. "Get off me! Get your hands off me! Don't touch me. Don't you ever, ever touch me!" My hands in front of me, I tore blindly at something—everything that hovered over me, shrouded me, tortured me for years. "Let! Me! Go!"

"I did." The deep voice came calm and low, reaching me as if from far away. "Sophie, you're free."

Realizing that the heavy weight of his body was no longer there, I stopped fighting, and my senses slowly brought me back to reality.

I stood with my back to the fence, my fingers curled through the links, flexing so hard, the metal cut painfully through my gloves.

My eyes were open, but the world remained out of focus. Everything was just a swirl of white snow streaked with the brown of the tree trunks, Monster's blurry shape a dark shadow at my side.

My knees gave in, and I slid to the ground.

I recognized the knitted thing on the snow in front of me as my hat, which I must have lost during my frenzy.

My chin trembled, and I closed my eyes again feeling two warm streams roll down my cheeks. I inhaled deeply, mentally counting while I caught my breath.

"I'm okay," I whispered, using every single bit of my mental power to will the black wave to retreat. "I'm free. I'm fine. It will pass. It always does."

"Always?" The soft fur of his knuckles brushed against my cheeks, soaking up the wet trails of tears. "How often does this happen to you?"

"I can't . . ." I shook my head vehemently, without answering his question. "I can't be held down. I can't be restrained . . . I have to move. I need to breathe . . ."

It was worse than that—any contact, with even a hint of being sexual, especially, if mixed with any kind of aggression, could trigger a panic attack in me.

No surprise that none of my boyfriends stayed for long. In fact, the two full months with Jason was the longest relationship I ever had. He just didn't seem to care enough to be bothered by my issues.

Monster remained silent for a few seconds as I focused all my attention on one deep breath after another.

"Since when?" He asked softly, and I noticed that he was now sitting in the snow next to me. "What happened?"

"Nothing happened," I replied quickly. "I'm fine because nothing happened," I repeated the same thing I'd kept telling myself for eight years now, shoving the dark memories deep into the pit of oblivion they had crawled out from triggered by his actions. "I'll be fine. A little air, and I'll be fine."

He shifted uncomfortably but, thankfully, didn't insist on an answer.

"I'm sorry, Sophie." His voice was rough and strained, as if it cost him a tremendous effort to utter the apology. "I didn't think—" Elbows on his knees, he raked his claws through his mane. "When I realized you were here . . ." He spoke slowly, choosing the words with care. "I spent the last days trying hard not to *feel* anything, hoping it would be possible. But one whiff of your scent—" He drew in a deep inhale. "And it all came back again—anger, memories, pain . . . things I don't even have a name for."

His voice sounded soft in the snow-filled landscape.

I thought back to the night I spent here and to the emotions he displayed then—rage, dislike, annoyance of having to look after me. I recalled him talking about the irritating feeling in his head every time someone came here, and a flush of embarrassment heated my face.

He had made it clear he didn't want me on the property. Last time, he couldn't wait to get rid of me in the morning. He'd told me just to leave the medicine by the fence.

Yet here I was, trespassing once again.

"I'd better go." I searched the ground for my walking stick.

"Let me take you to the house," his voice was rough, but with a note of unexpected concern. "You shouldn't drive in this state."

His fingers closed around my walking stick the moment mine did, and I lifted my gaze to his.

In the light of the bright winter day, I could see every single detail about him clearly. Everything I had missed before.

His eyes, for one. How could anyone miss those eyes? They were as complex and mysterious as the woods around us. There was the green of the moss, the brown of the bark, even the specks of gold and crimson of the autumn leaves—all the colours of the forest before the snow hid them from sight.

When he stared at me like this, I could even catch glimpses of sunlight filtering through, bathing me with warmth.

He still looked every bit the beast he was, but the thought and emotion in those brilliant hazel eyes were wholly human.

"I'll start a fire," he continued. "You can rest and warm up for a while."

I shook my head.

"You said you didn't want me here. There is a nagging feeling because of my presence."

He tilted his head, holding my gaze.

"Well, without anyone's presence there is just an empty void."

The brief flash of pain in his eyes, more than anything else he could have done or said, compelled me to nod in agreement. I didn't want to leave him just yet. Still, the little icy needles that had prickled my insides with trepidation I experienced in his presence prompted me to reply cautiously.

"You scare me."

The autumn forest in his eyes frosted over.

"I scare myself." Bitterness overpowered the sadness in his tone.

"Promise me that you won't hurt me, and I'll believe you."

"I promise," he said without hesitation. "I will not hurt you, Sophie."

He had proven to me that I could rely on his word when he helped me survive that night. I believed I could take the chance and extend my trust once more.

With another brief nod, I put my hat back on and accepted his hand when he rose to his feet, helping me up, too.

"I'll carry you." He picked up the bag. "It'll be faster that way."

I paused, unsure if I was ready for this much of a close contact with him again.

"Please, Sophie," he added, seeing my hesitation.

My eyes shot up to his in surprise—first a *sorry*, now a *please*. So different from his usual rudeness. Astonished, I couldn't form a reply right away.

He waited for a few seconds, shifting from foot to foot, then must have taken my silence for agreement and lifted me up in his arms.

The ends of his fur were frozen in sharp spikes, prickling my cheek when I leaned against his shoulder. I noted that the smell of wet dog was absent this time despite the dampness of his fur. Instead, the freshness of frost and the warm, earthy scent of his skin filled my nostrils. I believed I even caught a trace of something like a men's cologne or body wash.

"You smell nice," I smiled.

He cleared his throat and shrugged awkwardly.

"There was shower gel left at the house."

"You took a shower?"

"No, the water at the house is off. I bathe in the river."

"Even when it's this cold?"

"The river doesn't freeze all the way," he explained casually, as if the fact that he didn't have to hack through the ice to go for a dip made the whole winter swimming absolutely normal.

"The cold doesn't bother you?"

"I like swimming." He glided smoothly through the snow, maneuvering between the trees. "It does get too cold around here, even for me, but most of the year I'm okay."

"Do you live in the house at all?" I remembered the abandoned state of the place again, but he managed to make the fire that night, and he knew that the fireplace downstairs was in working order.

"No."

"Are there others, like you?" It was impossible not to think about where he came from and who he was.

"Others like me?" he scoffed. "I hope not."

"You *hope*? Would you rather be alone? Don't you have a family?"

"Sophie." He stopped suddenly but didn't set me down. "I'd need a promise from you, too."

"You won't tell me where you came from, will you?"

Slowly, he moved his head side to side.

"No. And I don't want you to waste your time asking those questions. Will you promise me not to ask them again?"

I paused, searching for a way to refuse. Not finding one, I nodded, with regret.

"I promise."

# Chapter 14

## Sophie

It was obvious Monster hadn't spent any time inside the house since my night here. The front door was half-open again, and the wind had blown enough snow on both sides to keep it frozen in that state until the first thaw if no one hacked it off before then. The heavy, red blanket was still hanging over the broken back door, stopping drafts from blowing through the house.

As soon as I limped to the couch, Monster took one of the bottles with painkillers out of the bag and dumped a few of the pills in his palm.

"They're extra strength," I warned. I couldn't tell exactly how many pills he had, but it was definitely more than the recommended dose of two.

"Well," he shrugged, "it *extra* fucking hurts," and shoved the handful in his mouth then went to get a fire started.

"You probably shouldn't take any more pills today," I offered tentatively, watching him quickly making the flames dance in the fireplace. "Or you might hurt your stomach."

"Couldn't be any worse than that rotten deer carcass I fed on once," he retorted gruffly.

"What?" I snorted, my eyebrows rose high in disbelief as my mouth twitched in disgust. "Why would you do that?"

"Obviously, I'm not what one would call *a picky eater*." He smirked and added, "I was pretty hungry. But yeah, it wasn't fun for a couple of days afterwards."

He shrugged. The movement jolted his head a little, and I noticed a slight wince in his expression when he came back to the couch.

"Is it the horns?" I asked as he sat on the floor with his back against the couch next to my knees. "The horns give you headaches?"

"Yeah. They are a pain. In more ways than one." He leaned his head back and closed his eyes. "It will get better soon. It usually does through the day."

He had said so before, but it was afternoon already and the pain was obviously still there.

Only because he happened to be exactly in the same position as he sat the last time, I ventured to offer again. "Did, um, did the massage help at all? I could try again. If you want."

As if he had just waited for me to offer, he shifted closer immediately and leaned against my knees, tipping his head back, into my lap.

Slowly, I raked my hands through his mane from the furry points of his ears up to his horns.

"Fuck, it's good," he groaned when I made the first set of circles along his temples.

"It's helping?" It was always so exciting to hear from people that my efforts loosened the hold of their pain.

"Mmhmm, don't stop," he murmured, his eyes closed. His long, thick eyelashes fluttered a little. The lashes seemed too beautiful and almost out of place on a beast.

Beast?

I felt a sharp jolt of shame, catching myself thinking about him as an animal. He might refuse to explain who he was, but I didn't need his answer to know by now that there was enough of a human in him to be treated as such.

Gently, I massaged around the base of his horns. Despite his occasional satisfied grunts, his whole body seemed extremely tense. Even through the snow pants I was wearing, I could feel the hard cords of the tightly knotted muscles in his back.

After finishing the basic steps around his forehead and horns, I raked my fingers through his mane again, applying even pressure here and there for a general head massage to relax him a little.

Thick and wavy, the golden-brown strands felt soft when I dipped my fingers into them. Even hopelessly tangled, the fur of his mane was surprisingly silky.

My fingers still deep in his mane, I leaned in and whispered in his pointy ear, "It's done. Are you feeling better now?"

It took him a moment to reply, as if my hands had put him in trance and he needed some time to come back.

"I better be," he smirked finally, "after the pile of pills I just took."

I flexed my fingers, tugging on his mane slightly. His promise not to harm me made me bolder.

"You have a hard time being nice, don't you?" I said sweetly, still leaning to his ear. "All you have to do is say *thank you*."

A smile curved his mouth, putting the sharp, snow-white canines on display.

"Thank you."

"See. It wasn't that hard, was it?" I beamed.

"You have no idea." He exhaled a laugh in return.

"It should get easier with practice." I patted his shoulder reassuringly. "You just have to do it more often."

"Practice?" he scoffed, turning more my way. "What for? There is no one around."

"Well," I suggested slowly. "You could do it simply for the inner satisfaction of being a decent human being."

"*Human*?" He lifted a bushy eyebrow in question. "Do you see anything human in me?"

"Yes," I nodded firmly. "You wouldn't tell me who you are, but—"

"I have no idea *who* I am myself," he barked out abruptly, leaping to his feet.

"Maybe you don't." I rose from my seat too. "But you have a conscience, awareness. You *know* right from wrong. Start from there—"

"Start what? *Being a decent human being*?" His voice rose, heavy with sarcasm, as he paced the room. His tail lashed at his legs with force. "When I look in the mirror, all I see is a beast. There is nothing left of a man, Sophie. Not a thing. There's no way back for me."

"Back?" I whispered, as realization jolted through me like a bolt of lightning. "What do you mean by *back*?"

He stopped in his tracks at my question, his back to me. His shoulders heaved as his tail continued to whip around his legs, but he wouldn't face me.

"Did you—" I took a few steps around him to see his face, but he turned his head away, refusing to meet my eyes. "Were you a man before?" I leaned to the side, needing to see his expression. "Were you born a human?"

Slowly, he moved his head my way, and his stare hit me from under the heavy brow.

Something in the way his eyes flickered between mine for a second made me hopeful that he might explain it all to me. At least he appeared to be considering it for a moment.

"You were, weren't you? What happened then?"

He blinked, his expression turned stony.

"You promised," he snarled. "No questions."

"Right. No questions." I nodded with a sigh of disappointment settling heavy in my chest. "I just hope that one day you will trust me enough to tell me."

"One day?" he asked quickly. His eyes squinted at me inquisitively. "Will you come back again?"

"Um," I twirled the end of my ponytail. Caught unprepared by his question, I realized now that I did want to come back, if just to see how he was doing. Any distant chance of solving the mystery surrounding him was an added incentive. "Well, I'm staying in town for a little while. I could come back. Is there anything else you need me to bring?"

"Yes." His answer was quick.

"Okay. What is it?"

"A lot of things, actually." His tone was lighter now, and his shoulders finally relaxed. "Come, we should get on our way if you want to make it back to town before dark. I'll tell you what I need while we're walking."

"IS YOUR LEG OKAY?" Monster asked again as we headed through the woods.

"It's fine. Honestly." I insisted on walking this time. The snow wasn't that deep under the trees, and there were still a few hours of daylight left. "It was just a sprain, nothing was broken."

"When are you planning to go home to Calgary?" He matched his pace to mine, which made him appear like he was on a leisurely stroll even as my own cheeks heated and my breath came out in pants as if from a strenuous workout.

"When my leg gets better," I answered mechanically, giving him the same answer I'd given to anyone who asked.

I tried to think if I ever actually told him that I lived in Calgary. Maybe I mentioned it sometime the night I spent here, but I couldn't remember it now.

There was certainly no rush for me to go back home. Sadly I had to admit there was no one and nothing that waited for me in the city.

All my volunteering positions were still there for me, but after exchanging emails with my supervisors, I had been reassured all my work had been covered for the time being.

I missed my mom, of course, but she was in the third month of her relationship with Jeff, the first decent man she had met in years. Even before my trip here, she spent more time at his place than ours, making me feel like I was the mother watching my grown-up daughter leave home to build a new life for herself, instead of the other way around. With her gone most of the time, our townhouse definitely felt a lot like an empty nest to me.

I was very happy for my mom. She, of all people, deserved to be loved. But I wasn't looking forward to coming back to the empty house. Not yet, anyway.

It wasn't that I had a lot going for me in Rocky River either, but I had been enjoying the quiet pace of life there.

"Actually, I'd like to start something at the school in Rocky River, so I may stay around for another couple of weeks at least. You know, to make sure it's all up and running properly before I leave."

"What is it?"

I didn't sense any real interest behind his question and could tell he was asking just to be polite. Still, he was making an effort at conversation.

"Well, you know it's not always easy for schools or parents to provide healthy lunches for kids. Around here it's especially challenging—fresh, healthy food is not cheap and not always available. I thought I could hire Melanie—she and her husband Bob own a restaurant in town—to cater hot lunches for the kids during school. Something simple but nutritious. Like soup or a healthy sandwich. Maybe a small salad and some fruit, too. Stan, the store manager, could get the necessary groceries on order." The idea took shape in my mind as I spoke. "Maybe just once a week for now. I can also talk with the owners of the charter company here, to see if their pilots could bring some fresh groceries whenever they fly to bigger towns nearby—" I cut myself short, realizing I was babbling, the way I often did in the company of a man, especially, if I found him attractive.

I blinked, surprised by the thought. Monster could hardly be called *attractive*, not by any stretch of imagination.

Could he?

I peered at him from the corner of my eye. Tall and broad, his shoulders wide, his head held high, he strode through the snow with ease. Each movement alluded to power and strength.

With his polished horns winding out of his head, tail swishing at his feet, thick, brown fur dusted with snow from the trees, no one would call him handsome by human standards. No one would even call him human, based on his appearance.

Could he still be considered attractive, though?

Why would I even wonder about it, at all?

I cleared my throat, annoyed at myself. "I'm sorry. I get carried away sometimes, talking about things that wouldn't interest anyone."

"I find it fascinating."

I glanced at him again, wondering if he was being sarcastic.

"Sure you do." I moved my gaze to the snow churning around my boots with each step.

A rather uncomfortable silence hovered over us, and I didn't trust myself to break it again—chances were I'd pick another boring topic anyway.

"What's in it for you?" Monster spoke first. The hostile note in his voice puzzled me.

"What do you mean?"

"You're paying out of your own pocket to feed a bunch of kids you don't know. What are you getting out of it? I don't imagine there are many PR opportunities around this godforsaken place. Or is your asshole photographer creating a documentary about your virtuous nature after all?"

"What are you talking about?" I shook my head, confused. "Jason left already. We broke up. I'm not sure what's made you angry this time. I have a charity budget for each month. And I just happened to be able to allocate some of the money for a school lunch program in Rocky River." I stopped walking to face him. "Why is it wrong for me to feed these children, in your opinion?"

"Don't tell me you're not getting credit for your good deeds here."

"I'm not interested in PR opportunities, if that's your concern."

"Fine." He met my gaze. "What are your reasons then? Simply good karma? Are you hoping to secure a place in heaven?"

The undisguised sarcasm in his tone was irritating. I hated to be put on defensive for doing something that felt right. The note of hostility behind his questions bothered me. I might not be perfect, but I didn't want him to think badly of me.

Deep inside, however, I knew what made me annoyed more than his tone. For the first time ever, someone questioned my true motives, forcing me to acknowledge them.

I could have voiced my annoyance or fake offense, brush off his questions or just ignore them all. But something about being this far away from my life in the city led me to believe that anything I told him here would stay between us, prompting me to explain.

"I've been doing charity for years now. I started volunteer work when I was still a kid. Then in high school I got more into it. And now, that's all I do." I kicked the snow with my boot, watching it fan out, as I tried to put into words things I never had to explain to anyone. "It gives purpose to my life. I don't feel alone—there're always people at the shelters or at the Soup Kitchen. No one asks me questions about me, everyone has their own problems to worry about." I inhaled, raising my gaze to the snow-covered branches behind his shoulder. "I like to think that I'm helping solve their problems a little just by being there for them. I wish I could do more, advise them in some helpful way. But really, people are grateful if you just listen. Even the ones who don't want to talk sometimes don't want to be alone. I stay with them, read them a newspaper. Sometimes, all you want is to hear another person's voice to keep away the loneliness . . ."

"Whose loneliness?" His voice came from above, calm and thoughtful. "Whose loneliness are you trying to keep away, Sophie? Theirs or yours?"

Both.

Definitely both. Because despite my mom and her friends, despite the occasional boyfriends I managed to have, I was always alone in my head—one on one with my thoughts and my nightmares.

I wasn't ready for this confession right now, though. My chest tightened with sadness that threatened to drown me, and I shoved it aside, refusing to dive any deeper in it.

"Theirs, Monster. I try to keep people at the shelter from feeling lonely. That's all I can do, really, in addition to cleaning or paperwork, as well as donations for food and maintenance. I wish I could be more helpful in terms of advice too, but I'm not a counselor—"

"You could be."

His scrutinizing expression made me feel like he could see right through me.

"Hardly," I scoffed. "I already have one failed attempt at higher education—"

"How did you fail?"

"I dropped out of medical school. I didn't pass the first-year exams, but really my grades were so low, I should've been expelled earlier. My father's influence was the only thing that kept it going as long as it lasted. Anyway, it's stupid to keep trying the same thing and expect different results. Right?"

"Bullshit." The conviction in his voice was startling. "You're not stupid, Sophie. The excuse *is*, though. Just because you failed at becoming a doctor doesn't mean you can't do something else. Did you figure out exactly why it didn't work for you? How come you had bad grades? Did you even want to be a doctor in the first place?"

I plucked at the fringe of my scarf, considering his questions.

In high school, I wanted to be a nurse, but Henri pushed a career in law or finance on me. Medical doctor was a compromise, one which Henri was not happy with—but for the first time in my life I had insisted on something and went against his plans for me.

Of course, when I failed, he was simply livid with rage. He claimed he'd always known I'd turn out to be a disappointment because there was too much of my mother in me. He yelled he never wanted to see me again.

It was the last time I saw him. Over three years ago.

"Honestly, it doesn't matter what I want, Monster. I don't think I could keep up with any program. I did okay until about the last couple of years of high school."

In fact, I had all A's and was going to graduate with honours. But then I started having trouble. I couldn't focus for long on anything. No matter how hard I intended to listen to the teachers, the meaning of what they were saying wouldn't register with me. Anxiety would kick in, paralyzing any comprehension. Eventually, studying became a real struggle and I began avoiding it at all cost. In university, I was skipping classes whenever I could, which made matters only worse of course.

"I can't concentrate on academic studies long enough to learn."

"You wouldn't know for sure unless you try studying something you really like," he retorted.

"Maybe."

I hadn't even noticed that we'd made it all the way back to the fence until it was right in front of me.

"You never told me what you want me to bring you next time," I reminded.

"Next time?" He blinked as if snapping back from his thoughts.

"Do you want me to drop by again?"

"Yes." He nodded quickly and raked the fingers of both hands through his mane. "Could you bring me some fuel?"

"Like gas?"

"Yes. Just make sure it's premixed with two-stroke oil. Tell them it's for a chainsaw."

"A chainsaw?" I raised an eyebrow. "Do you need a more efficient way to deal with trespassers?"

The corners of his mouth lifted in a smile.

"No. The sight of me is enough to chase them away. I just need to do some housekeeping around here."

"Okay. I'll bring you some."

"When you come, get on this side of the fence and stay by the opening here. Don't walk through the forest by yourself. As long as you're on this side of the fence, I'll know you're here and come to get you."

THROUGH THE REARVIEW mirror, I watched Monster's lone figure at the edge of the woods as I drove away.

He asked me about feeling lonely in a city filled with people. How desperate his own loneliness must be then, with not a soul to talk to?

How could one still hold on to any humanity inside, being this completely and utterly alone?

# Chapter 15

## Monster

She'll come back again.

Monster watched the old truck disappear behind the trees. The remnants of her tantalizing scent still tickled his nostrils. The memories of her light fingers in his mane teased his senses, sending a rush of blood to his groin once again.

Through a tremendous effort, he had been managing to control his feral lust around her, shoving the wild urges aside with everything he had.

Still forced to jerk off like a horny teenager when she was safely out of his reach, he held back any thought of ripping those puffy snow pants off her when she was near.

The trick, as he'd discovered, was not to get too close and not to breathe her scent in too deeply whenever he felt another rush of lust approach.

Slowly, painfully, he had been learning to control his raging desire for her body. However, the simple longing for her company proved to be so much more difficult to deal with.

When she left, his prison felt only more oppressive. The woods seemed colder and emptier without her here, the loneliness even more unbearable.

He couldn't go back to the simple existence of an animal in search of oblivion any more. As long as there was another chance to see her, he needed to hold on to any trace of human he had inside him.

With her, he wanted to be a man, regardless of what painful emotions and tormenting memories it brought to him. He would take the pain as long as it came with the pleasure of hearing her voice and feeling her touch.

It surprised him to discover that his yearning was not just physical. He'd never felt anything beyond sexual desire for a woman before. The glimpses of Sophie as a person, however, stirred his curiosity to know more.

Her genuine need to help turned out to be so different from the motivations of people in his past. Their actions were always dictated from outside, and their concerns were only about how they would be taken by others. Sophie's motivation seemed to be coming from the inside, and the benefits were also intrinsic.

A warm rush of excitement tingled along his skin at the thought of seeing her again soon. Even as a teenager, he never recalled feeling this much anticipation before a date.

Not a date, you moron. The girl is bringing you gas out of the goodness of her heart. Nothing else.

There never could be anything else.

He hadn't seen himself in the mirror for many years now—ever since he'd destroyed all the mirrors in the house—but he still occasionally glimpsed his reflection in the river and knew that one thing never changed. He was still a monster. On the outside, just as much as he had always been on the inside.

And here he was luring an innocent back into the den of the beast.

Guilt scratched at his conscience again, dousing any spark of excitement, and a black cloud of anger moved in from the far corners of his awareness.

With a snarl, he leaped to his feet and sped through the woods, east to the river, needing the icy water to smother the flames of impending fury.

As he dashed faster and faster through the trees, knocking the snow off the low-hanging branches, he realized that his anger was not directed at the world, at the circumstances or at other people, but at himself.

There was not one thing in his past that he could look back at with pride or satisfaction.

He had no one to blame for what he had become.

It was not his appearance that would make it impossible for Sophie to ever look at him with anything but disgust and revulsion if she only knew who he was.

He had hurt her long ago. And some things could never be repaired or forgiven.

# Chapter 16

## Sophie

I was busy with Jo the following day. Then another snowfall made all roads impassable, and I had to wait for them to be cleared. As it turned out, it took four days before I was able to head out to the house in the woods.

I got a couple of jerry cans full of chainsaw fuel at the general store, along with some tea bags and cookies. Stan gave me a funny look as he rang my purchases through the cash register, but thankfully didn't ask any questions.

I saw Monster behind the trees on the other side of the fence as soon as the property came into view. His dark, russet fur made a striking contrast to the white snow as he paced on all fours between the tree trunks.

Seeing him from a distance, I could fully appreciate his magnificent form. Large and powerful, he moved with a feline grace through the deep snow at the edge of the woods. His long, furry tail swished around his hind legs, fanning the snow in bursts of glitter that sparkled under the bright sunlight.

He held his head unnaturally still, even as he moved. I knew it was most likely to avoid aggravating his headache, however, it gave his movements an especially dignified appearance.

The regal poise with which he carried his long winding horns reminded me of a majestic elk with a full rack of magnificent antlers.

I'd promised not to ask him questions, but it didn't mean they didn't swirl around my mind almost constantly. Who was he? And what happened to him?

Somebody had to have taught him to speak English, had shown him how to start a fire, how to cook meat.

*"There is no coming back."*

The memory of his words tugged at my heart.

The fact that he was alone now, without any apparent contact with people except for me, was therefore only more heartbreaking. If something happened to him, no one would be there to help. Being possibly the only person aware of his existence, I might be the only link to the world for him.

He moved closer to the fence the moment I pulled the truck over, but he didn't climb through the opening to greet me.

"Have you been waiting here long?" I stomped through the snow with a heavy jerry can in each hand and a plastic bag with tea and cookies around my wrist.

"Four days. With a few breaks."

"Four days?"

"It's not like I have a super busy schedule." He shrugged.

I noticed a patch of packed snow by the nearby bush, as if a large animal lay there at least since the snowfall.

Did he really sleep here, waiting for me?

"I'm sorry. There was so much snow, I had to wait for the roads to be cleared—"

Still unsteady on my feet without the walking stick, I tripped over the snow bank and lurched forward. Dropping the jerry cans and flailing my arms in the air in a futile struggle to keep my balance, I leaned too far back.

"Careful!" I heard Monster's warning a moment before I landed on my ass.

"Shoot."

"Sophie. Are you okay?" Monster's strained voice reached me.

He stood in the opening of the fence, his fingers curled through the chain links, the claws fully extended.

"I'm fine. No damage done this time, just to my dignity," I assured him with a short laugh and climbed out of the snow bank with all the grace of a yeti packed in a puffy snowsuit. "I may need some help with these, though." I gestured at the heavy jerry cans, half buried in the snow wherever I dropped them.

"I can't." His grave voice drew my attention to his face. His expression was dark. "I can't get to you, Sophie."

"What do you mean?" I wrestled one jerry can out from the snow and carried it to the fence, holding it by the handle with both hands. "Why?" I sat it down by my side.

His eyes followed my movements, but he remained in place.

"I can't cross the property line. I can't leave the estate."

Puzzled, I considered his words.

"Is it psychological? Like when people can't leave the house?"

He frowned in reply and shoved away from the fence suddenly then slammed his fist at the opening. I jumped in surprise. His fist didn't go through. As if it had encountered some obstacle in the air, the force of his blow threw his arm back, jerking his whole body back, too.

"It's very much physical, princess," he growled.

"What was that?" I lifted both hands in the air and leaned into the opening in the fence in search of the invisible barrier that stopped Monster's fist. Not feeling anything, I almost lost my balance again, nearly falling through to the other side. "There is nothing here."

With my gloved finger, I traced the edge of the cut.

"Stay back," Monster bit out a curt warning, allowing me to stagger aside as he took a few steps back himself before lunging at the fence again.

He crashed into it with his shoulder this time. The full impact of his massive body sent him back through the air, and he landed heavily the good ten feet away from the fence.

"Stop it!" I leaped through the opening and rushed to him. It was painful to watch him thrash against his cage like a wounded animal. I couldn't even begin to imagine how it must have felt to him. "Oh, God, Monster, are you okay?" I sank into the snow at his side as he rose to his elbows, still lying on his back.

"It's real." He shot a hateful glare at the opening in the fence. "I can't leave." His gaze travelled to mine, and his features softened, as the rays of warmth made their way through the dark clouds of pain and rage in his eyes. "I'm trapped in here, Sophie."

"How?" I brushed the snow off his mane and shoulders. "What is this thing?"

"I don't know." He sat up. "But I do know that it's an impenetrable wall for me. All around the estate. I can't walk through it. Can't climb over it, no matter how high I climb. If I try to run through it, I get thrown back. If I run faster, I only get tossed back harder."

"How about the river? You said there is a river running through, right?"

He nodded.

"The river marks the western boundary. The property line must be right in the middle of the stream because that's as far as I can swim. I can't cross to the other side." He paused for a second. "I've tried it all, Sophie. Trust me."

I sat back, disheartened. I trusted he had explored every possibility of getting out of his invisible jail, but I struggled with the fact of its existence in the first place.

"Why is it here, Monster? How did it happen?"

"You promised not to ask questions," he reminded me quietly. "But even if you didn't, I couldn't answer them all anyway. I don't know exactly how all of this works."

"But this is not right," I argued. "You're being held a prisoner here. Who is doing this to you? And why? What crimes have you committed?"

"Many." He got up slowly. "I've done many things, none of which I'm proud of, and all of them I now bitterly regret."

"Are you saying you deserve this?" I exclaimed, scrambling to my feet, too, and pointing at the fence behind us.

"Yes." He grabbed my shoulders, his glare pinning me in place. "I deserve all of it. It took me years to realize it, let alone admit it to you now. But every single thing that happened to me I brought on myself, actively ignoring any path to salvation until it was too late. And here I am, a hideous monster, a pathetic creature from a nightmare, sitting like a dog by the fence for four days, waiting for you to return." His fingers dug into my shoulders as his gaze slid from my eyes to my lips. "And I didn't mind the wait. For the first time in years, I had something to look forward to. Will you still come to the house with me, knowing all of this?"

I couldn't reply right away, stunned by the passion of his admissions.

"I've told you enough for you to leave and never come back," he added.

Enough for me to understand how utterly alone he truly was, too—trapped in here by the fence and imprisoned inside his mind by his regrets.

I lifted my chin up. "I have no reason to run. Regardless of what happened in your past, I have no reason to fear you now. I have your promise not to harm me."

His chest heaved with a deep inhale as he broke eye contact.

"It is wrong for me to invite you here again and again." He shook his head as his shoulders slumped in defeat. "But I don't have it in me to refuse your company."

"Why is it wrong?" I hurried after him on his way back to the opening in the fence. "I came here willingly. It's not like you've forced me . . . I like being able to help. Besides," I added quietly. "I like your company, too."

He stopped abruptly, shooting me a surprised glance.

"You do?"

"Yes." My focus suddenly shifted to my fingers as I fidgeted with the edge of my scarf. "I like talking to you, despite all your growls and glowering. You're not a bad listener."

He cleared his throat, stepping from foot to foot, but didn't reply.

"I'll pass you the cans," I said to break the silence and slid through the opening back to the road again.

He grabbed the jerry cans when I lifted them through the hole in the fence. And I picked up my bag with tea and cookies.

"How is your leg?" he asked on our way to the house.

"Much better. Thank you." My limp was a little more profound when walking through the snow. However, there was no longer any pain and I didn't need a walking stick to get around.

We made our way to the house mostly in silence. I tried to start a conversation a couple of times, but it quickly died, as Monster seemed to be lost in thought, replying in monosyllables.

I noted that the front door was closed the moment we entered the front yard through the passage in the rose bushes. He must have cleaned the ice and snow that had held it half-open before. The porch seemed to have been cleared of snow, too.

Inside, the floors in the main room and the kitchen had been swept and instead of a blanket, several pieces of plywood had been nailed neatly to the frame of the broken back door. The cobwebs and dust had been swept off the remaining glass doors in the back, letting in more light.

"Wow, it's warm in here." I pulled off my hat and mittens, moving to the brightly lit fireplace.

"It takes a while to heat this house. I started the fire this morning." Monster's voice was gruff, but I sensed his satisfaction at my obvious pleasure.

"You did a good job. The place looks almost lived in. And I thought you didn't spend much time in here." I took off my parka, but left the boots and the snow pants on.

"I don't. Usually." He carried the fuel in the kitchen and then to the garage through the door there.

I followed him to the kitchen. The orange I got him last time was in a glass cookie jar on the island counter. Untouched.

"I brought some cookies," I announced when he returned. "And tea." I placed my bag on the counter.

He nodded then got the teakettle from a cabinet and filled it with water from the bucket nearby.

"Would you have some with me?" I watched as he carried the kettle to the fireplace and placed it on the wrought-iron stand over the flames.

"I'd rather not eat human food, Sophie."

"Why not? You don't like it?"

"It's not that," he heaved a sigh, rubbing the back of his neck. "It's just that it'd be harder to go back to eating raw venison again. You know . . . after you leave."

"Because there'd be no one to bring you cookies?" I whispered, lowering myself into the couch.

Without replying, he got busy getting my tea ready as I kept thinking about what he had just said.

I believed I could understand a little the reason for his initial hostility towards me now too. Over his time of being here, he had established a certain lifestyle. He'd learned not to *need* things he couldn't get. And here I came and disrupted this balance. Eventually, I would go back to Calgary, leaving him alone again.

"Monster." The name didn't make me wince anymore. Even as I wished he'd tell me his real name if he had one, I realized, this might be another one of his tactics to keep distance between us, for his self-preservation. "Could I help you in more ways than just bringing things for you? Can I do something that would last? Like, I don't know, something that would be helpful in the long run?"

He brought me my tea and joined me on the couch.

"A tempting offer, Sophie," he said softly. His eyes narrowed as he peered at me intently. His jaw flexed, the lips forming a thin line over the teeth—even the long canines disappeared from view—as he considered me for a moment. "I would love to bring the house back in order, but it may take some time. How long are you staying in Rocky River?"

"I haven't decided yet. I think I could stay until Christmas if it gives you enough time to get everything done. It's just over three weeks left. What exactly would you need me to do?"

"Three weeks is good," he nodded. "I'll take three weeks."

"What can I do?" I asked again.

He shifted on the couch to face me straight on.

"The house has been badly neglected, but I believe all services are still in working condition. I would like to bring them all up again. Electricity, running water, heating—"

"Are you planning to live here?"

"I used to. Until about three years ago. It hasn't been that long since everything was functioning."

"Alright, do you need me to call the utility company to turn it all on?"

"No. The house is completely off the grid. Solar power, geo-thermal heating, propane tanks outside, and a backup generator. I've learned to do a lot of things myself around here. But I need someone to call people to service the systems, to make sure it's okay to turn them on—an electrician, a plumber."

"Okay." My thinking processes finally got some traction too. "I could call someone to refill the propane tanks."

"A maintenance person should look at them first," he warned.

"How about sewage? Do you have a septic tank here? I'll find out who in town can pump it out." I swept the living room with my gaze quickly. "And the door—" I tipped my chin at the blanket.

"If you find a new one, I can replace it myself. Also, if you could send some mail to a law office in Calgary for me, I'll be able to pay for all these expenses."

"So, it is your house? You are the legal owner?"

His gaze slipped from my face, and he stretched his neck side to side, slowly, obviously stalling over his reply.

"Technically, my father's trust company is the owner. He's dead, and I'm the sole beneficiary."

I held my breath, welcoming any little bit of information about him and his past. I waited for him to continue, but he went quiet again.

"I'm so sorry, Monster. When did your father pass away?"

"Don't be sorry, Sophie." His tone hardened. "Not for him." He shook his mane. "Tell me about your family."

"My family?" He'd changed the subject so suddenly, I needed a moment to catch up.

"Yes. Are both of your parents still alive?"

"They are." I nodded. "I live with my mom. We get along very well, actually."

"Are your parents divorced then?"

"No. They were never married. My mom met Henri while back-packing in Europe after high school. Henri, well, he was on a rebellious streak at the time, I guess, travelling the world, looking for his purpose in life or . . . something. If there ever was a time for them to connect on any level at all, that was it. They had a few wild weeks together, before Henri's rebellion wore off and he returned home to France to take over his family business. My mom learned that she was pregnant with me several weeks later."

I didn't talk much about my parents. Normally, I didn't want my friends to know anything about my dad. His name and fortune only attracted unnecessary attention and seemed to cause people to form the wrong opinions about me too. And the few people who spoke to me in France didn't need or didn't want to know much about my mom.

Telling all this to Monster now felt different. He was so far removed from either Calgary or Paris that opening up to him was like making confessions in absolute privacy.

"Henri was not thrilled at the news of becoming a father. He had a vasectomy done the very same day my mom told him about me and refused to have any contact with us until I was about eight or nine."

"What changed then?" The genuine interest in Monster's expression prompted me to continue.

"Oh, nothing from our side. But that was when Henri remembered that there was a person carrying the legacy of his last name and became increasingly concerned about that legacy. He contacted my mom through his lawyers, demanding a custody agreement. My mom fought it at first but then gave up, realizing, I think, all the potential benefits I could reap by being accepted into the Morel family.

"Henri let us live where my mom wanted but insisted I come to his estate near Paris for one month each year."

I hated this part of their agreement the most. Instead of having a month of summer vacation like everyone else did, I had four weeks of grueling lessons with tutors hired by Henri to teach me French language, literature, and history.

"He was hardly around because he spent most of his time in a townhouse in Paris and came to the chateau only when he had a large company to entertain. When I visited, I was left in the care of his housekeeper and the Madame Morel of the month."

Monster snorted.

"You must have had an army of stepmothers."

"About a dozen, I think, not counting a few fiancées who didn't make it to wife status. All of them were pretty much the same—tall, slim and breathtakingly beautiful."

Unfortunately, their personality differed enough for them to have different and often confusing demands from me. Some of the Madames Morels assured me they wanted to be my best friend. Some treated me with the severity of a harsh schoolmistress. Some immediately had a set of external and internal makeovers planned for me. Honestly, I preferred the few who just chose to ignore me.

"Well, thanks to Henri's efforts, I speak fluent French. Despite his attitude and personality, though, I managed to fall in love with the country and its people. I still keep in touch with Madame Besson, Henri's long-term housekeeper." I smiled remembering Madame Besson's endless patience when I followed her around like a lost puppy all day, having nothing to do after my lessons and no one to play with in the huge and empty castle. "I turned eighteen, and I didn't have to go to France anymore."

"But you still went, didn't you?"

"I did," I replied with a short sigh. "I still went every year. It was stupid, I knew he didn't really care if I was there or not. But I felt like this was my one and only connection with him, something *he* wanted me to do after all, so I kept coming every summer until the fight over my failing school . . ."

I realized I had been talking about myself for quite a while and scanned Monster's face quickly. The way his eyes remained focused on me reassured me a little.

"I should be going back." I finished my now-barely-warm tea.

"Stay," he said quickly—his back straightened, his whole body suddenly visibly tense.

"It's going to be dark in a couple of hours," I reminded.

He blinked and nodded, getting up too.

"Sure. I'll walk you back to the truck." He held my parka open for me to put it on then wrapped my long scarf around my neck. "It's a long drive to do in one day, though, Sophie."

"It's not too bad once in a while. It's not like I'm here every day." I shrugged.

"Can you stay the night next time?" he asked unexpectedly, catching me completely off guard.

I couldn't think of a reply right away and just stood there for a moment, crushing my hat in my hands.

"Here?" I finally managed.

"I'll clean the fireplace upstairs," he continued, his eyes on mine. "The master bedroom will be warm. There are plenty of clean sheets in the linen closet, but you can take them to town with you to wash if you want, in case they smell moldy or dusty." His voice remained even, but the intensity with which he watched my expression betrayed his impatience for my answer.

"I—I'm not sure."

"I'll sleep down here or outside like I always do."

"What would I say to Bob and Melanie—?"

"Do you have to say anything at all? You're their tenant, not their daughter."

"I drive Bob's truck. What if he needs it for something that day?"

"What if he doesn't?" He tilted his head, cocking an eyebrow at me expectantly.

Bob and Melanie normally used a van for catering and delivering groceries. The truck was there for occasional larger hauls and driving out of town. Chances were I could keep it for two days if I needed it.

The truck was not my only concern, though.

"Are you still afraid of me?" His voice lowered.

I had been here alone with him for hours on a few occasions now, with no one to stop him from doing anything he wanted with me. Yet, I felt safe all this time. He acted as a gracious host lately, and I enjoyed our conversations.

"No. I'm not afraid of you anymore."

His expression remained somber, but his voice lifted.

"Have dinner with me next time. Then stay the night." He moved closer, invading my personal space. His warm scent suddenly made me want to bury my face in the fur on his chest, and I took a step back quickly, unnerved by my reaction to him.

"I—I thought you didn't want to eat human food . . ." I whispered, staring at my hat balled in my hands.

"I'll eat it, Sophie. With you." His deep voice grew softer and heavier at the same time, flowing over me. "Bring anything you like. Or I can roast another rabbit." He chuckled somewhere over my head, and I realized he'd come closer again.

I didn't move away this time. Instead, I closed my eyes and inhaled deeply, savoring his fresh, wild scent and reveling in the closeness of his large, powerful body.

A strong desire to drop the hat I was holding and rake my fingers through his thick fur, sink my hands into his mane and feel the softness of it on my face made me sway his way before I realized what I was doing. Quickly, I took another step back and cleared my throat, still avoiding any eye contact with him.

"I—I'll bring something. Something we could warm up in the fire . . . What is your favourite food? Is there anything you really miss?"

Not getting a reply, I cautiously lifted my gaze to his face.

His hazel eyes dark and heavy, his breathing shallow, his hands clasped behind his back, he stood in front of me like a mountain, obstructing everything else from view.

"Monster," I whispered. "Is there anything you'd like me to bring for dinner?"

His chest heaved, the long tongue darted out to wet his lips as the sharp fangs glistened in the afternoon sun.

"Beside yourself?" he rasped.

The feral note in his voice along with the wild glint in his eyes made me back up all the way to the door. Icy needles prickled along my skin. Only this time, there was a new warm tingle spreading from deep inside my chest down to below my waist.

"Maybe dinner is not such a good idea after all . . ." I breathed out.

"Popcorn, princess," Monster replied immediately. "Could you bring some popcorn, please? With butter."

"Popcorn." I nodded, relief stilling my trembling hands, as I sensed the tension in him ease and felt my own pulse slow down to a more normal rate. "I can do that."

# Chapter 17

## Sophie

We didn't set an exact date for our dinner. Mostly because I didn't know when I could have the truck for two consecutive days. Also, I started my work on school lunches with Jo, which needed my attention. As it turned out, I had to stay in town for the next three days.

Meanwhile, I found out all about the local services for Monster. Some technicians were available in Rocky River, but some had to be called in from other towns. I wasn't entirely sure how to go about it. On one hand, I had promised Monster not to tell anyone about his existence. On the other hand, I needed the owner of the property to give a formal work authorization to people to perform their services in his house.

All this time, the image of the large, furry figure would rise in my mind constantly. The warm, inviting scent of his body wouldn't leave my senses, wreaking havoc in my thoughts.

I understood the feelings of compassion and a budding friendship I had for him. What confused me were the tingles of excitement along my skin and the flutter of anticipation in my stomach when I thought about my next visit to the house in the woods. Was it normal to feel *that* way about someone covered with fur? Was it okay for me to find him attractive at all?

There was no one to answer these questions for me. I knew, however, that it was absolutely normal for me to doubt myself on everything. Ever since high school, I'd been having trouble making decisions and was constantly second-guessing everything I did.

Of one thing I *was* certain, though—I liked the way I felt when he was around. I enjoyed his company and was looking forward to our dinner together.

The first day I was available and could have the truck overnight, I drove to the Monster's house. I had washed a set of sheets from his linen closet, and packed a pot of Melanie's homemade stew along with some dinner rolls and salad.

I told Bob and Melanie that I was staying at a friend's house overnight, without explaining anything further. Melanie gave me a long penetrating stare and told me to be careful. I wondered if she'd assume I had a thing for a hunting guide from the lodge or one of the pilots. Without being able to tell her the truth, though, I had no choice but to let her make her own conclusions for now.

Monster waited on the other side of the chain-link fence for me when I approached. And my heart skipped a bit at the sight of him.

I noticed that the opening in the fence had been repaired, and Monster signaled me to drive further up the road before I had a chance to exit the truck.

A few hundred metres up, a section in the fence had been removed, and the impenetrable rose bushes had been cut down, revealing the long gravel driveway to the cabin.

I rolled the truck window down when Monster approached as soon as I turned onto the property.

"Did you do this all by yourself?" I gaped at the amount of work he'd managed in just a few days.

"No. I had a SWAT team of cute forest animals helping me, princess. Squirrels and rabbits are great at wielding a chainsaw." His light tone and the twinkle in his forest-coloured gaze sent a wide smile to my face. "Just drive up to the carport, Sophie, I'll meet you there."

Driving to the house along the cleared driveway was definitely much easier than hiking through the snow in the woods.

He caught up with me when I parked the truck in the carport.

"Are you trying to make it more enjoyable for me to come visit you?" I teased jumping out of the driver's seat.

"Sure." He started helping me unload the truck. "I'm well aware that my company alone is not that enticing. I need all the help I can get to lure you out here."

It was obvious he did more work inside the house too. The musty smell of an abandoned place was all but gone now. The furniture had been dusted and arranged properly throughout the living area. The freshly aired space, warmed by the flames from the fireplace, felt clean and inviting.

"You have a beautiful house, Monster. And you've made it warm and welcoming. Whenever did you manage all of this?" I glanced at him over my shoulder as he followed me to the kitchen with all the stuff from the truck.

"It was fun to be productive for a change." He rolled a shoulder. "It's not like I have a lot to do around here otherwise."

I noted that the kitchen cabinets had been wiped clean inside and out and started putting away some of the things I brought.

"Listen," I said. "Is there any chance you could talk to people from Rocky River? By phone, maybe?"

"To my knowledge, there is no cell phone reception here. And even if there was one." He leaned against the kitchen island, arms crossed on his broad chest. "How many people would actually believe *this* is a human voice," he flipped his thumb at his throat, "and not an animal growl."

I stared at him for a moment, the full comprehension of his situation hitting me anew.

"Maybe, you could write a letter of authorization or something? To allow me to act on your behalf in terms of making arrangements for the house maintenance?" Then a sudden thought crossed my mind. "You can read and write, can't you?"

He lifted a brow at me, tilting his head to the side.

"Yes, princess. I can read and write."

The beginning of a smile hidden in the corners of his mouth emboldened me to ask.

"Did you learn it in school?"

Despite his obviously lighter mood today, I was still half-expecting a rebuke from him for asking a question about his past.

"I was taught to read and write, Sophie."

This did not answer my question, but he didn't bark or growled at me either, I noted.

"Were you homeschooled?" I pressed on. This would make perfect sense, actually, since he couldn't leave the estate.

This time, he blatantly ignored my question and took the last bag from my hands.

"Popcorn?" He pulled two pre-filled aluminum camping pans.

"Want to have that as an appetizer?" I smiled, realizing perfectly well that he was switching the subject—leading me away from further questions—but unable to do anything about it.

One day, maybe one day, he'd tell me everything.

# Chapter 18

## Sophie

We sat on the floor in front of the fireplace. Monster held one of the aluminum popcorn pans over the flames, and I melted some butter in a stainless-steel ladle from the kitchen.

"I actually didn't mind school." I figured if he'd never been to one, maybe he would like to hear about what it was like, although my own experiences as a student were far from exciting, to say the least. "At the beginning, I even liked studying. High school was much harder, though, and I don't just mean its curriculum. Henri insisted I go to Sunny Ridge Academy, the most expensive private school in the city. And being raised by my free-spirited, down-to-earth mom, I just didn't fit in very well." I smiled and shook my head. "You should have seen the Sunny Ridge girls. At fifteen, they knew all about what labels to wear, what music to listen to, what places to vacation in. I couldn't carry a conversation on any of those topics to save my life. I wore the wrong clothes. Had my hair done the wrong way . . . Well, you know."

"Did you have friends outside of the Academy?" He shook the pan over the fire as the popping corn started to raise the cover into a dome.

"Not many. You see, the kids in our neighbourhood all went to the local public school and preferred to hang out together. I was the only one on our street who had a black limo show up at their door every morning to take me to school. I so envied the kids who took the bus. It seemed so much more fun than sitting in the dark back of the limo with no one to talk to."

"I know what you mean." He stared into the flames.

"You do?" I cocked my head.

He straightened his back and turned his ear to the fire. "Do you hear that?"

"What?" I went still too, not hearing anything beside the occasional pop from the pan.

"It's slowed down. I think it's ready!" The note of a genuine excitement in his voice made me smile.

"Man, this smells fantastic." He ripped the foil and dumped the warm popcorn into a glass bowl on the floor between us then moved it closer to me so I could pour the butter over it. "You know I used to think that's how it must smell in Heaven when I was a kid. Every time I'd walk into a movie theater—"

He cut himself short, apparently realizing that he'd said a little more than he had intended. I didn't use this opportunity to pry. Speechless, I felt dark and hollow inside from the realization that Monster had a childhood, with movies and popcorn. Someone took him out in public.

When and why did it all change?

"Would you like some?" He lifted the bowl to me, but I shook my head.

"I'm not hungry right now." Suddenly, I'd lost my appetite and just stroked his forearm lightly. "It's for you."

I watched him throw a handful in his mouth and close his eyes in pleasure as a low satisfied rumble vibrated in his chest.

How long had it been since he had popcorn? And when would be the next time, after I'd leave Rocky River?

Silent, I took my ladle to the kitchen and washed it in the bucket in the sink. The orange in the glass jar on the counter caught my attention again when I was putting the ladle in the drawer, and I took it out trying to distract myself from the gloomy thoughts.

The orange wasn't in top shape even when I bought it. Now its skin had begun to dry out, shriveling slightly. The inside should taste really sweet, though.

"Are you okay?" Monster's voice made me jump as he came up from behind me and placed the empty bowl on the counter.

"You don't like oranges?"

"I do. That's why I didn't touch it." He was so close—his breath got caught in the hair on top of my head. "I didn't want to remember how it tastes."

His tone was casual, even matter-of-fact, which made it sound only more heart-wrenching for me. I turned the orange between my fingers, not finding any words to reply.

"Here. Let me help you peel it." His hand came around me from behind, and he flexed his fingers, baring a full set of black, curved claws, which sliced through the orange peel with ease.

"These are impressive," I spoke in awe, taking his hand in mine for a better look. I'd seen his claws before, but never this close.

The skin on his palm was rough and calloused from running on all fours, I imagined. His hand relaxed in mine, and the claws disappeared completely.

I took one of his fingers and fully straightened it. The sharp point of the claw peeped out at the very tip, and I tapped it with the pad of my thumb.

"How do you make them come out all the way?"

He didn't immediately reply to my question, prompting me to look up.

He stood at my side, so close, the fur on his chest brushed my shoulder. The arm of the hand I held was wrapped around me halfway, my forearm flush against his. His fresh scent mingled with the warm, delicious smell of butter and popcorn.

The brilliant hazel of his eyes reminded me again of the wild woods that had become his home, and the emotions swirling inside them seemed just as untamed.

The intensity of his gaze made me forget about my question for a second.

Finally, he blinked.

"I—" he cleared his throat as his hand twitched in mine. "I have to flex my fingers to make the claws come out." He tensed his finger slowly and the slim, curved claw slid out again. "I'm not sure how it works myself, to be honest."

I slid the tip of my finger along the hard, polished surface of the claw. The top was smooth and rounded and the underside appeared to be razor-sharp, like a blade of a sickle.

"Dangerous . . ." A rush of cold prickled along my spine at the thought of how much damage could be inflicted with those.

Lethal.

Then I heard a low rumble somewhere deep in his chest, the vibration of it spread along my arm. His face sank into my hair, and I felt him inhale deeply.

"Monster?" I whispered.

He growled, and the hand I held in mine pressed to my chest, pulling me into him.

"I love the way you say it . . ." he breathed out into my hair. "It was supposed to be a derogatory name I called myself in one of many moments of self-loathing." His other arm went around me, as he hugged me from behind. "But you make it sound soft like a caress. So. Fucking. Sexy."

His heart thundered against my back as his face slid lower and he nuzzled my neck. My own heart sped up. The passion of his embrace washed over me in a hot, intoxicating wave.

The impact was almost tangible—my knees gave in and I braced myself with my hands on the cool granite of the kitchen island.

"Monster," I whimpered as his large body enveloped me.

With an animalistic growl, he pivoted me to face him then lifted me on the counter. I wrapped my arms around his neck, crushing the soft mass of his mane.

Frantically tearing at my clothes, he found his way under my blouse and slid his palms up my back, pressing me closer to him.

For an instant, the sensation of his rough hands caressing my bare skin was invigorating. A light shiver prickled my arms, settling in a pool of warmth somewhere in my lower stomach.

"I want you so much, it hurts," he groaned, rocking his hips into me. The hard bulge of his erection rubbed between my spread thighs.

Then, an icy flash shot through the budding desire in me, freezing my insides in a paralyzing fear at the sudden awareness of what was happening.

And the next moment everything felt wrong.

The strength of his arms around me turned from exciting to oppressively restraining. The touch of his hands on my skin twisted from caressing to intrusive in my mind. And the old hateful panic rose to the surface, suffocating any remnants of my arousal.

Hands on his shoulder, I leaned away from him.

"I can't," I rasped in a strangled voice.

I never could.

My throat began to feel like it was closing, making it hard to breathe as his hold on me didn't ease.

"Don't." I shoved harder against him mechanically, all my focus on my next breath.

"That's what I keep telling myself every fucking time you're here." His arms went even tighter around me, refusing to let me go. "*Don't touch her. Don't look at her. Don't breathe near her.*" He inhaled deeply, rubbing his nose against the side of my face. "But you're worse than a drug, my princess. Intoxicating and irresistible. More dangerous to me than any drug, too."

"Stop it," I managed a little louder, pushing against his fierce embrace. "I can't..."

The sense of what I was saying seemed to have filtered through to him, as his arms finally loosened, and his eyes found mine.

"You can't?" he echoed, his expression grave, the heavy fog of lust clearing from his gaze. "Of course you can't." He shoved away from the counter—from me—with force. "Who *could* fuck a monster?"

The real pain behind his crude words twisted my insides with sorrow for him.

For both of us.

"It's not you!" I jumped off the counter. "That's not what it is."

"What then?" He lunged forward again, looming over me. His whole body vibrated like a tightly coiled spring. "Why did you have to come here, Sophie?" His voice was dangerously low. "Why couldn't you just let me be the animal that I was? Why did you have to wake the man in me?" He slammed his hands into the countertop on either side of me. The sharp, black claws scraped against the granite with a screeching noise. "And now I have to see you, smell you, want you. Unable to touch you!"

His voice rose to thunder over me. I balled my hands into fists to prevent them from shaking. The tightness in my throat had turned painful.

"I may have the feelings of a man, but I don't look like one. Is that it?" He lifted a hand to my face, the rough pad of his palm brushed against my cheek, and the claws sank into my hair. " Why are you here, Sophie? What do you see when you look at me? A stray you found in the woods and felt pity for?"

"No, of course not..." I shook my head, but he didn't seem to be listening.

His eyes flickered between mine, but I didn't think he saw me. His self-hatred drove him so deep into despair, I wasn't sure he could be reasoned with at all at this moment.

"You'd love to keep me as a pet, but you're disgusted to have anything more!" he snarled wildly. "Isn't that why you're pushing me away?"

His fingers squeezed my nape, and I flinched inside.

All of this was happening too fast too soon.

But it didn't matter.

Whatever budding attraction I might have for him couldn't grow into anything more between us.

At the end of the day, I firmly believed it was my fault that all my relationships failed, often before they started. No matter what I felt towards a man, my response to his advances was never normal.

Because *I* was not normal.

Broken.

All emotions faded in me, leaving behind only panic and fear, along with the desire to flee that grew stronger by a second.

He saw my expression but misunderstood the reasons for it.

"The mere thought of fucking me repulses you. And now you look as if you'd just discovered your family pet has a much stronger urge to lap at your pussy than at your face."

"Oh, God . . ." I gasped, yanking myself from his grip, his last words filling me with disgust and turning the situation into more than I could bear. "You're right. I shouldn't have come." I exhaled, as my chest constricted to the point I wasn't sure I would be able to manage another breath.

The urge to flee was overwhelming.

I needed air—I had to get away from here.

Shoving past him, I ran for the front door and grabbed the car keys from the stand at the entrance on my way out.

An icy wall of snow blasted in my face when I pushed the front door open, but I hardly felt it. My heart squeezed tight in my chest, and my eyes stung with unshed tears of disappointment and pain as I ran through the snowfall to the carport.

The aggression in his behaviour didn't help. Although I had to admit something about the passion with which he expressed his desires felt alluring, the crude force of his actions seemed to be a sure way to set off a panic attack in me.

No matter what, it's all my fault.

Always.

I jumped in the driver's seat and started the engine, straining to see the driveway through the snowfall.

Everything inside me vibrated with nerves, and the view out of the windshield blurred as the tears welled in my eyes. Anger, disappointment . . . In him? In myself?

Sadness.

For the first time ever, I actually felt something for someone.

He'd called me his drug, but he had made me addicted to his company, too. He had made me want more—more of his presence, more of him.

I inhaled a shuddering breath, fighting the adrenaline shooting through my veins, and tried to make out the outlines of the tree trunks through the snow as I maneuvered the truck along the driveway.

A large shape jumped onto the driveway right in front of the truck.

I screamed, slamming my foot on the breaks. The truck skidded to a stop in the snow, but the dark figure didn't move from its way. Folded in half in the middle, Monster smashed his fists on the hood.

Did I hit him?

My stomach churned, I threw the door open and jumped out.

"What are you doing?" My knees shaking, I ran to the front of the truck, yelling at him through snow and tears. "Are you okay?"

Big, soft snowflakes landed on my face and shoulders. The chill seeped through the thin material of my blouse.

He shoved away from the hood, fully illuminated by the head-lights. His chest heaved—he had run to catch up with me—but he appeared unharmed.

I took a small step back.

"Don't go," he rasped, his big arms hanging limply at his sides.

"I should leave." I swallowed hard, speaking around the lump in my throat. "You're right. It would've been better if I never came here at all. I just make things worse . . ."

I put my hand on the handle of the driver's door, and his eyes followed my movement.

"No." He shook his head, snowflakes flying from his mane. "I shouldn't have said the shit I did—being near you drives me mad. When you pulled away, it hurt."

He stepped closer.

"I don't know how to fix this. Fuck, I don't even know how to apologize properly, but I am sorry."

Suddenly, he sank to his knees into the snow.

I gasped in surprise and swayed on my feet as his arms went around me.

"Please. Don't leave." He pressed his forehead to my stomach, his horns on each side of my waist, keeping me in place. "And you're wrong, Sophie," he gritted through his teeth as his arms tightened around me. "Everything—every single fucking thing—is so much better when you're around. With you, I feel alive again. You make everything better. Even the pain."

Shaking in the falling snow, I lowered my hands to the twisted spirals of his horns and wrapped my fingers around their bumpy surface, holding tight.

"I—I can never make relationships work, Monster, not even friendships, it seems. I always ruin things . . . I can never give you what you want."

He lifted his head, and I slid my hands down his horns and into the warm, silky mass of his mane.

"I'll take anything you give me, Sophie, for as long as it lasts. Every moment with you is worth an eternity alone here. Please, don't leave. Not now. Not like this." The genuine plea burning in his eyes gripped my heart. "Just say the word, and I'll never touch you again. I won't even come close enough for my breath to reach you." He drew in a deep inhale. "Dammit! I'll be your fucking pet if you wish—"

"No, Monster. Please," I exhaled, cupping his face between my hands. "It's not about it. Would you listen to me? That's not what you are to me. And it's not about your looks—"

I swallowed hard.

"It's me, Monster," I whispered with a sigh. "It's always me."

My whole body shook from cold or from nerves or both. Snowfall swirled around us, stealing whatever warmth my body still held.

"These panic attacks . . ." I said as my teeth began to chatter. "It's all my fault."

"No, it's not." He rose to his feet, without releasing me from his arms. Instinctively, I leaned into him to hide from the cold and wind. "You did nothing wrong. I did." His chest heaved heavily as he drew me closer, his chin pressed against the top of my head. "I am so, so sorry, Sophie. For everything I've done to you."

"It's okay," I whispered, burying the frozen tip of my nose into the fur on his chest.

My words, however, didn't seem to ease his thoughts, as his next sigh was just as heavy.

As I thawed slowly, wrapped in the warmth of his arms, a shudder ran through my whole body.

"Jesus, Sophie. You're freezing." With his arms around me, he walked me towards the driver's door. "Get in the truck. I'll meet you at the house." He cupped my chin, lifting my face to his. "We *will* have that dinner."

# Chapter 19

## Sophie

Wrapped in a blanket, I was slowly warming up on the couch by the fire. Melanie's stew simmered on the wrought-iron stand inside the fireplace. A side table was set with bowls, water glasses, and a plate with dinner rolls.

Monster went upstairs for a minute, and when he came back, he wore a pair of jeans. Unused to see any clothes on him, I might have kept my gaze a little too long on his powerful thighs, admiring the way the material hugged him in all the right places.

"Um," I cleared my throat, catching myself staring. "Those look . . . nice on you."

"Well, I figured it would be *nice* to get dressed for dinner. Right? I had to cut a hole for the tail." He turned around, his bushy tail whipped across the back of his thighs. "What do you think?"

"Dashing." I smiled.

He took a bowl of salad and sat on the other end of the couch.

We ate mostly in silence. My thoughts kept going through the argument we'd just had. His words wouldn't leave me.

'I may have the feelings of a man, but I don't look like one'.

He did not look like a human, and there was no point pretending otherwise. However, as shocking as I initially found his appearance, it didn't frighten or repulse me anymore.

In fact, I even wondered if his looks were one of the reasons why I was able to feel at ease around him, despite his volatile temper and gruff attitude. Normally, I felt rather self-conscious and uncomfortable in the company of men, especially the handsome ones.

Besides, over the short time I knew him, I'd grown to appreciate the size and strength of his body and even found it attractive in its own fierce, untamed way.

"I just need you to know one thing," I started after we had finished dinner and took our dishes to the kitchen to wash. "You may want me to call you *Monster*, but I don't see you as one. When I look at you, I see a person, and it's what you do that defines you."

"What do I do?"

"Yes." I nodded and handed him a rinsed bowl to dry with the towel in his hands. "I see good in you, no matter how hard you try to hide it. There's a struggle inside you, but I know you want to do the right thing."

He placed the dish and the towel on the counter and propped himself with his arms against it. His head dropped between his shoulders.

"Do you, Sophie? Do you really see anything good here?" He shook his head and moved back to the fireplace. "*Monster* is not just my name," he threw over his shoulder. "It's who I am. Who I've always been, even when I looked like a man on the outside."

"You did?" I hurried after him. "You *were* a human?"

He nodded, with a sad smile. "No fur, tail, or horns. A family, or something like it. School . . . You know." He dismissed with a wave of a hand and sat on the couch.

"What happened?" I climbed over the back of the couch to sit next to him. "Did you get sick?"

"Sick?" He lifted an eyebrow at me incredulously, the familiar mocking expression returning to his face. "With what? A beastly form of chickenpox where your body gets covered with fur instead of a rash?"

"Well, what then?" I insisted, undeterred. "How did you grow horns?"

"Overnight." He shifted to face me.

"Really? Overnight?" I repeated, stunned.

"When I had every opportunity in the world, I made all the wrong choices, Sophie. Back then I might have looked human on the outside, but the way I am now would have been much more suitable all along. I drank, fought, and fucked all the way through high school. And in college, it got even worse."

I clasped my hands in my lap and closed my eyes, trying to imagine his human form. If I shut his current appearance from my mind's vision, it was actually fairly simple to visualize Monster as a wild college student on the path of self-destruction.

He would be one of the *cool* kids, I imagined—angry, sarcastic, self-assured, hiding the insecurities of youth well enough to appear confident.

"In my second year, I met a girl at a party." He raked his fingers through his mane. "One of many parties, one of many girls. I, um, took her upstairs to the bedroom. She spent the night." He cleared his throat. "In the morning, I was still asleep when she woke up and started cuddling, waking me up, too. I remember a hideous hangover—with raging thirst and headache—and the strong desire for her to leave me alone."

He rubbed his forehead.

"I said something along those lines to her."

# Chapter 20

## Monster

Then.

"**I** thought we shared something special!" She seethed with anger, sitting up in bed.

Her small, perky breasts with dark nipples bounced enticingly, making him consider another round after all. However, the mere thought of moving made his head hurt, forcing him to abandon the idea as soon as it came.

"I felt something for you," she wouldn't quit. "You know I don't normally jump into bed with the first guy I meet. I'm not some skanky ho."

"Could've fooled me," he groaned and grabbed her pillow to place over his ear in an attempt to muffle the noise she was making.

"You. Pig!" She jumped out of bed.

Her rapid departure jerked the mattress and jarred his headache. His stomach also lurched from last night's liquor.

Great!

She flicked the lights on.

"Fuck!" he pulled the pillow lower over his eyes to block the bright light that flooded the room.

"Don't tell me you felt nothing! Last night was magical. No one has ever fucked me the way you did. It was wild! And . . . crazy. I love crazy. Isn't it obvious? We're made for each other."

His irritation chased the remnants of sleep away. He rose on his elbows and opened his eyes again, wincing from the blinding light that pierced through his head with another stab of pain.

"That's the way I fuck, babe. Glad you liked it, but it was no magic. And it meant nothing." He rubbed his face. Now that she woke him up completely, maybe he should go get some water. Maybe throw up and take a piss, too.

Slowly, so as not to aggravate his stomach any further, he got off the bed.

"If it makes you feel any better, you're not alone." Blinking in the light, he turned towards her naked figure at the foot of the bed and met her furious dark amber eyes. "Chicks beg me to fuck them. All. The. Time."

She jerked at his words, grabbed a throw pillow from the chest at the bed and hurled it at him.

"Asshole! You're a disgusting animal." Another cushion followed, hitting him straight in the chest. "Just because you're good-looking, you think you're so irresistible? You think you can get away with shit like this?"

"Hey!" He ran his fingers through his tangled hair, massaging his achy skull. "Good looks don't hurt, but we both know it's more than that, babe. Nobody forced you to throw yourself at me. Yet here you are. Thoroughly fucked and begging for more." He smirked. Despite the raging hangover, he couldn't resist taunting her. "Just like any other *skanky ho* before you."

She looked outright furious. Rage shook her slender body, her ink-black hair messy and wild.

But she stopped yelling insults at him. Instead, she clenched her fists and took a deep breath. Her eyes narrowed, the amber-brown in them deepened.

"How many?" She asked gravely.

"What? Hos?"

Arguing with her didn't seem so funny anymore. She wasn't just angry, now she was a picture of a barely contained fury ready to erupt in something outrageously insane, and he really didn't want to deal with the meltdown.

"Yes!" The loud shrill of her voice cut like a knife through the pain in his head. "How many girls have you slept with? You, asshole!"

"Fuck if I know!" He yelled back. "Lots. It's not like I keep a record somewhere. I don't even remember their names. A shitload of them. Okay?" He turned towards the bathroom, suddenly feeling tired of all of this. "Why are all of you so annoying in the morning?" He mumbled, deciding to go back to bed whenever this one left. "Just . . . welcome to the club, babe. And get out of here. I gotta take a piss."

She didn't appear to have heard him.

"You slept with the wrong girl this time, *babe*." Her voice was dangerously calm, prompting him to glance her way one more time. Angry specks of gold flashed in her eyes as she set her hands on her hips.

"No kidding," he muttered sarcastically under his breath. "What the fuck was I thinking?"

"Well, I'm going to fix this." Her grave, strained voice demanded to be taken seriously. "No more misunderstandings. Now, you're going to look on the outside the same disgusting animal you are inside. So no *chick* will ever mistake you for her Prince Charming again."

"Whatever, babe."

Psycho!

"It's Cecilia! You asshole! And I'll make sure you remember my name as you sit in the middle of nowhere with your tail between your legs, wishing there were at least one woman in the world who could still love you—all of you—just the way you are, when she is no longer blinded by your pretty face."

# Chapter 21

## Monster

Now.

Cecilia.

She was right. Out of all the names of random girls he'd been with, hers was the one he couldn't forget.

"It was horrible. The way you treated her." Sophie's somber voice reached him.

He didn't embellish that morning, didn't leave anything out. He didn't try to paint himself in a better light or make up excuses for his behaviour, laying himself bare to her judgment instead.

Yet the grave note in her tone filled him with dread. Had he shown her too much of his real nature, his true ugliness? Enough to send her running in fear and disgust once again?

"It was awful," he agreed wholeheartedly. "It took me years to realize it though, even longer to feel any kind of true remorse." Now, he would give anything to turn back time. And not just back to that night. He'd have to go way, way back to start anew.

"Do you really think Cecilia did this then? As revenge or punishment?" She leaned over and touched his knee—in an impulsive gesture, he was sure of it. Her touch burnt, scorching his skin with the now-so-familiar pleasure and pain.

Her movement sent a fresh whiff of her tantalizing scent his way, washing over him with another heat wave of desire. And he held his breath, counting the seconds until the wave receded, lest he lunge for her again.

"How could Cecilia, or anyone, do something like this?" Her voice held more concern than judgment, he noted with relief.

"Beats me, princess. I have no idea how she did it. As soon as she stormed out of the bedroom that night, I went back to sleep and woke up here, looking like this.

"For days, I was convinced I was still dreaming, having some super long nightmare that would have to end sooner or later. I couldn't walk on these." He kicked out his clawed foot. "My neck was sore and shaking after just hours of carrying these on my head." He swung his horns her way. "None of it felt like it could be real.

"On top of it all, I was starving. So ravenously hungry, I felt I could eat a horse. Then I did. Not a horse, but an elk. I hunted it, and killed it with my bare hands and teeth. That's when reality slowly started seeping in. The animalistic satisfaction from the hunt, the contentment I felt as I tore the meat off the bones—convinced me I was no longer human."

"Why here?" She asked, peering at him intently with those inquisitive grey eyes, as if he held all the answers, as if he could help her make sense of it all.

"I honestly don't know, Sophie. Of the dozen or so properties that my parents owned all over the world, why did I have to get stuck here? My best guess would be because this is the most remote of them all. The only place where hiding someone like me would be possible."

"How long have you been here?"

"Just over six years. Almost three of them entirely alone, save for an occasional hunter wandering in."

The first year of being alone was the hardest. Between gnawing hunger during the months when game was scarce and the excruciating loneliness and despair, there were moments when he didn't think he would last much longer. Sitting on the riverbank, he had caught himself wondering a few times how tall a tree he'd have to climb to make sure the fall onto the rocks below would break his neck at once.

Sophie shifted on the couch, wrinkling her nose in that adorable way when she concentrated on something.

"Melanie, at the restaurant, mentioned that someone used to come to check on the property regularly."

"David." He nodded. The old grief of loss tightened around his heart like a band of steel. "He was our family chauffeur. My one true friend. David found me a few weeks after I turned into this." He gestured at his chest. "He came up here with my father's hunting party."

He winced at mentioning this. His father's death brought him some kind of a closure. However, none of the memories of him were pleasant.

"They hunted here?" Her eyes went bigger, entreating him to lose himself inside her gaze simply to bask in her concern for him.

"There never was any actual *hunting*." He attempted to give her a calm smile, even though it probably just looked like him baring his fangs at her. "My father built this place to take his drinking buddies and random women out of the reach of my mom's lawyers. The last thing he wanted was to give his wife a solid reason for a divorce."

"Did your mom want a divorce?"

"Only if she caught him red-handed and could take him to court for everything he had. She came from a prominent British family and hated Calgary, couldn't stand Canada, and loathed being married to my father, but she loved his money. And he was good at creating golden shackles to manipulate people into doing what he wanted. Money was just another form of control for him."

"Did David tell your parents about you?"

"Mom never came here and knew nothing about what happened to me, but my father did. He knew. I was stupid enough to hope he could help, or at least care."

"He didn't?" There was a clear note of compassion in her voice, but no surprise. From what she had told him about her own father, parental indifference was nothing new to her.

"No." He shook his head. "We had an argument. It didn't go well. He left, and I knew he'd never be back. He died in a car crash not long after. Mom passed away, too. They said it was heart disease, but I knew before David confirmed it that it was a drug overdose. She'd been using whatever stuff she could get her hands on since I was a little kid. Everything, just to forget what kind of monster she'd married."

He paused, exhausted by the dark memories. For years they had been collecting inside him, weighing him down. There was something oddly liberating in being able to bring them out into the light. Talking to someone about all of this, he realized, lightened his soul.

He shot a cautious glance at Sophie's face again, needing to see her expression. Feet tucked under her, she sat facing him, her attention seemingly fully on him, waiting for him to continue.

"How did you manage here?" She prompted when he remained silent a moment too long.

"David taught me everything I know about how to survive out here alone. Survive in a human way, I mean. He showed me how to skin and butcher a kill properly, how to operate and maintain all machines and tools on the property. He even taught me how to cook. Before that I had no clue how to boil an egg for myself. Then one day he left, promising to return in a couple of weeks, and never came back."

He swallowed hard at the memories of waiting for David by the fence—day after day for weeks that turned into months—before the inevitable realization that something horrible must have happened to David fully settled in his mind.

"Oh, Monster . . ." Sophie inched closer to him, and his arms ached to pull her into a hug. "David. He passed away, too."

He inhaled sharply, fighting the spear of pain her words sent through his gut.

He guessed this had happened—David wouldn't have abandoned him just like that. However, hearing the confirmation of the death of the only real friend he ever had—the true father figure in his life—still came as a shock of overwhelming sadness and pain he could barely cope with.

Her soft voice reached through the cold wall of grief, ringing with sincere empathy and concern, "Bob said David had a heart attack. I'm so sorry, sweetie."

She leaned even closer his way, and he couldn't hold back any longer. The hug had become a necessity.

He grabbed her by the upper arms and dragged her into his lap. Wrapping himself around her delicate warmth, he breathed deeply, reveling in the genuine compassion of another human being.

She stroked his mane, whispering something kind and soothing in his ear.

Crushed by the avalanche of sorrow, he didn't even attempt to comprehend the meaning of what she was saying. He simply allowed the soft cadence of her voice to slowly carry him from the dark abyss of grief back to the light.

# Chapter 22

## Sophie

"It's warm here." Still, I hugged myself, as if the air of the room brought the chill to my arms. My skin prickled along my spine from the uncomfortable feeling of being in someone else's bedroom.

"I cleaned the fireplace yesterday. It's been on since morning."

"Thank you." I clutched the folded, clean bedding to my chest. I had washed it and brought it back with me with the full intention of sleeping in this bedroom. Now, however, I was wondering if I should sleep downstairs, on the couch, ripped upholstery and all.

Monster seemed to sense my doubt.

"This room is smaller than the living room. It will stay warm through the night. The bed is very comfy, too."

"You've slept in it?"

"I did. At the beginning."

He moved to the bed and tugged the cover off, helping me change the sheets.

After the bed had been made, I washed my face and brushed my teeth using the bottled water I brought with me. Monster then escorted me to the outhouse on the other side of the rose hedge.

It was quite a walk from the main building, as the outhouse was probably built for the workers maintaining the grounds. But it was either walking all this way or going in the bushes somewhere, which Monster probably wouldn't allow me to do anyway for fear of the cougar.

"The cat doesn't adhere to any strict hunting schedule that I'm aware of, but he seems to be more active late in the evening or early in the morning," he explained when I wondered out loud whether the cougar was around.

"Has he attacked you before?"

Monster's wounds seemed to have been healing well, not that he would let me inspect them to make sure of it, but the fur had smoothed out over them, giving no sign of the injury underneath, and I hadn't noticed him wince from pain or discomfort when he moved.

"Just once. He jumped on my back out of a tree when I was passing underneath. I fought him off, but he still lurks around quite often. You wouldn't even notice he's there until it's too late. Don't ever walk out here by yourself."

Afterwards, I lay alone in the massive bed in the master bedroom.

In the dark, the deep shadows created by the tall flames in the fireplace danced between the wooden beams of the ceiling, making the room appear like something straight out of a horror movie.

I closed my eyes to shut out my unnerving surroundings and focused on my breathing instead, willing pleasant thoughts to trickle into my mind.

Monster's story stayed with me, though—unsettling, incredible, and unbelievably sad. His deep voice still rang in my ears, filled with anger, pain, and remorse bringing back the overwhelming desire to comfort him.

As I finally drifted to sleep, my last conscious thought was the memory of his soft fur under my palms as I patted his wide back and the feeling of safety from his strong arms wrapped around me.

HE WAS ON TOP OF ME. His heavy weight on my chest pinned me to the ground. My face was shoved into the ravine floor. The dead grass and dirt stuffed my nose and mouth, forcing me to fight for my next breath as I thrashed under him.

The feeling of complete helplessness rushed all my senses, immediately turning to panic. I couldn't move. I couldn't scream for help.

The terror inside me built up to the power of an explosion, threatening to rip me apart without finding a way out.

Every last modicum of my awareness focused on one single task.

Scream.

And I fought to pass any kind of sound out of my strangled throat.

Scream!

Then I felt it before I heard it. The liberation of the air rushing out of my lungs in a loud, desperate cry coming, it seemed, out of the bottom of my very soul.

The crashing noise of a door flying open followed my scream.

"Sophie!" Monster's voice, filled with alarm, brought me back into the bedroom and reality.

I was in bed, on my back, with no one on top of me.

It had all been just memories coming back as nightmares.

I sat up, rubbing the remnants of tightness out of my chest.

"Sophie?" Monster leaned his knee on the bed and grabbed my shoulders.

"I'm fine," I mumbled. "Sorry, just a bad dream."

"Jesus, Sophie." His massive shoulders slumped in relief as he lowered his forehead to mine. "That scream . . . That fucking scream."

"Sorry, I woke you up . . ."

With his hands still firmly on my shoulders, he leaned back to catch my gaze.

On this moonless night, the crimson glow from the fireplace cast grotesque shadows across the beastly features of his face. Blood-red highlights streaked his mane, and the hellfire itself appeared to glance off the polished points of his horns and off the sharp canines peeking from under his upper lip.

In the dim, red light of the room, he appeared much closer to the creature from a nightmare than to somebody who came to save me from one.

Yet the sight of him no longer scared me. On the contrary, a wave of relief and gratitude flooded me in his presence.

"What was your dream about?"

"Nothing. Really . . . Just an uncomfortable feeling . . ."

He shook his head slowly.

"This was not a scream of *discomfort*, Sophie. More like of utter terror."

My gaze wandered up to the tip of his ear peeking out of the mass of his mane.

"It's not important. And it's normal for me. I have them once in a while . . .They're just dreams—"

"Nightmares. Not just dreams." He let go of my shoulders and shifted in an easier position next to me. "How often do you have them?"

I let out a sigh at his insistence. My usual tactic of dealing with nightmares was to sweep them out of my memory as soon as possible, or to stuff them deep into the graveyard of my mind if they refused to disappear for good. I definitely didn't feel like dragging all their ugliness out into the light right now.

"Please, princess." His voice softened as he moved a strand of hair from my face and tucked it behind my ear. "Tell me. What horrors torture you at night?"

The somber sincerity of his tone, the warmth of genuine concern in it was tempting. Except that even if I wanted to open up to anyone, I had no idea where to begin. I simply didn't know how to talk about it after so many years of silence.

"You don't want to know," I exhaled with a short, nervous laugh.

"I *need* to know, Sophie." His hard stare reflected the conviction of his words. "But this is about you, not me. You have to tell someone. Even if not me—"

"It *has* to be you," I interrupted quickly. The truth of my words registered with me the moment I said them out loud.

With me sitting in this eerily lit room, facing Monster in the middle of the night, the real world didn't exist. And the story of my past was just that—a story. Something about him—big, strong, and kind—stole away the power the past held over me, if just for a few moments.

"The nightmares don't happen that often," I said quietly. "And I deal with them one by one as they come. I keep telling myself I can do it on my own—I'm functioning okay, trying to make myself useful to the people around me . . . But sometimes," I found his hand on top of the covers and squeezed it in mine. "Sometimes I wonder if they'll ever go away. Because if they don't . . . I just don't know how to go through the rest of my life fighting this."

"How long have you been having them?"

"Eight years," I replied without having to think about it because I knew exactly when the nightmares started and why. "Ever since that night . . ."

His hand twitched in mine, but he remained silent, so I continued.

"I was sixteen, and I took a job tutoring a girl from my class. Her housekeeper drove us to her house after school, and my mom was supposed to pick me up afterwards on her way from work. My mom works shifts, and she was really late that night. I waited way past dinner. When she finally called me to tell she was leaving work, I told her I'd meet her on the way.

"It turned dark by then, but it was a quiet part of town and I wasn't afraid of being on my own.

"I walked along a side road running through a ravine—the same road my mom would be taking to pick me up—when a dark vehicle pulled over next to me and the driver asked if I needed a ride.

"I recognized him as a boy from my school. He was the older brother of the girl I tutored. Still, I declined the ride, telling him my mom would pick me up soon. Then I saw *him* staring at me from the passenger's seat."

I stopped for a moment. It'd been years since I said his name out loud, since I'd even allowed myself to utter it in my mind.

"Hunter Reed," I whispered. "The golden boy of Sunny Ridge. God, I had such a crush on him! Everyone did. How could you not? Golden brown hair. Moody, soulful eyes. A smile . . . Well, I didn't actually see him smile that often, but when I happened to catch him grin once or twice, it was as if the day got brighter and the sun moved closer to earth, bathing the world in bliss.

"At eighteen, he was already taller and broader than many adult men. Any sports—you name it—he was the star of the team. I think hockey was what promised a really big future for him.

"Add to all of this a prominent family, basically the uncrowned royalty of the city, and no wonder every girl was swooning over him.

"I fell head over heels for him, in total secrecy of course. He was this semi-god in my eyes, unable to do anything wrong. Getting to ride in the same vehicle with him was as close as I could ever hope to get to the deity. Stupid," I shook my head. "But then and there it felt exciting, and I got in the car."

Monster sat so still, if it weren't for the feeling of his hand in mine, I wouldn't be able to tell he was here at all.

His eyes glistened in the dim light, his attention fully on me, prompting me to go on.

"There were more boys in the back seat. The strong smell of alcohol hit me as soon as the door closed behind me. Suddenly, everything felt wrong, but the boy behind the wheel took off, and when I begged them to let me out at the end of the ravine, they just laughed at me."

The humiliation, the hopelessness, the terror of that night washed over me as if it all happened yesterday. It had never gone away, buried under layers upon layers of years and silence.

That night kept following me, hitting me full force over and over again when I least expected it.

I moved my gaze from Monster to the glass balcony doors behind him and rushed through the rest of my story, afraid I might run out of courage before I finished it.

"They turned into a narrow road along the river. Everyone got out of the car. The guys, they were drinking, laughing. They started to push me around . . . groping. Hunter told them to stop, and for a moment I thought he truly was my knight in shining armor. My rescuer," I scoffed. "Then he tossed aside the bottle of whisky in his hand and grabbed me . . . I fought him, got away and ran."

I inhaled, reliving everything, hurrying to get it all out before the memories suffocated me into silence once again.

"I tripped and fell, face down, and he crashed on top of me. With my face pressed into the ravine floor, I couldn't move, couldn't breathe. My mouth filled with dirt—" I shuddered, remembering the smell of dry grass and dust suffocating me, making me sick. "I thrashed, struggling for air . . . The moment I had a chance to lift my head and spit the dirt out, I screamed . . . And when his hold on me eased, I ran again.

"I ran through the ravine until a ray of flashlight danced in my face, blinding me. It was my mom. She hadn't seen me on the road as we agreed and went searching for me. She brought me home."

I realized I had been squeezing Monster's fingers in a tight grip. It had to be painful for him.

"Sorry," I loosened my hold.

"What?" He frowned, blinking.

"I'm hurting you. Am I not?" I patted the furry back of his hand. "Anyway," I continued with a sigh. "These are my nightmares—the pressure on my chest, suffocating me, pinning me down, making me unable to move . . . or scream. As if *he* were still here . . ." My voice trailed off, and for a few moments we sat in silence interrupted only by the faint crackling of wood in the fireplace.

He stared somewhere behind me.

"You never reported him." It wasn't a question.

"Nothing happened . . ." I repeated my mantra robotically.

"You were attacked!" The sudden anger in his voice, booming through the dark room, startled me.

"I wasn't raped," I argued. "There were no big injuries. No one calls the police over some ruined clothes—"

"It was an assault," he retorted gravely. "A crime—"

"I didn't want to talk about it!" I yelled. An uncomfortable feeling put me on the defensive, reminding me why exactly I never told anyone what happened. "I told my mom I took a shortcut through the ravine and got lost. I never told her the truth. All I wanted was to forget, pretend it never happened, and move on."

"Have you moved on?"

The silence dragged out, as I made no answer.

"It's not just nightmares, Sophie, is it?" he continued. "You're so smart, and you did great in school until this, didn't you? And I know I did it all wrong every time I touched you—you had every reason to run away from me—but has there ever been anyone, a man, in your life whose touch you enjoyed?"

I closed my eyes, unable to tolerate the burning intensity in his gaze.

"No," I breathed out my confession. "Never."

"Oh, Sophie," he whispered with so much sorrow, my heart couldn't take it and tears burned my eyes.

"It's all my fault, Monster." I swallowed the painful tightness in my throat and opened my eyes again. "All of it is my fault. If I didn't get in that car, if I just waited at the house for my mom, none of it would have—"

The wild look on his face made me stop mid-sentence.

"*None* of it is your fault." He grabbed my shoulders and gave me a slight shake. "Do you hear me, Sophie?" he repeated slowly, his voice deep and powerful. "*Nothing* that happened to you that night was your fault. Please, believe me."

I stared at him, shocked by his severe expression.

"The asshole, who attacked you is the only one to blame," he gritted through his teeth. "That pathetic excuse of a human being is the one responsible. You should have reported him. He deserved to be punished. Maybe then you would've had justice and moved on."

I dropped my gaze to my lap.

"I'm not sure there would've been any justice, Monster. The Reeds, they were a very powerful family. They would've made sure that Hunter walked away without any punishment whatsoever. I would've only been forced to talk about that night over and over again for no reason, to complete strangers . . . I didn't want to go through that." I shivered, suddenly feeling the chilly air through my nightgown. The flames in the fireplace had been dying out, plunging the room into darkness.

"You're talking to me now," he pointed out softly.

"You're not a stranger," I protested. Though I might not have known him for long, it felt like I knew enough to consider him a friend. "And you're not from *that* world. You wouldn't force me to do something about this, like I'm afraid my mom would have, had she known." I moved closer to him, seeking the warmth of his large, furry body, but he wrapped the blanket over me, instead, keeping his distance.

"I am practically a stranger, Sophie. God knows, I would do anything to help you, but I can't. I don't know what to say and have no clue what to do. So far, I've fucked up everything I've touched. But you do need to talk to someone who can help."

Gently, he took me by the shoulders and lowered me back to bed, tucking the comforter around me.

"Please." He patted my arm through the cover. "You have been dealing with this shit on your own all this time. You're strong, but it's been sitting inside of you for so long, it can't be good. You've told me now. Could you talk to just one more person? Someone who'd know exactly how to help you to move on?"

His voice was calm now, soothing, as he kept stroking the covers over my arm.

"Because you need to move on from the past, Sophie. You deserve to have a beautiful life, full of true happiness. You deserve to find joy in the world."

The warm comforter kept the chill of the room away, and the deep rumbling of Monster's voice held the promise of keeping me safe.

"Monster." I hid a yawn behind my hand, unable to keep my heavy eyelids open. "Would you stay here? Please?"

I knew I wouldn't be able to fall asleep if he left—I never slept after the nightmare if I was alone.

"If you wish," he whispered, laying down on top of the covers next to me. "Sleep, princess. I'll be right here."

# Chapter 23

## Hunter

Eight years ago.

"You're a little piece of shit!" William Reed yelled, spit flying out of his mouth. A thick vein bulged across the angry burgundy of his forehead, and Hunter idly wondered how much longer before his father had a heart attack. "Where did you steal the money for this?" He shoved a piece of crumpled paper in Hunter's face.

"I didn't steal it," Hunter muttered gruffly.

That was true. He'd sold the rifle he got for his birthday last year to get the few thousand dollars he needed for the donation. Not that his father would see it Hunter's way, even if he told him.

Either way, it didn't matter. Sooner or later his father would find out about the rifle. Hunter knew it was impossible to hide from William Reed.

A safe place simply didn't exist.

"It was my money."

His words seemed to have set another explosion inside William Reed.

"There is no such thing as *your money*, you shithead! Everything you think you own is mine! It's all *my* money. All of it! Do you hear me?"

Hunter heard him. The whole house must have heard him. Except maybe for Hunter's mother, who lay upstairs in her rooms, *in-*

133

*disposed*, which was code for 'passed out drunk' or 'stoned out of her mind.'

"I really don't enjoy having to part with my money just because you got a soft spot for some fucking dogs for some fucking reason!"

"They were going to kill them," Hunter objected angrily, knowing as he spoke that the euthanasia of a dozen dogs meant absolutely nothing to his father.

They were mix breeds rescued from an abandoned farmhouse. Hunter visited the shelter with his mother to deliver a charity cheque during a Public Relations event organized by his father's company.

Bored by the endless speeches and posing for pictures, he wandered off to the back rooms where the dogs were being received at that moment.

Dirty, rail-thin, with haunted eyes, the image of their terrified faces wouldn't leave his mind long after he'd left.

He knew his father would never let him have a dog of his own, especially a mutt. But when he called the shelter, unable to stop wondering about the fate of the rescues, and was told that most of them needed serious medical attention before they could even be considered adoptable—meaning that they'd be most likely euthanized by the end of the month—he had to do something.

His donation was meant to pay for the dogs' veterinarian costs and give them the chance of a home with people who'd care for them.

"The mutts are dead, by the way." His father tossed the crumbled 'Thank You For You Donation' letter from the shelter into the wastebasket.

"What?" Hunter exhaled in shock. "How?"

The flash of satisfaction in his father's expression made him immediately regret exposing his true emotions, even for this brief moment. He made an effort to school his features back to the look of cool indifference, even as his blood heated with anger and pain.

He'd known his father would find out about the donation sooner or later, and he'd expected to be punished. He didn't expect, however, that all of it would turn out to be completely useless.

All he wanted was to give those animals a fair chance, but he accomplished nothing.

"I told the board your cheque was meant to cover our regular funding for the next three months—the secretary made a mistake and sent it in a lump sum early. Our regular donations are therefore being cancelled. Unfortunately, there wasn't any left to cover vet fees. Those dogs are dead." Each word his father spat his way was laced with deep resentment. "Let it be a lesson for you. If you have to spend a penny on a bunch of dirty mutts, make sure you get publicity and tax breaks. This money, *my* money!" His face slowly turned the darker shade of burgundy as his voice rose again. "It was outside of our charity budget for the year! You wasted my money, you piece of shit!"

Hunter guessed that wasn't just the money spent that fueled his father's rage—the amount of the donation was less than what William Reed spent on cigars in a month. More than the money, it was the fact that he did something independently, behind his father's back. Hunter strayed from the path laid by his father for him, which was simply unacceptable.

"It's not what you do!" his father raged on. "It's what people *think* you do that matters!"

William Reed demanded absolute obedience, and Hunter learned early on that the only way to stop his father's fists was to cower and beg. He knew from experience that the best way to deal with his father in this state would be to keep quiet. Let him rage until the fire had burned out.

Except that anger simmered hot inside him, clouding his better judgment, depriving him of common sense and self-preservation.

"*You* should know." A crooked smirk stretched across Hunter's face. He couldn't hold back, even as he knew this would cost him.

William Reed's face turned an even darker shade of red, and his eyes narrowed into two glowering slits burning with hate.

Adrenaline buzzed hot under Hunter's skin, charging every nerve in his body, fueled by the rising anger coursing hot through his veins.

This time, he was ready for a fight.

Now well over six feet, Hunter was as tall as his father. He still lacked in body mass compared to the older man, but he felt that one on one in a fist fight he had a fair chance. A sense of wired excitement shot hot through him. The anticipation of being finally able to return a punch was intoxicating.

His father must have realized Hunter's strength now equaled his own because he walked from around the heavy oak desk holding the baseball bat he kept in his office.

"I thought I'd taught you how to keep your mouth shut by now! I thought I'd taught you respect!"

Hunter wasn't watching the bat—his glare was glued to his father's eyes. Anger had drowned fear, and all he wished for was to throw one punch into the hateful face. Just once to feel his own fist connect with the flesh and bone of the man he had feared and despised all his life.

"You don't teach respect, asshole. You earn it," Hunter gritted through his teeth, his legs braced in a wide stance, hands fisted tight ready to swing.

His father swung first. The bat hissed in the air above Hunter's head when he barely managed to duck in time.

Fuck you.

He straightened, leaning back to gain momentum for his own blow, but his father proved to be more shrewd. He stepped to the side out of Hunter's reach and used the advantage that the length of the bat provided to him to land a blow on his son.

The bat slammed into Hunter's upper arm then slid along his shoulder and connected with the side of Hunter's head, just below his temple.

He didn't even feel the pain right away, just a deafening ringing inside his head, like a church bell, resonating through his entire being. Momentarily disoriented, he stumbled forward, struggling to regain his balance, when another blow of the bat threw him to the floor, blinding him for a moment.

"Don't you ever take a swing at me again! You, little shit." A kick in the ribs made Hunter curl up on the expensive Persian rug on the floor. The side of his head where the skin must have split open from the blow stung, rubbed against the prickly surface of the rug. "You're nothing but what I've made you! I own you. You do *what* I tell you *when* I tell you! Do you hear me?"

The baseball bat, tossed by his father, landed on the rug next to Hunter and rolled to the wall. Then he heard the door slam shut loudly as his father left the office cursing under his breath.

The bitter failure of his rescue attempt, complete with the frustration of the unfulfilled revenge, crippled Hunter more effectively than the throbbing pain in his head and ribs.

He rolled onto his stomach then staggered to his feet, pressing his left arm against his bruised side. His eye caught the baseball bat by the wall, and anger boiled over, erupting into madness.

With a deep growl he grabbed the bat and swung it in the air, searching for a target.

Nothing felt worthy of his wrath, though. Not one thing in this hated place would give him the satisfaction he craved if destroyed.

His wild gaze fell on the framed portrait of the perfect family his father had displayed on his desk. The Reeds in formal attire—both men in suits with ties, his mother in an elegant cream dress. Carefully choreographed fake smiles plastered on all three faces, including his own.

Suddenly, he had a target. He swung the bat, putting the force of his whole body into the motion. The blow propelled the picture into the air and across the room, shards of shattered glass raining down on the rug.

"Fuck!" He bellowed—rage churning like a black hurricane inside his chest—and tossed the bat across his father's desk. "Fuck!" His hands shook with uncontained fury.

He tore off the door of the liquor cabinet in the corner and grabbed an unopened bottle of Crown Royal. Twisting the cap off, he gulped the burning liquid straight from the bottle, trying to douse the flames of rage that consumed him.

His phone buzzed in the back pocket. He yanked it out and flung it at the wall, without a glance then stormed out of the office and slammed the door behind him with the force that made his mother's delicate crystal wall cones clink vehemently in protest.

Vince's black Hummer was parked on the circular driveway, in front of the mansion, with Vince hanging halfway out of the open window on the driver's side.

"Hey, Hunter." He tipped his head towards the passenger's side seat, prompting him to hurry. "Move it, man, while the beer is still cold and chicks are still hot."

The idiot guffawed at his own joke, and for a moment Hunter envisioned Vince's stupid mug with a few teeth missing and blood dripping from his broken hose after a good punch in the face.

He savored the picture in his mind as he climbed in the Hummer, taking another huge swig from the bottle of whisky he still held in his hand.

"It's fucking early," he snarled, completely ignoring the two others in the back. He was picked up last, but the front seat was kept for him. Hunter didn't ride in the back, unless it was a limo, and his friends knew better than to piss him off.

Right now, though, he wished they didn't. He craved a fight, wishing for someone to give him a reason to land a blow, so he could have an outlet of the anger gnawing at his insides.

As the Hummer roared through the streets towards Macleod Trail—the highway that ran through the city—Hunter focused on the burn of each scorching gulp of whisky as it ran down his throat, numbing the pain of the bruises on his body.

What hurt the most, though, weren't the physical injuries.

Just a few more months.

That was how long he still had to share a roof with his father. In September, Hunter was starting university. Of course, it could only be Ivy League—nothing else would ever be acceptable to his father. That meant he would be on the East Coast, in another country, thousands of miles away from here.

His father's minions were all lined up to keep an eye on him there and to report everything back to his father. However, it would be the most freedom Hunter had been allowed in his entire life.

In Calgary, he couldn't breathe without his father's permission. He couldn't even fuck without William Reed knowing whom and where.

Hunter got his driver's licence years ago, but had no car in his name. If he ever wanted to use one from The Reeds' expansive collection of luxury vehicles, he had to beg his father, who would unfailingly use the situation to his advantage, striking another debilitating bargain with his son.

One couldn't get something for nothing, and his father used every single leniency to gain the upper hand. Each 'favour' cost something or was a reward for better grades in school, for winning a game in sports, for leaving a good impression on important people at some social event.

This was one of William Reed's many *talents*—he routinely used money to construct invisible chains for everyone in his life. Yanking at these chains at will, he always got what he wanted, manipulating people around him like his very own circus of marionettes.

No matter how much Hunter craved freedom, he couldn't easily run away from home. Without his father's money, Hunter had no idea how to support himself on his own.

It was another way of control on the part of William Reed. Hunter was born with a silver spoon in his mouth and raised in luxury. He didn't work a day in his life, and knew little about how to survive in the real world without the allowance from his father. He didn't know where to begin looking for a job. Even the most basic things in life like cooking a meal or doing laundry were outside of his skills and abilities.

Even if he took a chance and ran away in hopes to make it on his own, his father would simply pull the strings of the intricate web he had constructed over the course of his long and shady life, and Hunter would be back in the mansion in no time, facing the consequences of his disobedience.

But Hunter had a plan.

Over the course of several months, he worked out the details with the help of David, their chauffeur, during the fifteen-minute rides to and from school each day.

David was a simple and honest man, and he listened. Hunter took special care to hide his bruises from him, because, out of the many people surrounding him every day, David cared enough to figure out the reason for them. And if he did, if David found out of his boss's physical abuse of his son, Hunter couldn't predict the outcome of his possible actions then. He couldn't risk getting David fired and removed from his life.

It didn't escape David's attention, however, that the relationship between Hunter and his father was strained. His tactful questions and endless patience, along with an ability to listen, finally coaxed Hunter out of his protective shell and compelled him to open up.

Together, they had concluded that hockey was Hunter's best ticket to freedom. Of all the sports, he loved playing hockey the most, and he excelled at it. The plan was to join a team at university and work his ass off to make it to the pros.

Signing a big league contract would not only ensure his independence, but would also give him the means to keep his father out of his life for good.

Hunter experienced a flash of satisfaction every time he thought about the fit of rage his father would have when he'd find out that his son was not going to lead the carefully planned life he'd arranged for him.

Maybe that would be the time when that angry, burgundy vein on his forehead would finally burst, and the rage would end William Reed.

"We're gonna go to Kevin's house first. Drink his dad's booze." Vince's annoyingly cheerful voice brought Hunter back to the moment. "Looks like we need to catch up with you, man." He tipped his chin at the bottle of Crown Royal in Hunter's hand.

"Why wait?" Hunter rasped and shoved the bottle at Vince. It's not like they needed to worry about DUI charges—Vince's dad would get his son cleared of them in no time.

Just like if Hunter were to commit a crime, William Reed would promptly deal with it. Hunter's crime would be his father's problem.

*'My name is your legacy'* his father loved to repeat. And there was nothing in this world that he seemed to care more about than his name.

See how you'd like it if I soiled it. If I ripped to shreds your pristine reputation, which is built on lies. If I shoved your legacy into the mud where it belongs.

The poison of deep-rooted hatred, mixed with whisky, flowed through his veins. Anger and hate kept building up, churning hot, with nowhere to go.

"Hey, I know that girl." Vince pointed ahead. "It's Sophie Morel, she tutors Riley. Not that she could make my dumb sister smarter. No one could," he snorted.

Hunter's focus narrowed on the lone figure walking along the road. Lost in his troubled thoughts, he noticed just now that they had gotten off the highway and were driving along a ravine on the road going through the park by the river.

It was well into spring, the time when the ever-fluctuating weather in Calgary was the most volatile. The bright Alberta sun would warm up the air well into the double digits during the day, only for the temperatures to drop to below zero after the sunset.

Illuminated by the Hummer's headlights, the girl walked swiftly, huddling into the thick, light-brown sweater and hiding her face from the wind behind the fuzzy collar.

Sophie Morel.

He recognized the name from his mother talking about some charity events he always only half listened to. His mother seemed to be most impressed by the girl's French father, especially by his financial success and vast influence in Europe.

His stare glued to the girl's back.

Another one born with a silver spoon in her mouth.

"I know her, too. She's weird." Jared's deep voice chimed in from the back seat. "She volunteers at the shelter that my mom wrote an article about last month."

The small figure fighting against the wind on the deserted road didn't seem entirely unfamiliar. Hunter must have seen her around the school somewhere. As exclusive as Sunny Ridge was, it didn't have that many students.

Another fake.

As if the world wasn't full of them, people like his mother, who handed out checks to charities for photo-ops, publicity, and tax write-offs for his father, who murdered animals that didn't fit into his fucking budget.

"It doesn't look like she's going to the party. Must think she's too good to hang out with us," Vince snickered. "Let's bring the party to her!"

There was something about the girl that irritated Hunter as Vince pulled the Hummer over. The fog of alcohol clouding his senses made it hard for him to put his finger on what it was.

Her skirt?

It was wide and long, the hem brushed the top of her ballet flats, the wide frill on the bottom embroidered with small blue flowers. The rest of the skirt was pure white.

Pristine, untouched, innocent.

Fake.

There was nothing pure or innocent left in this world. Only dirt and lies were real.

He hardly heard Vince offer a ride, was barely aware of the girl accepting it and getting in the Hummer.

His eyes straight ahead, he gulped whiskey from the now half-empty bottle, his chest heaving, straining to contain the intoxicated rage that had a whole world as its target now.

It barely registered with Hunter that Vince turned from the road and drove along the riverbank.

The girl protested the detour from the back seat, but no one paid her much attention. Her voice, melodious and sweet, supported the illusion of an angel on Earth, which only increased Hunter's fury.

A sick feeling churned his stomach, and he jumped out of his seat as soon as Vince stopped the truck. He slammed the door shut with force that made him stagger, unsteady on his feet.

Somewhere in the periphery of his impaired awareness, his friends were laughing at their own crude jokes. Someone, probably Jared, pushed the girl. She stumbled backwards, only to be caught by Taj, his arms around her middle.

The whisky had reached his brain and took over completely. The muddy cloud of intoxication reduced all his thoughts and emotions to a fuzzy tunnel. His perception narrowed to one single focus—the pure white of the girl's skirt. No one had the right to look so pure and innocent, because the whole world around him was built on hatred and lies.

She begged them to let her go, but it wasn't her pleas that made him yell, "Stop!" to his friends. It was the sight of Taj's hands crushing the soft material of her skirt. Soiling its purity with his touch.

She was Hunter's to crush, to soil, to ruin. Only his. In his twisted mind, flooded with alcohol, the world owed him, and she was the one to pay.

He lurched forward, struggling to keep his balance.

"Mine," he growled, tossing the near-empty bottle away with force, and grabbed her.

The sweet girly smell of her skin caught him off guard and overwhelmed his senses, making him pause for a second.

She used the moment and twisted out of his arms.

The sight of her fleeing ignited a predatory urge. He tore after her, his gaze glued to the soles of her ballet flats kicking up the hem of her skirt as she ran from him.

Even in her shoes with slippery flat soles, even with her legs shorter than his, she ran faster than him. Fear gave her speed, and the amount of alcohol he consumed left him unfocused and clumsy.

Desperate to get away from him, though, she tripped over her own feet and fell, crying out in defeat, because she must have known then that she had lost.

He fell on top of her, trapping her under his larger body. Her delicate scent, the warmth of her slender body under him did not escape him, but it was not about that. The lust that made his dick rock-hard the moment his crotch connected with her ass thrashing under him had little to do with the person he was assaulting and had everything to do with the intoxicating sense of power that rose from a dark pit of anger and overtook his entire being.

The painful memory of the defeat he felt laying on the floor in his father's office—the helplessness of that moment—had finally receded under the onslaught of invigorating sense of power and control. Crushing another into the ground made him feel strong, his head reeling from his own dominance. For once, the victim wasn't him.

Right now, he was the one on top, like his father.

Father.

That was what Hunter was doing right now—he was acting exactly like William Reed. The thought pierced through him like an icy arrow, momentarily sobering his foggy brain and paralyzing his body.

This was his father's true legacy.

The legacy of blood he couldn't fight.

There was no escape for Hunter, his father's son. Sooner or later he would turn just like him. Judging by what he was doing—the transformation had already begun.

The girl's desperate scream solidified the horrifying awareness of the monster he had become, shaking him to the core.

She pushed up from the ground, rolling his now limp body aside, and glanced his way. Her large, grey eyes, wide with terror, met his just for a fraction of a moment. In the moonlight, they glistened bright and wild on her face covered in dirt.

The next moment she was gone. But the memory would remain forever.

His eyes closed, he pressed his forehead into the dry grass, wishing he could just stay here until the earth took him like a pile of old leaves.

All emotion vanished, drained into the cold ground below him, leaving behind just a black hole in his chest, in the place he had once believed he had a heart.

# Chapter 24

## Monster

Now.

Propped on an elbow, he leaned over the sleeping Sophie. The moon rose outside the balcony doors. In its soft light mixed with the warm glow from the fireplace, Sophie's face seemed peaceful. She trusted him to keep her safe in her dreams, without realizing what kind of a monster she'd allowed close to her.

For days after that night, he'd waited for her to report him, expecting the doorbell of the mansion to ring any minute, with the police standing on the other side to arrest him.

The punishment he was waiting for never happened. And the gnawing guilt inside turned into a deeper form of torment.

His partying increased, helping him make it through those last months at home. Alcohol had become his trusted tool for coping with guilt and trying to forget about the monster he had glimpsed inside himself. But whiskey made it impossible to control the anger.

The suppressed rage had been seething inside him for years, fed and nurtured by his father's regular attacks. With alcohol weakening his defences, the anger sprang out in fiery outbursts that no one could control, definitely not Hunter himself.

Somehow he still made it through high school, and flew to New York State for his first year of university. Being away from home gave him a new hope.

Initially, he was even able to stick to the life plan that he had devised with David. He made it into the university hockey team and for a while kept up with the rigorous training and discipline. He even maintained his grades at the required level.

Eventually, however, the monster caught up with him. And the parties, the fights, and the booze took over his lifestyle once again with a vengeance.

His grades started slipping. After a while, he was barely able to keep up with his team's practice times, turning from one of the most promising athletes into a wild card that the coach didn't want to bet on anymore.

Just a couple of months into his second year, it became clear even his father's money and influence wouldn't be able to keep him from being expelled at the end of the semester.

That was about the time when he met Cecilia, and then all his problems became trivial when faced with the impossible.

Scared and alone, he ended up revealing himself to David when he came to the remote estate in the woods with William Reed's party.

David, overwhelmed with the realization of what his charge had become once he finally accepted the fact that the wild beast in front of him was indeed Hunter—insisted they tell his father.

If anyone could do anything about his situation and find a way to undo what was done to him, Hunter still believed it was William Reed. The faith that his father's powers were limitless had been with him since childhood, compelling him to ask for help.

As expected, his father had an extremely hard time believing Hunter's story, even more so accepting his son's new appearance.

When David recounted their conversation, Hunter feared that his father would actually decide to use one of the brand new, never-fired rifles from the house to hunt his own son.

A rifle was slung over his father's shoulder when he met Hunter on the riverbank for the last time, but at least he wasn't pointing it at him. He threatened Hunter in every other way, though. Furious, he accused him of every sin under the sun, cursing him and the day he was born.

As the grey, icy water of the river tumbled past—the noise barely masking the filthy abuse and threats spewing from his father's mouth—the blinding rage rose to the surface again, annihilating commonsense.

Hunter rose to his feet. The maddening fury that made him go against a baseball bat once, propelled him into an attack when his father yanked the rifle off his shoulder.

He knocked the gun out of his father's grip. His monstrous paws wrapped tight around the man's throat, the tips of his claws piercing the delicate human skin. He saw the flash of terror in his father's bulging eyes.

Just like that, the balance of power shifted. The childhood fear beaten into him during years of abuse fell away. And the god he had believed his father to be, turned out to be nothing but a sniveling old man.

Hunter could have had his revenge right then and there. He had nothing to lose—he was already a monster. By killing his father he would just become a hunted one. But he refused to take the last step in abandoning his humanity by killing this whimpering excuse of a man hanging limp in his hands.

He let William Reed go and ran back into the woods, belated rifle shots at his back whizzing by his horns.

Less than a month later, his father was killed in a car accident. David brought him the news, along with some supplies and groceries.

Hunter sat alone on the riverbank after hearing about his father's death. Watching the rapids churning among the rocks, he searched for any satisfaction or triumph inside him and found none. There wasn't any sadness or grief either. *Nothing* was the only thing that his father left behind.

Hunter's mother finally got her heart's desire—her husband gone, leaving all his money in her sole possession. Either carried away celebrating the unexpected fortune, or simply from the effects of long-term substance abuse, she passed away from an accidental drug overdose just a few months after her husband's death.

As a final courtesy to her memory or maybe just out of habit of cleaning up the Reeds' mess, even after their deaths, his father's lawyers ensured that the official cause of her passing was a heart failure.

Hunter mourned his mother. Not the woman who spent his school years upstairs in a drug-induced dream trying to hide from the nightmare of her marriage, and not the one who would clean up and dress up once in a while to show her face in public at some important social function.

He mourned the much younger woman he still remembered. The one who told him stories about her childhood vacations in the sunny Mediterranean and even sang him lullabies when he was very small.

After the death of his parents, all of their possessions, including this hunting estate, became his. The only problem was that he couldn't assume any of it in person. He was trapped in this place, physically unable to leave. Little good would it do, even if he could travel to Calgary to visit a lawyer's office, looking the way he did.

Through David, he was able to receive all of the legal correspondence. Together, they managed to arrange a lease of the house for David. Thus making it easier for him to oversee the maintenance of the place and obtain whatever supplies necessary as well as hire help when needed.

With David around, even as a beast, Hunter still led a civilized life. With him gone, the last link to society had been severed for

Hunter, leaving him to spend his days as nothing more than an animal.

Until Sophie.

As starved for human company as he'd been, he tried hard to resist her. He told her to go back to live her life. Only now he knew, the life she'd been living was nowhere as full and vibrant as he'd imagined.

She had been trapped in the prison of her own mind. Like a bird with clipped wings, she had been struggling through life, unable to take off because of his actions on that one drunken night.

Her soft, even breathing moved a lock of hair that had fallen across her face. Carefully, he lifted the strand on the tip of his claw and moved it behind her ear.

Being this close, her gentle scent enveloped him, but the wild lust was easier to tame—her fear of his touch kept his desire for her locked in a cage of self-control. The simple joy of being near her was all he allowed himself to feel.

The slightly musty smell of the air in the room tainted Sophie's scent. If she were to stay here more often, he'd definitely need to make it more comfortable for her somehow.

Was it her pity for his pathetic ass that kept bringing her over here again and again? Or did she find something in him that compelled her to seek his company? She told him things she claimed she'd never told anyone, not even her mother. For some twisted reason, fate sent her to this god-forsaken place and he became her confidante.

Watching a faint smile flutter across her lips, he wondered if this could be his chance to undo at least some of the wrongs he'd done.

Maybe there could still be a purpose to his miserable life?

What if he could be the friend she so desperately needed? Would it help her find her wings and feel the joy again?

# Chapter 25

## Sophie

I opened my eyes to bright sunlight behind the glass doors of the balcony. It took me a moment to remember where I was and then a little longer to realize that I had fallen asleep after having a nightmare. Something that never happened before when I was in bed alone.

Right, I wasn't alone last night, was I? Monster had been here.

I got up quickly. The fireplace had been lit again, making crawling out from under the cozy comforter much more pleasant. After throwing on my jeans, clean top, and a sweater, I ran downstairs.

"Good morning." Monster's deep voice greeted me from the kitchen, and I returned his greeting, glad to see his scruffy figure hulking over the counter. He took a towel off a pot of tea and poured a cup.

A plate of leftover dinner rolls sat in the middle of the kitchen island. I took one before sitting down on a barstool and realized that the roll was sliced in the middle, slightly toasted, and buttered.

"You made me breakfast?" I smiled. "Again?"

"Yeah." He rubbed the back of his neck, sliding the teacup my way. "No rabbit meat this time."

"Thank you." My smile grew wider before I bit into a roll. "And thank you for staying with me last night."

He nodded silently and sat at the other end of the counter with a glass of water for himself.

"How long are you staying at Rocky River, Sophie?"

"Um. I would definitely have to be home for Christmas . . ."

"Would you stay until then?"

Christmas was still a few weeks away. There was no real reason for me to leave before then. In fact, I could come up with a few very compelling reasons for me to stay. One of them was staring at me now expectantly.

"Yes, I believe I could stay until Christmas." I smiled.

"Good." He exhaled with visible relief.

"You want me to stick around?"

"Very much. Actually, I have a favour to ask of you."

"Do you need me to bring anything?"

"Not this time. I was wondering if you'd sign a lease for this place."

"What?" I almost choked on my tea. "A lease?"

"Yes. If you were legally leasing the house, you could call maintenance people, right?"

"Right, but . . ."

But I'm not local to the area. I will be leaving to go home, eventually. I'm already renting an apartment in town.

There were many more *'buts'* I could come up with. The thing was, though, Monster was asking for help from the only person he could. He had no one else.

"Sure. I'll do it."

"Good." He rose from his seat and brought a black folder from the dining table. "Here is the lease agreement for you to sign." He placed the folder next to me, and I opened it immediately.

"The lease is for a year," I said quietly.

"It's a standard form. You can cancel it any time without a penalty. I've put a clause in there."

"Okay." I nodded, continuing to read. "The monthly payments will be made from a trust account?"

"It's the trust fund that the lawyers set up for me after my parents' death."

"So, basically, *you'll* be paying yourself?"

"Sophie, I'm asking you for a favour. I wouldn't expect you to pay to lease a house you don't need. An agreement requires some money exchange. So there it is."

"There is no owner's signature."

"I'll sign it after you do." His voice was quiet now, his tone even more serious than before.

"You don't want me to know your name?" An accusatory note slipped into my voice. "You're leasing me your house, but you don't trust me with your name?"

His broad chest heaved with a sigh.

"It's not a trust issue, Sophie. Please believe me."

"What is it then? Will you ever tell me your real name?"

"Honestly, I don't know. I'm not sure what is the right thing to do here." He seemed to consider something for a moment, the velvety fur on his forehead wrinkling in a frown. "What if I told you that I want you to get to know *me,* without any names? The name I used as a human belonged to the man I was then. I'm still trying to figure out who or what I am now, but it's definitely no longer him. Would you just call me *Monster* for now? Until I figure out who I truly am?"

I searched his eyes for any teasing or even sarcasm and couldn't find any. His expression remained very serious, somber even.

"If that's what you want . . ." I would've loved to know his name. Not because calling him *Monster* bothered me—but because I now knew he had a *real* name. His past life was a part of him, and I longed to know all about him. However, I also understood his desire to start anew. "Okay."

"Thank you." He lowered himself back onto the barstool.

I almost finished my tea, when I noticed that he hadn't touched his water at all. Thinking back to our dinner last night, I remembered him eating with me but never drinking anything either.

"Is something wrong with your water?" I asked, taking another bite of my roll.

"No," he replied quickly. "Why?"

I inspected his face for a moment, his mouth, to be precise. The thin, dark lips stretched over the teeth on his long snout. And I wondered if the shape of his face made drinking out of a glass uncomfortable, if not impossible.

Next, I got up and took out two bowls from the kitchen cabinet.

"What are you doing?" he asked, with a wary note in his tone.

"I'd love to have another cup of tea if you don't mind." I reached for the teapot. "Only I'll drink it from the bowl this time." I poured some tea into one of the bowls then slid the empty one his way. "Would you join me?"

"Why?" His back straightened.

I returned to my barstool then took a sip from my bowl of tea. Fresh from the teapot, the liquid proved to be way too hot. I gasped and spat it out immediately. The bowl burnt my hands too, and I nearly dropped it splashing the tea all over the counter.

Monster watched me with a raised eyebrow.

"Okay, what was that?" The confused expression on his face was way too funny for me to feel mortified.

"*This*," I snorted, unable to hold back a laugh, "was how I make a fool out of myself. Come on, Monster." I shoved the empty bowl closer to him. "There is no way you can do worse than me."

"Wanna bet?" His voice sounded sulky, but the lines on his face smoothed out, as his general expression lightened. He poured the water out of his glass into the bowl and lapped at it with his long, wide tongue a couple of times. "How was that?" He asked carefully, raising his head.

I eyed the few drops on the counter around his bowl then pointed at the puddles of tea around mine.

"What do you think?" I laughed. "No wonder I've never been invited for a bowl of tea by anyone."

Despite the sharp points of teeth peeking out from under his parted lips, the lopsided grin he gave me was very human.

"I'll always have a bowl of tea ready for you, Sophie." A warm, velvet note in his voice sent a tingling sensation through my chest. His smile grew wider. "Here, you have been invited."

# Chapter 26

## Sophie

I mailed the copy of the lease agreement to the office of Monster's lawyer as soon as I drove back to Rocky River that morning. As soon as it was done, I let my friends in town know that the heir of the estate in the woods had asked me to take care of the place.

It was a relief to finally have an honest explanation of my drives to the forest and a valid excuse for my odd purchases.

In response to questions of how I knew the owner in the first place, I still had to lie, though, to keep Monster's existence a secret. I told everyone that it turned out our families knew each other.

I hated the uncomfortable feeling that scratched inside me when I told the lie, and I could only hope that the day might come when Monster would no longer have to hide from the world.

In the weeks before Christmas I visited him several more times, bringing him groceries and house maintenance supplies. I also had a few appointments with trade people on the property. They inspected the services around the house and started working on bringing them back to life.

Between my visits, Monster continued making improvements on the house and surrounding grounds. He replaced the broken patio door with the new one I'd ordered. Together, we scrubbed the kitchen inside and out, getting rid of years' worth of dust and grime. Then started out on a thorough cleaning of the rest of the house.

While we worked, we talked.

Despite him opening up to me, Monster was still reluctant to talk freely about his past. I struggled to piece together his previous life from the tiny glimpses he had shared with me so far.

On the other hand, Monster seemed to be hungry to know everything about me. It continued to amaze me how good a listener he turned out to be. He asked thoughtful questions and didn't seem to be bothered by any amount of detail I provided.

Encouraged by his attention, I told him all about my own childhood, my parents, and every single pet I ever had.

Scrubbing the walls of the living room, I described in detail everything I loved about France and how different it was from Canada. And while rolling the huge, filthy rugs to get rid of them, I talked about the travelling I had done.

"There is so much of the world I still want to see," I said wistfully then remembered that *he* no longer had a chance to see any of it.

"Travelling completely on my own was something I was never allowed to do, and now can't do anyway." The bitter resignation in his voice tugged at my heart.

"Do you really think it was Cecilia who did this to you?" I asked quietly. Since he told me his story, we hadn't spoken of it again.

I sensed he didn't like remembering that part of his life, but I couldn't stop thinking about his incredible physical transformation and the possible reasons for it. There must be an explanation as to what happened to him, and if he could figure out exactly why and how his appearance had changed, maybe he could reverse it?

"I don't really know what to think, Sophie." He heaved the rolled rug over his shoulder, dirt and dry pine needles dusting his fur. "But do you see any other explanation?"

I pondered his question for the few minutes it took him to carry the rug out to the driveway to be picked up by a junk removal truck I planned to call later.

The picture he painted of his behaviour that night was far from flattering. In fact, I had a very hard time reconciling the image of that arrogant, cold-hearted college boy with the person I had been watching emerging from under Monster's beastly exterior during these past weeks.

"Do you think Cecilia would still be angry at you?" I asked when he returned.

He crouched on the floor next to me but paused before rolling another rug. "The way I treated her?" His voice was gruff. "I believe she had every right to turn me into a frog and feed me to a snake."

"Would you like to find her and maybe apologize? It couldn't hurt . . ."

"Fuck." His chest heaved. "There are so many people I need to apologize to, Sophie. So many I wish I could say sorry to and beg for their forgiveness. The list is a mile long. Cecilia is way up there. And you . . ."

"Me?"

He propped himself with a knee against the floor and faced me. "I'm so sorry for all the harm I did to you."

Unnerved by the intensity of his stare, I patted his hand.

"It's fine. It's not hard to forgive. I realize I had to deal with a feral beast the first time we met, and I know you wouldn't want to hurt me now. Not intentionally. Do you think if you apologized to her too, she would forgive you? Maybe undo what she's done?"

He grabbed my hand.

"Would *you*, Sophie?" His voice was low, and his focus on me hadn't wavered. "Do you think an apology is all it takes? Would you forgive Hunter Reed if he said sorry?"

The mere sound of that name made me wince. My breath hitched under the heavy wave of resentment, making everything inside me harden to ice.

"Hunter Reed." I swallowed hard. "He would never apologize, Monster," I said quietly. "I watched him in school. It was like the blindfold fell from my eyes after that night and I saw his actions for what they were, no longer fooled by his good looks. His arrogance. The way he treated other people. I never noticed any remorse in him. He certainly never apologized to anyone."

I rubbed my forehead with a shaking hand. The memories were always hard, and normally, I'd avoid them at all cost. But I sensed the reasons for Monster's question were important to him and wanted my answer to be useful and real.

"When you mistreated Cecilia, she must have wanted to punish you, making you regret what you did. That's why I wonder if she knew that her punishment worked, would she reverse whatever she'd done to you? In my case, I never wished ill on Hunter Reed. I'd rather he'd never come into my life in the first place. All I've been trying to do is erase him from my mind, hoping with everything I have that our paths never cross again."

THE DAY BEFORE I HAD to leave for Calgary, I drove to Monster's house again. By now, talking to him had become almost a daily necessity. I caught myself having conversations with him in my head even when he was not around.

The topics didn't need to be deep or personal. I would wonder if he'd like the new dish Melanie had added to the menu. Or wished I could ask him something about a movie I'd watched with Jo.

Christmas was the time I was supposed to leave Rocky River for good. My leg had long healed. The lunch program at school was up and running smoothly. As long as I wrote the monthly cheques for it to continue, I could arrange for others to place grocery orders. My presence was no longer required. Even Jo, my closest friend in town, was set to leave in a few months, as soon as her contract was up.

Monster was the biggest reason why I extended my rental agreement with Bob and Melanie until the end of January. I told myself he needed me, at the very least to help him finish bringing the house back to life. By now, the heating was functional, but the electricity was not on, and the plumbing still needed some repairs.

However, I couldn't lie to myself—I needed him too. I was leaving to spend Christmas with my mother, but I had already promised to come back for New Year's to celebrate it with him.

On my last day, we roasted marshmallows in the fireplace in the living room and drank hot chocolate.

We said goodbye at the house before I left that afternoon, but driving to the road, I caught a flash of brown fur between the tree trunks—Monster obviously decided to see me off.

I pulled over to the side of the road and walked back to the end of the driveway.

"You should have told me you wanted to see me off, I would've given you a ride." I called into the trees.

"I wouldn't fit in the truck." He pointed at his horns, stepping out on the driveway from behind the tree line. "Anyway, I like running."

His chest heaved, but his breathing had slowed down as he came closer. Placing a hand on the chain-link fence on the side of the driveway, he remained behind the invisible property line.

"Did you want to say another goodbye?" I smiled.

"Honestly?" He rubbed the back of his neck. "I was hoping for a goodbye hug."

I studied his now familiar face, the way the corners of his eyes crinkled when he looked at me, the warmth of his expression.

Did I really use to find him scary?

Even his size, the imposing height and bulk of him no longer felt intimidating to me. If anything, his appearance promised safety and protection.

I stepped over the invisible barrier and into his arms.

"This will help me make it through the week without you," he whispered above my ear, holding me close.

Warm and firm, it was a hug that, for as long as it lasted, made everything right with the world. I pressed my face into the fragrant softness of his fur, wishing we could just stay like this forever. It felt so wrong leaving him behind, especially at Christmas.

"I'll come back."

"I know." His voice didn't hold much conviction, though. And I remembered that he must have heard the same promise from David.

I leaned back to catch his eye.

"Is there anything you'd like me to bring for you this time?"

The afternoon sun brought out warm orange flecks in the brilliant mix of green and brown in his gaze.

"Just you, princess." A faint low rumble in his voice resonated through me as his eyes flickered between mine.

If only I could take him with me somehow.

Curling my fingers in the fur on his biceps, I rose to my toes impulsively and planted a kiss on the tip of his nose.

The rumble in his chest grew louder, and his arms tightened around me.

"Please, come back," he pleaded.

"I will," I promised.

# Chapter 27

## Sophie

Christmas at home was fun and chaotic as usual. My mom and her friends made every gathering special, if a little crazy at times.

Jeff spent two days with us. Watching him dote on my mom filled my heart with gratitude. And seeing Mom bloom with happiness under his attention, made me happy too.

Jeff's Christmas gift to my mom was a weeklong cruise in the Caribbean. And Mom squealed like a little girl when she unwrapped the tickets.

They left a couple of days after Christmas to ring in New Year's on the cruise ship, and I was supposed to leave for Rocky River two days later, on the earliest flight available.

Thoughts of Monster wouldn't leave me. I wondered what he was doing almost every minute of the day. His future, spending the rest of his life as a prisoner on the remote estate, seemed tragic. And the fact that he never had a chance to right the wrong he'd done felt unfair.

Once I was left alone in the house, with all the craziness of the holidays behind, I found myself in front of my laptop, trying to figure out a way to search for Cecilia.

Monster couldn't give me much information about her when I asked. To his chagrin, he didn't remember anything about her beyond her name and appearance. And I was worried that trying to find her now would be like looking for a needle in a haystack.

On the other hand, wouldn't the ability to turn a man into a beast make Cecilia a rather unique woman?

I typed '*Cecilia, the magic witch*' in the browser's search bar.

The search results that came back were ordinary and benign—video games, children's books, fantasy illustrations. No women with that name who supposedly possessed magical powers either.

Clicking on one result after another, I delved deeper and deeper. Witchcraft, demonology, rituals of summoning spirits, magical spells, life beyond death—things that appeared at once fascinating and unbelievable, and sometimes even disturbing.

It amazed me how vast that world seemed to be, how many people had an active part in it, and how many believed.

After hours spent sifting through pages of information, the most promising result I could come up with was a woman named Cecilia, who was listed as a guest speaker at a witchcraft fair held in New Orleans in March.

Unsurprisingly, there was no contact information available for her on the website, but after opening an account with the organization and paying the small membership fee, I was able to email the event organizers.

In my message to them I attempted to be as specific as possible to catch Cecilia's attention, without providing too much personal information, to make her understand I was not just a random person. I begged for her to get in touch with me, desperately hoping that it was indeed the right Cecilia.

If it was, and if she really cursed Monster somehow, then maybe after all these years her wrath had worn off? Maybe if she knew of Monster's remorse, she could reverse what she'd done and release him from his prison?

DARKNESS SUFFOCATED me. The crushing weight pinning me down . . . My silent scream helpless in its desperation . . .

With a loud gasp I sat up in bed, doubling in half, as my heart beat high in my throat.

Another nightmare.

I touched my forehead beaded with sweat.

Again.

I stared into the darkness of my bedroom in Calgary, unseeing. A long breath in. Pause. A slow breath out. Waiting for my pulse to slow down and the panic to recede.

With another deep inhale, I got out of bed and flicked the lights on. Without Monster here to keep the darkness at bay, I knew I wouldn't be able to sleep any more tonight.

I walked into the kitchen and filled the kettle with water to make myself a cup of tea. My gaze fell on my shaking hands.

It will pass. It'll all pass soon.

Only it hadn't passed, had it? It'd been year after year of the same—living in fear of another nightmare, always scared to go to bed alone as evening approached.

And after years of fighting it, I still hadn't made any real progress on conquering it on my own. On the contrary, the fear had spilled from my nightmares into reality, taking over many aspects of my life.

Anxiety filled my brain, rendering me unable to focus on anything for long and often making it impossible to make a simple decision.

How many relationships had I started, only to have them fail almost as soon as they'd begun because almost every attempt at intimacy with a man brought on the same devastating panic. Fear made me unable to relax in a man's arms and enjoy his touch.

The water in the kettle boiled, triggering the automated shutoff switch. Still, I sat there, staring at it, without making a move.

How long was I going to let fear dictate my life? And could there ever be a way to stop the nightmares? I was so tired of being afraid of the night.

I longed to feel a man's weight over me one day and have my heart fill with excitement instead of dread.

Determined, I got up and found my cell phone.

I knew the number by heart. So many times, I'd given it to women in shelters, urging them to call for help whenever they needed it. There was always someone on the other end of the line, ready to listen, day and night, and they had a whole list of resources for further assistance.

Yet I had never dialed it myself. I believed with all my heart that there was help out there but had spent years alternating between being afraid to ask for it and being in denial that I needed any.

Just the thought of setting the dark memories free by talking to someone about them used to paralyze me with fear.

Now that I had opened up to Monster, I knew I was capable of doing it again. I could be stronger than the nightmares, and dialing the number was my first step on the way to win over them.

"Crisis line," a friendly female voice greeted me. "How are you doing tonight?"

With a bracing inhale, I said the three little words that proved to be nearly impossible to say out loud, "I need help."

# Chapter 28

## Sophie

As I approached Monster's estate, I almost swerved off the road, searching for a glimpse of russet fur between the tree trunks behind the chain-link fence. I missed him while away. The need to see him now was almost painful.

I left Rocky River immediately after a very early breakfast, and it was still morning when I got to the fence, a couple of hours before my usual arrival time.

The gate was open, but I couldn't spot Monster's shape anywhere as I drove Bob's truck up the driveway.

I parked in the carport and opened the back of the truck to get out the supplies I brought with me.

"Welcome back." The gruff, familiar voice behind made me jump in surprise, immediately filling me with joy.

"There you are!" I turned to face him, happiness from seeing him again floating weightlessly through me.

He stood a couple of feet away, the wide grin on his face left his snow-white fangs on display.

"I was by the river." He gestured east. "It's so, so nice to have you back, Sophie." His voice strained, his hands twitched at his sides, but he didn't come closer.

"Oh, Monster," I exhaled, closing the distance between us and wrapping my arms tightly around him. The happy feeling radiated through me. "I missed you."

"You did?" The note of disbelief in his voice made me squeeze him more.

"Very much."

His big, strong arms went around me, his large body surrounding me. The fresh smell of winter on his fur and the warm spice of his skin underneath enveloped me, and I drew in a lungful, unable to resist the invigorating mix. I splayed my hands on his back, enjoying the feel of the hard planes of muscles under his fur.

"I missed you too, Sophie." He tucked my head under his chin and buried his face in my hair. "I've waited for this." He drew me in closer until there was no space left between us at all. "Just to hold you again."

"YOU HAVE A CHRISTMAS tree!"

The fresh scent of pine needles filled the air, coming from the decorated tree standing in the living room next to the fireplace.

"It's gorgeous." I walked closer. The strings of red and yellow lights on it turned out to be outdoor patio lights, shaped like pineapples and miniature red plastic cups.

"These were all I found in the attic." Monster had taken the grocery bags to the kitchen and now stood right behind me.

"Well, this makes it by far the most unique Christmas tree I've ever seen. Too bad I wasn't here to help you decorate it. We should've done it before I left."

"Nah. I didn't want it here while you were gone. But it feels right, now that you're back."

I smiled, turning around to face him. "I brought champagne for me and popcorn for you, Popcorn Monster."

"A true celebration then!" He laughed heartily.

Watching him, I realized it was the first time I'd ever heard him laugh. Not chuckle or snicker, but laugh. Open and happy.

"A true celebration, Monster."

HE HELPED ME ORGANIZE the supplies and groceries. The heating at the house was functioning well, the propane tanks outside had been filled before Christmas, and Monster had a generator supplying electricity for now because the solar panels and their connection were still in the process of being repaired.

Through our combined effort of the past weeks, the house was warm and cozy, despite its gargantuan size. The cold and snow outside made me appreciate the warmth inside that much more.

"The ice along the river is the thickest I've seen," Monster remarked, sweeping the floors in the kitchen while I did the dishes after lunch.

"Hopefully, you'll get running water here next week, so you'll never have to go swimming in the icy river again." I shivered at the thought of having to bathe outside in the winter.

"Oh, I'll still be swimming, princess. Running water or not."

"Really?" I placed the last cup on the rack to dry and turned to face him. "Even on a day like today?"

"Sure." He dumped the garbage from the dustpan into the bin and put the broom away. "I was going to swim this morning, right before you came."

"Did I interrupt you on your way for an icy dip?"

"Something I didn't mind at all." With a tip of his claw, he carefully moved a strand of hair away from my face.

"Do you really enjoy it?" I dropped the dishcloth on the counter.

"Very much." He slid his gaze to my lips and swept the sharp points of his teeth with his tongue.

"Swimming in the river, I mean," I clarified, unsure if we were still talking about the same thing.

He closed his eyes, swallowing hard.

"Sure." He glanced my way again, taking a step back. "I love swimming."

"Okay then. Let's go to the river."

"Together?"

"Yep, I'll come with you. Just give me a minute."

I quickly threw on my winter clothes then ran to the closest bathroom to grab a towel.

"Do you want to swim, too?" He eyed the towel in my hands.

"Oh no!" I laughed. "I'll walk to the river with you. I'm not jumping in, though. At least not as long as there is still any ice in the water."

"Why the towel then?"

"For you," I replied, on my way to the front door.

"For me?" Monster followed. "Really? You think I need one?"

"Come on, it's freezing." I shuddered as we stepped outside.

It was cold even for the end of December. Dressed as warmly as I was, the frost still nipped at the exposed skin of my face as we followed the well-worn path to the east end of his property.

"One of many advantages of having thick fur—I rarely get cold."

"One of many? What are other advantages of having fur?"

"Um . . ." He stared at the sky above us for a second then exhaled a laugh, making me smile too. "I really can't think of any others."

After a while, the noise of water rushing between rocks announced that the stream was close. In a few more minutes, I glimpsed the riverbank between the trees.

"This time of the year, I can only swim in that part over there." Monster pointed at an area of relatively placid water. "Everywhere else there are either too many rocks here or the ice is too thick. The rest of the open water is on the other side of the property line—I can't get to it."

The reminder of the invisible but impenetrable boundaries of his prison dampened my easy mood.

Please, let it be the right Cecilia, I prayed, thinking of the email I'd sent. And please, give him a chance to be free again.

To avoid giving him hope only to possibly disappoint him later, I'd decided not to mention anything about the email to him for now.

"Watch this, princess!" Monster's excited voice brought me back to the moment.

He ripped his jeans off quickly and dashed for the open pool of water with a clear layer of thin ice formed over it.

He jumped from the rocks at the edge. His body stretched into a graceful arch in the air before crashing through the ice and entering the freezing water in a smooth dive.

A wave of shivers ran along my spine as I watched the loose shards of ice close over him once he'd fully submerged into the darkness of the pool.

Crazy man.

I shook my head, clutching the towel to my chest.

His long spiraling horns re-appeared first then his head rose over the surface, shaking the water out of his mane. He waved at me and swam with long, confident strokes towards the icy edge.

His hands on the rocks, he heaved himself up and out of the river. The water flattened his fur, plastering it to his body in a thin layer clinging to the muscle underneath.

I watched, as if in slow motion, the thick biceps and the ropy muscles of his forearms ripple and bulge. His massive shoulders rolled as he pushed off the rock, straightening to his full height.

My heart sped up, threatening to jump out onto the ice-covered rocks beneath my feet.

Broad chest. Perfectly flat stomach. The layer of wet fur could not disguise the hard edges of the well-defined squares of his abs. Trim waist. The sharp V of his lower stomach, narrowing down to . . .

I should've looked away. He had come too close by now, close enough to see exactly where my gaze was directed. I should not have continued staring, but I couldn't tear my eyes away from his body.

Obviously, the cold didn't bother him in any way whatsoever. Despite the freezing water and only at half-mast, his erection still appeared massive, bobbing between his thick, muscular thighs with every step he took.

Heat flushed my face and pooled between my legs, as I stood there, my eyes wide and my heart racing. My lips parted when he reached me, his heavy gaze on my burning face.

"Don't look at me like that, princess," he rasped. His eyes flickered between mine before settling on my mouth. He lifted his hand to my face—his thumb a hairsbreadth from touching my bottom lip—then moved back from me. "Please. It makes it impossible to stay away from you."

"Stay away?" I whispered, my whole body swaying his way as if under the influence of a powerful magnet.

With a low growl, he tore his stare from me then took a few steps to the side and lowered to all fours. His paws in a wide stance, he shook the water out of his hide, looking very much like a humongous dog.

Water flew through the air in every direction. A few of the drops hit my face, bringing me out of my stupor.

The next second, he bolted past me—still on all fours—and disappeared into the forest.

After a moment of confusion, I realized what he was doing. For whatever reason, he was reminding me of what he was—a beast, an animal.

Only, it was too late. I had already discovered the man underneath his rough appearance—fur, horns, and all. For me, he had been a person more than a beast for a long time now. He was a friend, who listened, whose company I enjoyed. Someone who made me feel safe.

And someone who, apparently, could render me speechless and make me weak at the knees.

When it came to Monster, I craved being close to him. I didn't want him to *stay away*.

The affection for him that had warmed my heart for weeks grew impossibly hotter—exciting but unfamiliar and a little bit scary in its intensity. I'd never felt this way about anyone before and needed time to absorb it all.

Clutching the useless towel, I picked up his discarded jeans and started on my way back to the house.

I was sure Monster was near, watching me from the woods somewhere. I knew he wouldn't leave me to walk alone. With a cougar on the property, he never let me out of his sight. But his reasons for staying hidden worried me.

At the house, I got everything ready to make dinner, wondering if Monster would join me, or would he hunt just to prove that he was indeed an animal?

An hour dragged by, and I was beginning to really worry about him. True, the woods had been his home, but there were dangers out there, even for him. The cougar. Slick, icy rocks at the river, leading to deep, treacherous water. Occasional bears and wolves . . . My overactive imagination was coming up with more and more perils as the time passed.

I paced in front of the fireplace, wondering if I should go out there in search of him, when the door finally opened and Monster walked in, on all fours.

I twisted around to face him, an overwhelming sense of relief flooding me.

"Where have you been?" I rushed to him. "Are you okay?"

He didn't reply, sitting down on his haunches, like a giant dog. For a second, I almost envisioned him scratching behind his ear with his hind paw to complete the illusion and really drive his point across.

"Is it more comfortable for you?" I asked quietly since he continued to remain silent. "Is it easier to walk on four legs instead of two? Do you force yourself to stay bipedal for my sake?"

"It's not a matter of comfort. Some things are easier done on two legs, others on four." He wasn't looking at me when he spoke. Instead, his eyes were diverted somewhere behind me.

"Why do you insist on remaining on all fours now?"

"I—" He drew in a lungful of air and finally glanced my way. "I'm unsure who I am, Sophie. Around you, I have this uncontrollable urge to be a man, the best man I could be—"

"Then be one."

"But I'm not. Look at me!"

His eyes met mine, challenging me to disprove what I saw.

"It's not about looks." I got down on my knees in front of him, since he wouldn't get up. "It's not about your appearance to me, not anymore, and you know it. Why are you trying to convince me otherwise?"

"Because you *have* to see me as nothing else but an animal, Sophie, a monster." His chest heaved and his hands fisted at his side. "I can't give you up anymore, even as I know it would be the right thing to do. The *only* right thing to do. But I need you, more than anything in this life. Every time you leave, I exist only knowing that you'll come back."

My breath hitched, and my hand rose to cup his face, but he leaned back, evading my touch.

"Having you near is torture of another kind, though. When you look at me with this tenderness, this longing . . . when you touch me—" his eyes closed for a moment, a grimace flashed across his face. "I can't stay away," he groaned. His voice dipped lower. "I want you. I want *everything*."

"Is that why you have to stay away? Are you . . . are you afraid I'd run again?" I thought about the last time he lost control around me and I fled in confusion and fear. I could hardly blame him for pushing me away now, could I?

"I have no right to feel upset about that night, Sophie." He shook his head. "I can only be grateful that you came back."

I was unable to tear my gaze from the green-brown forest in his eyes.

"Why stay away then?" My voice was barely audible. "And what do I do if I want you close?"

"Sophie." His voice held a warning, and his whole body vibrated with tension. "You have no idea who I am—"

"But I do." I stared at him in my own challenge now. "I know who you are *to me*. You're a man I care deeply about. A man I missed terribly when I was away. You make me feel the way no one else ever has. With you, I'm not afraid to be myself. I don't have to pretend. You make me feel safe. When you're close, I can breathe easily, the world is no longer a scary place, and life itself seems to be simpler and manageable. Don't you see, Monster?" My voice shook, and I took a deep breath to steady it. "I *need* you. I need you just as much as you need me. Maybe more. Please, don't push me away," I pleaded, raising my hand back to his face again.

A sigh of relief escaped my chest, as he leaned into my touch this time.

"It can't be wrong for you to want me if I want you too, can it?" I asked quietly.

The growl in his chest resonated somewhere deep inside me, making all my limbs warm and weak at once.

"Do you really want this, Sophie?"

I cupped his face with both hands now, smoothing his mane away.

"What I feel for you is like nothing I ever felt for anyone else. It's so very new. I'm not sure I can explain it, but I want more of it. More of your words, your touch . . ."

Finally, his fists relaxed, and he placed his hands on my waist, holding me carefully, as if I were made of glass.

I slid my hands through his mane to the back of his neck.

"I want more of your hugs," I whispered, as he drew me closer with yet another deep growl. "More of your smell." I buried my face in his mane at his shoulder. "Please, give me more of you."

"You'd be appalled by what you may uncover," he warned in a whisper.

"The more I learn about the man hiding inside the beast, the more I like him," tightly wrapped in his embrace now, I replied with certainty.

A deep, shuddering breath heaved his chest and shoulders.

"As you wish, Sophie. I can't deny you anything. I can never be the man you deserve, but I'll die trying."

WE HAD DINNER SIDE by side, at the kitchen counter.

"Would you stay with me?" I asked hesitantly when he walked me up the stairs to the bedroom.

"If it'll make you happy," he replied simply.

"It will." I smiled, taking his hand in mine.

The room seemed more cozy than scary this time. Thanks to the generator, the lights went on with the click of the switch, and the flames in the fireplace appeared warm and inviting rather than intimidating.

"Sleep, princess." Monster tucked the covers around me after I had changed into my nightgown in the bathroom and climbed in bed. "I'll sit right here."

"You can lie down. Under the covers. If you want," I suggested hesitantly, unsure of his reaction.

He seemed to ponder my offer for a moment then silently flicked the lights off and climbed in bed, leaving his jeans on. The mattress dipped under his weight, and the massive bed frame groaned.

"Are you a cuddler?" I whispered in the semi-darkness of the room.

"I've no idea," he snorted. "I haven't had many opportunities to find out."

"I guess I should warn you—I cuddle. A lot."

"Do you?"

"Yep. I love spooning. And I prefer to be the big spoon."

He rose on his elbow, facing me.

"What on Earth are you talking about, Sophie?"

"Come, I'll show you. Turn your back to me."

He shook his head but did as I told him.

"Here we go," I exhaled, settling at his back and throwing one arm around his middle. "This is my favourite way to fall asleep," I murmured, pressing the side of my face to the thick fur on his back.

His torso vibrated with a chuckle.

"So, you're basically using me as a body pillow."

"Mhm." I nuzzled between his shoulder blades. "A big, scruffy body pillow. Do you mind?"

The long, silky fur of his tail brushed against the back of my leg as he wound it around my calf, anchoring me to him.

"Not at all," he replied softly and added after a small pause, "I might even get used to this."

# Chapter 29

## Sophie

"**A**re you sure you don't want any champagne? It's New Year's," I asked, holding up the bottle after pouring a glass for myself.

It was still a few minutes before midnight. Without a radio or a television in here, I had my phone alarm set to ring in the New Year on time. Now, Monster and I sat on the couch in the living room, waiting.

"No. No alcohol," Monster replied firmly.

Tonight, he'd helped me with dinner. And after we ate, we made popcorn and played the board game I'd brought from my apartment in town.

"More for me." I grinned, stuffing the bottle back into the bucket of packed snow we'd used instead of ice. "I have to warn you, though, alcohol has some weird effects on me too. Champagne especially."

"Really?"

"This is my second glass," I waved the flute in front of me. "If, after another couple I start singing Bonny Tyler's *Holding Out For A Hero* off key, please, *please*, take the bottle away from me."

"No way." He shook his head, leaning back. Amusement spread wide on his face. "*That* I've gotta see."

"No, you don't." I almost choked on the huge swig I took from my flute. "Trust me." I laughed with him. "I'd do the whole shoulder-shaking, hair-tossing, arm-sweeping thing. No!" I let a shudder ripple through my body, even as we both were choking on laughter now. "It's terrifying—"

The sound of the alarm broke the moment.

"It's here!" In my haste to give Monster a New Year hug, I tripped over my feet and crash-landed in his lap instead, straddling his thighs awkwardly. "Happy New Year," I whispered, immediately subdued by his sudden closeness.

"Happy New Year, princess." He put his hands on my waist. We stared at each other for what felt like an eternity, ignoring the alarm ringing nearby. His gaze caressed my face before landing on my lips. "I'd give everything in the world, just to be able to kiss you right now," he whispered.

Something fluttered inside me, like a kaleidoscope of some fuzzy-winged butterflies, and I realized I would've died to have that kiss from him. Gently, I stroked the short velvet of his fur on the side of his face. Letting the tips of my fingers trace the line of his muzzle.

The mouth of a beast, impossible to kiss in a human way.

"Kissing is not everything," I offered soothingly. "Besides, I could still kiss you, like this . . ." I placed a small kiss on the corner of his mouth. "And like this . . ." I trailed a few more light kisses towards his nose.

He moved his hands from my waist to my hips and slid me closer in his lap.

"Sophie." He shifted under me. His mouth parted, exposing the long, sharp canines.

"Monster," I exhaled, brushing my lips against the side of his face, his short fur soft against my skin.

My arms went around his neck, sinking into the thick mass of his mane. And I felt the rough pads of his large hands slide under my shirt and up my sides. I whimpered when he cupped my breasts, his thumbs brushing my nipples through the bra.

The warmth from his hands seemed to be seeping into me, flooding me with heat, head to toe. I pressed myself closer into him, unable to stand any distance between us.

Growling, he lowered his face to my neck, and I felt a slight nibble of his teeth right before his warm tongue soothed the sting, sending a flock of sweet, tiny shivers along my skin. A soft moan came from the back of my throat.

His breathing turned ragged.

"What are you doing to me, Sophie?" He rasped with a pained groan, rising from his seat with me in his arms, then lowered me on my back. "It's maddening."

He dragged his tongue down my neck in small flickering caresses then tugged at the bra under my shirt, ripping it apart and catching my naked breasts in his palms.

Desperately, I tried to ignore the weight of his body pinning me to the couch, forcing myself to focus on the invigorating passion of his body moving against mine.

The moment my chest tightened and my throat felt like it was closing in, I yanked my mind back to the amazing sensation of his warm, rough palms on my skin.

I wanted him so badly. I wanted this between us. Monster was like no other man I'd ever known, and the things I felt for him made me hope that with him everything could be possible. That maybe, just maybe, I could go all the way this time.

Even when my breathing turned shallow and my mind dove full speed into panic, I still struggled to fight through the black smog shrouding my vision. Clinging to his shoulders, I still tried to search for my way back to the moment, to him.

"Sophie?" Monster's concerned voice found me in the fog. He cursed under his breath. "I'm so sorry, princess." Strong hands lifted me up. "Just breathe. Please." He petted my back in long, soothing strokes, holding me in his lap. "It's all gone now. Nothing will happen, I promise."

"I . . . I want it to happen," I panted, drawing the air through my protesting windpipe. "Dammit," I groaned and bent over in his lap, hiding my face in my hands. "Just once, I simply want to make love, without ruining it for everyone."

"You ruined nothing." His voice was firm. He combed his fingers through my hair, matching the rhythm of my calming breathing. "I did." A grave note rang through his tone. "And I keep doing it. I do everything wrong, even when all I want is to make you happy."

"That's the thing!" I sat up, facing him. "You do. You do make me happy." I shook my head in frustration. "I'll just have to work on it one day at the time, I guess. Some days will be better and some worse, but I can make it. That's what my counselor said. And I believe her."

"Who?" He dried the wetness from my cheeks, making me aware of my tears.

"I got a counselor referral through the crisis phone line." My voice strengthened, and my breathing finally settled back to normal. "I told her everything. It was hard." I winced. "Very hard, but it feels much lighter here now." I rubbed the middle of my chest.

"You did it?"

"Mmmhmm." I leaned my head against his shoulder. "I told her about *him*. And you know what I've realized? He doesn't matter. It's not about that one night, not about the past. It's about the future, about gaining control over my life again. That's what I'm going to focus on in my weekly phone sessions with the counselor now. I just want to live a full life, and I need to figure out a way to do it. For myself, you know. Because when I'm happy—truly, fully happy, it's so much easier to make people around me happier too."

He nuzzled my hair.

"And you are helping, by the way, very much," I mumbled, melting into his warmth surrounding me. "Before I told you, I could've never even imagined talking to anyone about it at all. Thank you for that. For being there for me."

# Chapter 30

## Sophie

The ray of sunlight on my face woke me up late the next morning. Then came the awareness of the warm, large body under me. The spooning position we fell asleep in last night again had rearranged, and Monster's chest lay under my cheek.

He was on his back, his arms spread wide, and I ended up halfway on top of him.

For a moment, I remained still, listening to the even sound of his heartbeat. A light, happy feeling curled inside me like a warm, fluffy kitten. It felt simple, and real, and so very right to wake up next to him like this.

I spread my fingers on his chest, sinking them into the thick, brown fur, and watched them disappear completely in the soft lighter undercoat underneath. Suddenly, I became aware of the same softness under my thigh on top of his hip.

The realization of what that meant hit me—Monster wasn't wearing any pants.

I distinctly remembered his jeans being on when the two of us finally went to bed last night. Did he take them off sometime later? I imagined sleeping in jeans couldn't be very comfortable.

Him being naked was hardly unusual. After all, it hadn't even been that long since he started wearing pants around me in the first place. Still, having him completely naked under the covers with me sent my thoughts in another direction.

I recalled our encounter last night in vivid detail, before my meltdown ruined everything. The hot intensity in his eyes, his hands on my breasts, the tingling heat of his tongue on my neck . . .

The memories of those sensations made me lightheaded all over again. I slid my gaze down his stomach to the edge of the sheet covering his lower body. It tented high with his morning erection. The sight of it sent another rush of tingles through my skin.

I remained still for a moment, halting even my breath.

There was one thing I knew for sure I could do without worrying about a sudden panic attack.

Afraid to sleep alone, I'd always been glad to have a boyfriend to share a bed with. Unfortunately, for men, *sleeping together* had a different meaning, and I used oral sex as a tool of distraction with the few men I'd dated.

I'd discovered that some men considered a blowjob a good enough substitute for intercourse, and I would resort to it every time the things would get too heated in the bedroom for me.

Going down on a man had turned into my way of avoiding having to explain anything about my past or risking a panic attack during another failed attempt at intercourse.

Here with Monster, oral sex simply felt like a safe path to the intimacy I craved with him.

As if having a will of its own, my hand inched along Monster's lower belly towards the tenting sheet. The finer fur covering his abs slid between my fingers, tickling my skin, while the dark hair covering his groin felt more springy to the touch.

I pinched the edge of the sheet between my fingers and tugged carefully. It slid off immediately, making me gasp at the sight of his massive cock springing free—tall and proud, leaning up towards me ever so slightly.

"What is it you're trying to do, princess?" Monster's deep voice, rough from sleep yet with a distinct tone of amusement, made me freeze in my spot. Still holding the sheet in my fingers, I realized I'd been caught red-handed, looking very much like a pervert.

"Sorry," I squeaked, dropping the sheet.

"Don't be sorry," he rose on his elbows. If anything, his erection only seemed to get harder, bobbing in the air, urgently. "Tell me what you want."

I lowered my gaze to his abs.

The thoughtful note in his voice cut through the initial amusement in his tone, prompting me to give an honest answer in return, no matter how mortifying or awkward it felt.

"I wanted, um, to see it."

"Well, you have." He cocked his head. "Now what?"

"I want to touch it," I blurted out. "With your permission, of course."

"Are you sure?" His eyes narrowed at me, and his voice dropped a few notches deeper.

I nodded then added quickly, "Just. Stay where you are. Okay? Don't move. Like, at all."

"I won't," he promised then tipped his chin down his body, granting me his permission. "He's all yours."

I felt his stare on me, as he probably monitored my reaction. After all, I hadn't given him much confidence in my attitude towards sex. As far as oral sex went, though, I didn't doubt my abilities and that gave me all the confidence I needed. I knew from experience that as long as I held a man's most sensitive part of his body between my teeth, I didn't need to worry about him climbing on top of me or pinning me down—*I* was in control.

Fingers trembling, I reached for his shaft. My chest rose with a sigh of relief the moment my hand wrapped around him. I could at least give us this.

He was impossibly hard—so engorged, it must've been painful. The skin felt warm and silky, delicate in contrast to the hardness underneath.

Slowly, I slid my fingers up and down his length, enjoying the feel of it. He hissed and stretched through his whole body, thrusting his hips up, into my hand. A low growl reverberated through his chest, and I felt the vibration through the side of my body pressed to his.

"I want to taste it," I demanded, emboldened by his response.

"Anything—" he rasped, his voice strained and stilted. "Anything you want. Just, don't stop."

I pulled myself up and over his pelvis then lowered my mouth, taking as much of him in as I could manage.

Sliding my lips up and down his length, I felt it twitch in my mouth with every stroke of my tongue.

He stiffened and his back froze in an arch, his whole body vibrating with strain.

I realized it'd been years since anyone touched Monster this way. His deep growl sounded tortured, and his groans appreciative, even reverent. I knew that at that moment it was just me for him—my lips sliding up and down, my tongue twirling, my teeth grazing. And for these few minutes, he was absolutely mine.

The noises he made, the shudders of his body under my hand, the pulsing of his shaft in my mouth channeled the pleasure I made him feel back to me.

The warm feeling enveloped me, swirling in a languid vortex inside my chest all the way down to my lower stomach.

Unexpectedly, I felt my own control slip. Suddenly, I became aware of the sensations my own body was feeling.

His musky, wild scent tickling my nostrils, making me want to bury my face in the springy, dark fur between his legs. The warmth of his thigh seeping through my nightshirt as my breasts rubbed against it with my every movement. The tingling in my nipples as they hardened against the soft fabric.

I tucked my knees under me and arched my back, pressing my thighs together, against the achy pressure building up between them.

"Sophie—" Monster gritted through his teeth. "I—"

He was attempting to give me a warning, I assumed, but I only moved my head faster. His heavy breathing hitched for a second then broke into a roar as his hips jerked up and his shaft pulsed, filling my mouth with his release.

The roar grew stronger and continued to resonate through the house. I could have sworn the glass panes in the balcony doors shook.

Milking every last drop of orgasm from him, I glanced up, enjoying the sight of the bed covers fisted in his hands, his claws deeply embedded in the silk. His head was thrown too far back for me to see his face, but the two deep, long grooves left by his horns in the timber logs of the headboard gave me the pleasure of my own kind of satisfaction.

His undoing was my reward.

"Fuuuck!" One last convulsion ran through his large body, horns to toes, like the aftershock of an earthquake, and his tail lashed the mattress with force.

I waited, as the shudders of his climax subsided. Only then I let him slip out of my mouth as I sat up, propped on one arm, my hand on the bed between his spread legs.

He panted, coming down from his high, then rose on his elbows reaching for me, grabbed me under my arms and dragged me up along his body.

"If only I could, I'd kiss the shit out of you right now." He sank back into pillows, holding me close to his chest.

"Most guys avoid kissing after a blowjob." I smiled and buried my face in the mane between his neck and his shoulder.

"Most guys are idiots." He lifted my head to face him. The pad of his thumb caressed my bottom lip. "I would never stop kissing you. Long and deep."

I stroked the short, velvety fur on the side of his snout and kissed his nose.

"There is nothing I miss," I whispered to comfort him and myself.

His mouth stretched in a smile.

"Oh, but you must be missing something, princess." His hand slid down along my spine to squeeze my bottom as the fluffy end of his tail stroked the back of my leg from the heel to the thigh.

Anxiety flickered somewhere at the back of my mind already, stopping me from exploring any tantalizing possibilities his words and his caress could bring.

"Don't worry about me," I breathed out as he slid his tail under the hem of my nightshirt, tickling the sensitive skin of my inner thighs. "I'm good, really."

"Are you?" A small inquisitive smile played across his lips. He continued to gently cup my ass as he remained still—relaxed. Except for his tail—flickering in short, teasing strokes, the tip inched further up between my thighs, reviving the sensation of achy pleasure. "Say *no*, and I'll stop." Monster's low voice held a challenge.

Unexpectedly, his demand eased the threatening anxiety. His words reminded me that I did have control. Sooner or later, I knew I'd still have to say *no*—I had no choice, but it was up to me *when* to stop it.

"Not yet," I whispered, closing my eyes and spreading my thighs wider for him. "Don't stop yet, please . . ."

Following my invitation, his tail dove deeper, stroking my folds now. I realized just how wet he'd made me only when I felt the tip spreading the slick wetness in tantalizing circles around my opening.

Lying on top of him, with my legs on each side of his waist now, I moaned and buried my face in his shoulder.

"Just a little bit longer . . ." I rocked my hips against his hard abs, seeking more contact.

"There are still places where I *can* kiss you, my princess," Monster's hot whisper came next to my ear.

For a second, every muscle in my body tensed, as I realized *what* he was suggesting, then a deep sigh escaped my chest as fear, doubt, and desire warred inside.

"I can still kiss you," he repeated, pressing the side of his face to mine. "Long and hard." His deep voice slowly coiled around me like a velvet ribbon, making the fine hair on my arms stand on end as my mind dissolved into the possibilities offered by his words. "And I won't stop until you tell me or until your legs shake, your mind explodes, and you beg for mercy."

His words brushed against my skin like the caress of silk then coursed through me in a waterfall of scorching hot lava, down to the place between my thighs.

With a gasp, I lifted my head, needing to see his face.

His hands slid up and down my back. His tail continued drawing circles—enticing, tormenting, and suddenly not enough.

"Please, let me, Sophie." His eyes seemed even more imploring than his voice. "I want to hear the sweet, breathy moans that you'll make. I want to feel your body flush hot as you come around my tongue."

Breathless, I was afraid to move, lest I chase the moment away, lost in the speckles of amber glowing among the moss-green of his eyes.

I watched his tongue wet his lower lip, grazing the tips of his sharp, gleaming canines.

"Let me," he begged, his arm tightening around my waist, bringing me closer.

I lowered my gaze to his chest and nodded briefly, giving him my silent permission. Still unsure if I could go through with this, but wanting so badly everything he'd just said.

The next moment, he slid me up his body by my hips, all the way to his chest.

"Hold on to the beam." He tipped his chin up at the horizontal log between the two posts of the massive timber frame bed.

My emotions scattered, I stretched my arms up and grabbed the wooden beam above my head.

"Hop on." He winked at the invitation. "I won't bite." Two rows of long, white, pointy teeth bared in a wide smile didn't help this assurance.

His teeth were not the reason I hesitated, though, and he knew me well enough by now to guess.

"I won't grab you," he promised, letting go of my hips. "Here." He turned his open palms to me. "My hands will be right here the whole time." Lying on his back, he stretched his arms over his head and took hold of one of the logs in the headboard.

Slowly, I rose on my knees over his chest. My thighs shook with trepidation as much as with anticipation of what was to come. Walking on my knees, I shifted forward, holding on to the beam over my head. His long snout still peeked from under the hem of my bunched up nightshirt.

"Close your eyes, Sophie. Don't look at me," he whispered, before diving under my shirt.

Seeing the pair of his thick winding horns between my legs was intimidating, as was the knowledge that his sharp teeth were now a breath away from my most delicate place. However, this was not what caused my concern.

My gaze shot to his hands, holding firmly onto the log, as my mind already calculated the possibilities of his grabbing me, flipping me over, pinning me down . . .

The contact of his cold nose with my hot, sensitive folds was startling. Followed by the wide sweep of his warm tongue, though, it turned into an exquisitely invigorating sensation.

My eyes closed, his hands immediately forgotten, I focused on the new wave of desire spreading between my legs.

His chest rose with an audible inhale as he nuzzled between my legs in the most intimate way. The slight prickle of his whiskers on my inner thighs shot tiny sparks of pleasure through the wave of liquid heat that engulfed me as his thick, long tongue lapped at my core.

With my knees on the pillow on each side of his head, I swayed my hips slightly, following the motions of his tongue and slipping into the pleasure he created. My fingers flexed around the beam I held on to for my dear life, nails scraping at the wood, and a groaning moan tore from my chest.

Floating in the speeding current of bliss, I felt his tongue dive inside me, swirling in and out with increasing intensity. The waves of pleasure rose higher with every twirl, each swell more intense than the other, until they swallowed me whole.

Monster lapped at me in long firm strokes, and the hot pressure inside me erupted in violent shudders against his relentless tongue, the intense ecstasy of orgasm blinding me.

My fingers gave up, letting go off the beam, and I collapsed in a boneless heap. Monster's hands caught me around my waist and gently lowered me next to him.

He met my dreamy gaze with a smug smile, his tongue licking his lips. The satisfaction on his face was that of a cat that just ate the canary. The comparison brought a lazy smile to my face.

Only then I realized that I never ended up saying *no* after all.

"I can't believe it," I exhaled slowly.

"Was it good?" He traced the side of my face gently.

"Good? It was simply amazing, Monster. Incredible." I settled my gaze on his eyes that had more green than brown in the bright late-morning sunlight. "My first orgasm ever," I whispered and added shyly, "That I didn't give myself, I mean."

With a deep inhale, he gathered me in his arms.

"No one ever made you come, princess?"

"No one was this caring and patient."

# Chapter 31

## Sophie

It was almost noon by the time we got out of bed and had break-fast. And before long, the sun started to move closer to the hori-zon. The evening seemed to approach way too fast today.

"I have to leave soon, Monster," I said, reluctantly. Here, on the couch, next to him—with my head on his shoulder and his arms around me—was the only place I wanted to be at that moment.

"Do you?" he replied slowly.

"Mmm." I raked my fingers back and forth through the fur on his forearm. "Bob needs his truck first thing tomorrow morning. I promised—"

"Is it simply the truck?"

"What do you mean?"

"Well. What else holds you in town?"

"Um," I inhaled, wondering what he was after. "You know. Jo and Melanie, my weekly phone appointments with the therapist, and I have the apartment there—"

"How often do you need to see your friends? And, technically, you have the lease of this place too," he reminded.

"The lease is just to help you out, isn't it?"

He lifted me off the couch and turned me around to face him, setting me down in his lap to straddle his thighs.

"How long are you planning to stay in Rocky River, Sophie?" His eyes narrowed, and his voice grew more serious.

"I . . . well. I haven't really organized anything." In fact, I hadn't planned much in my life for years now. "I've been just kinda drifting with the flow here." I gave him a small, awkward smile.

Most people had life goals and tried to follow through on them, didn't they? Wasn't it an adult thing to do? My own life had been just happening, without much control or preparation on my part. I used to be much more proactive when I was in grade school. But then, many things used to be different.

"Okay." He nodded with somber focus. "When do you have to go back to Calgary? I mean when is it that you absolutely have to be back?"

I dropped my gaze to his chest where I started to twirl my finger in his fur.

"There really isn't a deadline for my return . . ."

"Your mom? Does she need you in Calgary?"

"Mom would love to have me close, of course. But no, she doesn't *need* me there to help her or anything. And now that she has Jeff . . ." I gave him a small shrug.

"How about your volunteering positions?"

"They're fine. For now. There is always a need for volunteers, and I'm sure they'll be able to find something for me to do when I come back—"

"How about the school lunches here?" he kept questioning me in what began to feel like an interrogation. At the same time, I realized, by making me organize a list of everything going on in my life right now, he was helping me to get a grasp of the big picture.

"The school lunches are good." I smiled broadly. "Both children and their parents love them. I'm working on increasing it to twice per week now. That's the other reason I should be in Rocky River tonight—I need to review next week's orders for groceries and make some payments."

"So, technically, there is no need for you to live in Calgary. Right? You could always go visit your mom whenever you want. And there are more than enough opportunities for your charity work up here."

"Well, I may change my rent agreement to a yearly lease." I'd started thinking about it ever since I made the January payment. All the reasons that Monster made me name right now had been bouncing in my brain for some time now.

"What if you stayed here instead?"

My gaze snapped up to his.

"Here?"

He released a long breath and sat up straighter, radiating nervousness.

"Move in here until the end of this year."

"What?" I exhaled. "Is that what you want?"

He shook his head slowly.

"I'll tell you what I want in a minute. First, think if that's something *you* would want."

"Me?" I blinked, considering his offer. Forced to make a decision, my thoughts scattered in disarray.

It would make more sense for me to drive to Rocky River once or twice a week than coming here every moment I had the use of the truck. The truck . . . Moving in with Monster, I would have to figure out how to get a vehicle of my own, which wouldn't be easy up here. I'd probably need to place an order for one to be delivered, if no one in town was prepared to sell theirs . . .

"I'd have to get my own car somehow."

"Forget about a car." Monster waved off my concern, a slightly impatient note entering his voice. "Besides that, would you *like* to move in here?"

Right. This would be the most important question to answer, wouldn't it? Did I want to live here with Monster? Every day?

Lacking a plan, I'd been extending my rent in town on a weekly, then on a monthly basis. I still paid a small rent to my mom in Calgary, too.

Through the distorted chaos of my thoughts, one emerged with a refreshing clarity. I truly felt at home only here, with him.

I inhaled deeply, and settled my gaze on his face again.

"Would you make me tea every morning?"

"Promise." The corners of his mouth twitched up slightly.

"And we'd talk by the fire like this every day?"

"Yes."

"Would it mean I'd get to sleep next to you every night?"

"Absolutely." His tone was firm.

"Then yes, I would love to move in with you, Monster."

"You would?" His voice was filled with disbelief, relief, and excitement—all at once.

"Only if that's what you want, of course," I added, just in case.

"What do I want?" He shifted under me. "Let me tell you what I want, princess. I'm sick of having to watch you drive away, knowing I'll spend my time pacing along that damn fence waiting for your return. Because when you're gone, I can't think about anything else. I want you here," he wrapped his arms tightly around me, pulling me closer, "because this feels like where you belong."

"Then right here I'll stay," I murmured, inhaling his familiar scent as his fur tickled my face.

He tucked my head under his chin, his fingers stroking my ponytail along my back.

"At first, all I wanted was to chase you away because I thought we'd be better off as far away from each other as possible. But now .. . Is it selfish of me, Sophie? Wanting you here in my jail with me?"

"No, Monster." Normally plagued by doubt about everything, I felt an absolute certainty about my decision this time.

"Do you think you could be happy here? Really happy?" Something still seemed to bother him.

"I feel very happy right now," I reassured him.

He stirred suddenly.

"Come." He lifted me off the couch then pulled me towards the door leading from the kitchen to the garage, and I followed.

"What?" I wrapped my arms tightly around me, shielding myself from the cold on the other side of the door.

"I should've done this earlier. Come here," Monster led me to the wall of the garage, furthest from the door.

There, behind the fleet of landscaping and maintenance equipment, including the ATV with a plow that Monster used to clear the snow off the driveway, was a long shape covered with an enormous grey tarp.

"When you're in town, can you get a mechanic to come look at this please?" He pulled the tarp off, revealing a black Dodge truck underneath.

The vehicle appeared to be almost brand new, even if considerably dusty. Its chrome detailing glistened in the semi-darkness of the garage.

"I can pump air in the tires and do an oil change, but I'd rather get a mechanic to look at it before you drive since it's been sitting here all this time unused."

"Wow. Monster. Whose truck is this?" I slid my fingers along the tailgate, leaving behind a shiny trail in the dust.

"My father's. He kept it here." Monster folded the tarp, setting it aside. "Occasionally, David drove it to and from the airport when he came to check on me. More often than not, though, he had someone from Rocky River to pick him up on their way to the hunting lodge. That's how he left last time. So the truck has been here ever since."

The vehicle was simply beautiful. And it was definitely much more than what I was going to get for myself.

"I'll do a proper Bill of Sale in your name, to make it easier for you."

"Monster, this is too much." I shook my head. "I could get something smaller . . ."

"You can't go much smaller around here, Sophie. You need the four-wheel drive at least, on these roads. Besides, she needs to be driven, too. It's not good for a vehicle to sit idle."

I considered his words for a moment.

"I'll give you money for it—"

"Sure." He chuckled. "Write me a cheque. I'll take it to the bank one day."

"I'm serious." I swatted at his hand as he swept my hair away to playfully nuzzle the side of my neck. "I'll sell my car in Calgary and do a bank transfer to your account. You can't just give it to me for nothing."

"How about all the supplies you have been bringing here for me? Count them as a payment if you want."

"A truck? In exchange for some gas and a few bags of groceries?"

"Fine," he exhaled with exaggerated frustration. "Feel free to keep bringing groceries, especially popcorn. I'm sure we'll be even over time."

"So, essentially, you're selling me your truck for a lifetime supply of popcorn?"

I said in amusement, absentmindedly drawing my initials in the layer of dust on the tailgate.

"I'm getting the better part of the deal here, in my opinion." He wrapped his big, furry arms around me, pressing my back to his chest. "As long as you're always going to be the one to bring it."

He reached from behind me and drew a plus sign between S and M of my initials in the dust on the tailgate.

Sophie plus Monster.

The charm of this childish gesture made me smile, warming my heart.

"Stay," he whispered without a shade of humour in his voice this time. "Just stay with me, princess."

# Chapter 32

## Sophie

It took me a couple of days to get things sorted out in Rocky River. I let Bob and Melanie know I wouldn't renew the rent agreement for February and refused to accept the remaining balance for January they kindly offered to refund.

"Are you sure you want to live all alone in that place, honey?" Melanie's expression was that of genuine concern when I told her *where* I was moving. "There're bears and cougars all over that area. And how would you call for help if you need it?"

When I told Jo that I was moving out of town but would still come to Rocky River once or twice a week to help her at the school, her jaw dropped.

"Why?" She stared at me in obvious shock and bewilderment. "It may sound like a great arrangement to look after the place in exchange for rent, but there is no internet, Sophie. No cellphone reception. It's like burying yourself alive! Not to mention that it's not safe. A girl living alone in an abandoned house deep in the woods? Just think about it—it's a perfect horror movie scenario."

Their concerns were valid of course. Especially since I couldn't tell them about the almost seven feet of hard muscles enclosed in fur, topped with horns, and equipped with sharp teeth and claws that I'd have to protect me in the house in the woods.

In the end, I had to promise to research every communication option available, from radio to a satellite phone. I told them that it'd be easier for me to look after the property if I lived there and assured everyone that I would come to town regularly, agreeing to a search party being sent to the house if I ended up missing for over a week without advanced notice.

A plumber and his apprentice coming to work on the pipes gave me a lift to the estate, leaving me alone afterwards, as Monster kept to the woods while people worked on the house. I knew he'd come back as soon as he sensed them cross the property line on their way out of the estate.

I had dinner almost ready when he came in.

"Yay! We have running water," I cried out triumphantly, rinsing my hands in the kitchen sink. "Hot and cold."

Silent, he stood on the other side of the island, leaning against the nearest wall with his shoulder.

"Is something wrong?" I asked. "What are you doing?"

"Enjoying the view." A smile played on his lips.

"What view?"

His grin got bigger.

"You, in my home."

I smiled, feeling my cheeks heating with pleasure from the affection in his expression.

"I'll never get tired of it." He closed the distance between us, wrapping me in his arms. "Thank you for being here, princess."

"NOTHING MAKES YOU APPRECIATE a working toilet like having to use an outhouse for a while. I'll never take functioning plumbing for granted ever again," I announced to Monster, who sat on top of the covers in bed wearing nothing but his fur.

"Come here." He reached for me, when I climbed in bed on the opposite side, and pulled me into his lap to straddle his legs. My nightshirt rode up, and a flock of small flutters rushed through me from the tickling sensation of his fur against my inner thighs. "I'll see if I can get the hot tub clean enough to fill it again."

"A hot tub?" I gasped. "I had no idea there was one."

"You can't see it. It's built into the back deck, and everything has been covered with snow out there for weeks." His hands slid up and down the top of my thighs, the rough skin of his palms in contrast to the softness of his fur beneath me.

"Hot water *and* a hot tub. You're all set for a life of luxury." I raked my fingers through the fur on his chest, tracing the hard ridges of his pectorals underneath.

"*We*," he corrected. "We're all set."

"We." I nodded, enjoying the sound of the word.

He moved his hands up to my hips, and I slid my fingers to his shoulders threading them through his mane.

"Say it again," he whispered.

"We," I repeated, leaning my forehead to his. "You and I." He shifted me closer until our bodies ended up being flush against each other.

My core slid along the solid ridge of his erection.

"You're so hard," I gasped before I could stop myself.

He chuckled into my hair.

"A very common occurrence when you're around."

A soft, deep rumble in his voice vibrated through me all the way down to my lower stomach, igniting desire inside.

I buried my face in his mane, savoring the fresh smell of frost on his fur from his daily swim in the icy river. I had grown addicted to his wild scent and inhaled a lungful now, getting my fix.

"Mmmm." I rocked my hips against the hard bulge underneath me, needing to feel the ripples of pleasure it sent though my body.

"Sophie," Monster groaned and threw his head back—with a thud, the tips of his horns embedded into the wood behind him.

"Now, you've damaged the wall," I whispered, glancing up.

"Fuck the wall." He jerked his head forward, yanking the horns out of the timber. "You're a damage to my sanity," he growled, his eyes darkened with lust, his hands suddenly between us, his claws bared.

I made a small noise of surprise, as he sliced my nightshirt open in one lightning-fast movement without leaving so much as a scratch on my skin.

"Yesss," he hissed, sliding aside the ripped edges of my shirt and exposing my breasts. With an arm under my backside, he lifted me up, bringing my chest to his face.

His long, thick tongue lapped at my nipple as he kneaded my other breast with gentle insistence. The sensations fanned my arousal from delicate tendrils into flames.

"Perfect," he growled against my skin. The vibrating sound intensified the throbbing heat between my legs, and I rocked my hips against him searching for contact.

A teasing bite of his teeth on the sensitive bud of my nipple reaped a soft whimper from my lips. The whimper ended on a moan as his tongue soothed the sting right after and I arched my back leaning closer to him for more.

"God, it's so good." There was no place for fear or panic here. Somehow, I'd had no chance to be afraid this time, completely swept away into the heat of the moment by him.

I gripped his horns, my whole body trembling with the intense pleasure spread by his tongue and hands.

"Hold on," he ordered, and I obeyed, clinging tighter.

His arms firmly around me, he flipped us onto the bed, my back to the mattress, then inclined his head, nudging his horns and prompting me to release my grip.

He cupped my breasts and rubbed the rough cushions of his thumbs over my nipples, sending a new wave of scorching need rushing down through me.

Slowly, he dragged the tip of his tongue between my breasts. "Delicious." His hot whisper hit my skin then the flicker of his tongue continued down to my stomach and lower.

With a sharp exhale, I grabbed on to the winding spirals of his horns again when he dipped his tongue between my thighs. I raised my hips to meet the invasion. Eyes closed, I rolled my head on the pillows, lost in the onslaught of sensations swirling through me.

How could it feel so insanely good? How could he know this well every nerve of my body, better than I did myself?

Breathless, I dug my fingers into the grooves on his horns when the tight spring of pleasure inside me finally uncoiled with the blinding force of climax released by his skillful tongue.

A series of sharp moans left my parted lips as my hips jerked in blissful spasms against his face.

"Oh, God . . ." I whispered on exhale, basking in the warm, languid waves of afterglow rolling through me. "How can it be so . . . so—"

"Amazing?" He propped himself on an elbow at my side. "Magical? *Fanfuckingtastic?*" His magnificent tongue darted between his teeth, licking his lips after each word as if he'd just had the most satisfying dinner.

"All of the above, darling." I smiled as a warm tide of intense affection for him rose inside me. "All of the above."

He brushed my hair from my face, sliding his thumb along my cheekbone.

"I love this thoroughly satisfied look on you." He traced my lower lip. "It suits you."

"How about your own satisfaction?" I murmured. His rock-hard erection nudged my thigh. Emboldened by my body's unusually wonderful response to his touch, I daringly slid my hand down to trace his length with the tips of my fingers.

"Sophie," he rumbled a warning at the contact, thrusting his hips into my hand.

His jaw flexed, and his eyes gleamed dark from under the thick eyebrows. A flash of feral lust crossed his features. With a low groan, he grabbed my wrist and threw my arm over my head then heaved his massive body over mine, thrusting his hips against me.

The warm haze of arousal receded as soon as he was on top of me. My stomach fluttered with nerves, but the panic never had a chance to get hold of me, as Monster stopped immediately. With a loud exhale, he dropped his head between his shoulders then rolled off me to his back.

"I swear you've taken me to the very edge of my endurance—" His whole body shook with tension as he closed his eyes and took another deep breath, obviously struggling to rein in his lust. "Ever since you came along, I've been learning the virtue of endless patience among so many other things." He exhaled a strained laugh and met my gaze again as his muscles relaxed a little. "The sweetest torture of having you near. I wouldn't give it up for anything in the world."

The passion of his confession melted my heart. I raised a hand to touch his shoulder but held back, unsure of his reaction to my caress at the moment.

"I want to do it," I said quietly instead. My desire to go all the way with him became only more intense when voiced out loud.

"What do you mean, princess?" he asked cautiously.

"I want to have sex, Monster. Real sex."

"You've never done it." He wasn't asking. Based on my reaction to any attempt at intimacy, it was easy enough to figure out by now that despite the number of boyfriends I'd had, I was still very much a virgin.

I swallowed hard and focused on my fingers clasped in my lap. "No. But I want it. With you. I don't want to be afraid any more."

It could only be him, or no one at all. He was the one capable of making me forget everything. Only he could bring me to ecstasy the way he did. I trusted his patience, and I wanted him to help me fight the fear.

"Are you sure, Sophie?" He sat up, too. The thoughtful attention in his voice gave me the courage to look up.

"It has to be you." My breathing came in shallow pants. My hands trembled with nerves, but my determination didn't waver. "If I can't do it with you, I doubt I ever will . . ."

"You can do it." He said firmly, raising his hand to my face, and I leaned into his touch. "And you will. *We* will." His thumb caressed my temple, and his voice dropped to almost a whisper. "Tell me what you want and how you want it, and I'll make it happen. Anything."

My breath hitched, excitement now mixed into my apprehension. Overwhelmed, my mind suddenly drew blank.

"I don't know," I confessed.

"Have you tried being on top, my sweet?" Monster's voice came soft and gentle.

I nodded in reply.

"And it still didn't work. It's not just the position then?"

I shook my head.

"What then?"

"The hands . . ." I croaked.

He considered it for a moment.

"I'll hold the headboard then, like the last time. Okay?" He tipped his head searching my eyes.

I nodded again, with a small, hopeful smile.

"Here you go, Sophie." He lay on his back and grabbed the log of the bed frame. "I'm all yours."

The submissive Monster was still a new sight to me. He looked both strong and sweet, and tantalizingly enticing, lying there, inviting me to take my pleasure in his body.

His erection jerked up, demanding my attention, tempting . . . I slid my gaze along its length, wishing to glide my hand over it, flick my tongue along it.

"Go ahead." Monster's voice was soft and hypnotic, entreating me to take a chance.

Slowly, I shuffled on my knees along the mattress to his side, the remnants of my ruined nightshirt hanging off my shoulders and dragging behind me.

"You're in control," he reminded me.

I wanted to believe him. So much. With all my heart, I wanted to be with him. But this was not like the last time when I had my mouth on him.

He'd be inside me, lost in his own pleasure, chasing his own climax . . . It might be easy for him to forget himself and his promise.

My mind whirred along the path to panic, going through all the ways he could grab me, flip me over, pin me down, shove my face into the mattress, making me unable to breathe . . .

"Sophie," Monster's voice found its way to me. "I will not touch you. No matter what. You're safe."

But the excitement was quickly fading already, replaced by fear and disappointment. The feeling of shame and failure choked me with unshed tears.

"Sorry," I whispered.

Damn you Hunter Reed! Damn you and that night.

I dropped my gaze to my lap, and collected the torn sides of my nightshirt. With shaking hands, I tugged the material together in front of me, suddenly feeling the need to shield my naked body.

"Look at me." His voice was low but firm and commanding, prompting me to obey. My hands stilled, and my eyes snapped to his immediately.

"I swear," he gritted through his teeth, yanking the top sheet from under the duvet.

"On my life." He curled his fingers, forcing the claws out, and slashed through the material.

"I will not touch you."

In quick, forceful movements he tore two wide lengths of silk from the sheet then threw them around each of the bedposts, tying the ends to make a big circle of fabric around each post.

Quickly, he made a loop out of each strip and threaded his hands through.

"I swear," he repeated firmly and flexed his arms, forcing the loops to tighten around both of his wrists simultaneously.

He sat facing me now, arms spread wide, each wrist tied to a bedpost. His chest heaved. His hands balled into massive fists. His focused gaze watched my every move, every change in my expression.

He did this for me. Not only had he tamed the beast inside him, he physically tied himself to the bed to calm the feverish panic in my brain and help me go through with what I wanted.

Deep in my mind I knew that the silk would never really hold him. But his willingness to do this for me proved to be enough.

The full meaning of his gesture melted any remnants of hesitation inside me, making me want to be as close to him as possible. As close as only having him inside me would be.

"Come, Sophie," he called. "Come to me. Because I can't come to you now."

There was just Monster here with me, my Monster, no one else. And I wanted him. So much.

I shrugged the nightshirt off my shoulders and threw my leg over his thighs, straddling him.

He released the breath he held and sank back into pillows when I wrapped my fingers around his shaft again, shifting my hips closer.

With fear gone, the sensation of his pulsing erection in my hand brought back the excitement of anticipation. His open expression gave me all the reassurance I needed.

I rose on my knees and hovered over him.

"You look like a warrior princess, ready to go into battle." The stern focus on his face melted into an affectionate grin.

I gave him a smile in reply and dragged the head of his shaft through my folds.

He inhaled with a hiss, the grin quickly replaced by an expression of tortured bliss.

Tension left my body, filling it with languid warmth instead. Slowly, I circled his tip around my opening, feeling my channel swell with liquid heat.

"I want you, Monster," I whispered, aligning us perfectly together. "So, so much."

I slowly lowered my hips, letting the tip slide in.

"Fuck, Sophie!" he groaned, his body vibrating with restrain. "It's . . . heaven."

I tried to sink lower, but sudden pain made me gasp and bend over. I fisted my hands in the fur on his chest and jerked my hips up, away from what was hurting me.

"You have to do it fast, princess." I heard Monster's reassuring whisper. "You're in control. You have to do it yourself."

Right.

Myself, because his hands were tied, literally.

I squeezed my fists tighter, closed my eyes, and took a deep inhale.

Fast.

The sharp pain blinded me for a moment when I thrust my hips all the way down, making me cry out.

"It'll be okay, Sophie." His words filtered through, comforting and distracting me from the pain. "It won't hurt for long. Just breathe."

He was right. The pain was receding quickly. It already felt like a distant echo of itself, reduced to a dull ache.

Still gripping the fur on his chest, my head down, I focused on the sensations inside me as I began to slowly move my hips up and down, sliding along his shaft.

The smooth gliding felt soothing to the ache inside me, prompting me to move with added confidence. Up and down, gradually increasing my speed.

"Sophie."

I glanced up at his sharp exhale.

"Too fast," he groaned. "I won't last."

"Then don't. I'm on a pill." I smiled and circled my hips, enjoying the tingling sensation it caused, further alleviating the remaining ache. "Let go, my Monster," I whispered softly.

The excitement bubbled in my chest, making me slightly light-headed. "Please, let it go." I moved faster, willing him to explode.

He arched his back and roared, baring his teeth. His biceps bulged under the fur, as his arms flexed in the restraints. The silk ribbons tore to shreds, unable to contain the beastly force, the moment he shuddered and his climax erupted inside me.

My own body shook, arms and legs trembling, but not from orgasm—there was no way I could have one this time, overwhelmed with emotional and physical sensations as I was—but from the receding adrenaline and excitement.

A light, sunny feeling floated through me, as I leaned forward, propped by my hands still fisted in the fur on his chest.

"Fuck. Sophie, being inside you . . . It was everything." With a long groan, he stretched under me. "You can let go now."

"What?" I sat straight and held my hands in front of me.

Unclenching my fists, I watched in horror as the thick clumps of Monster's fur fluttered from my palms to his stomach and onto the sheets around us.

"I'm so, so sorry," I whispered, mortified. "Did I hurt you?"

"Well." He sat up and circled my waist with his arms, the strips of silk dangling from his wrists. "I can honestly say that I *felt* your pain."

Humour lightened his tone as I guiltily smoothed the fur on his chest, mechanically trying to cover up the small bare patches by brushing the remaining fur over them.

"I'm so sorry."

He lifted my face, cupping my chin.

"Don't worry about it." His eyes grew more thoughtful, the twinkle of humour slipping aside. "How are you feeling?"

"How?" I felt a wide smile stretch across my face, letting the radiance inside me shine through. "Happy." I threw my arms around his neck, crushing his mane. "You make me feel so very happy, Monster."

"Can I finish it for you, though?" His voice dropped down suggestively as he added with confidence, "I can make you come again."

"No," I giggled, shaking my head. I didn't doubt his ability, but I felt so deliciously tired and still a tiny bit sore. "Later, darling. After we rest." I relaxed into him, leaning my head on his shoulder. "Apparently, having real sex can be rather exhausting."

He lowered us onto the pillows, throwing the covers over. The thick cloud of his fur enveloped me in a soft caress against my naked skin as I drifted asleep in his arms.

# Chapter 33

## Sophie

Monster made good on his promise the very next day—making me come again and again.

In fact, since our first time, he'd made love to me almost every night. Sometimes with humour but always with tenderness and end-less patience, he exorcised the darkness from my mind.

The horrifying memories that had been forever associated with a man's touch in my brain drifted into oblivion, as Monster replaced them with his own gentle caresses.

Soon, instead of dreading the night, I looked forward to it. It wasn't that fear had disappeared completely. Panic would still raise its ugly head, even during my most blissful moments with Monster.

Only now I knew how to fight it.

Allowing his touch and his voice to lead me out of the dark, I al-ways found my way back to joy. To him.

I couldn't help but wonder, though, if our nights could be as ful-filling to him as they were to me. Not that he ever complained. On the contrary, he made me feel like being with me was the best thing in the world for him. Still, I sensed the intense passion Monster held in out of concern for me. I felt his arms shake and his body tense as he imposed invisible restraints on his desire, his focus always on me. And I yearned to release him from that.

As much as the unknown force intimidated me a little, the glimpses of the wild passion I'd caught deep inside him enticed me. I wanted for him to be able to make love in his own way, wild and free. With time, I was afraid that lying on his back for me would get old for both of us. And I wished he'd come undone.

Unfortunately, being pinned under him still remained one of the major triggers of a panic attack for me.

One snowy morning at the end of January, I padded in my thick, woolen socks into the living room, fingers wrapped around a warm coffee mug.

It was nice and cozy in there, now that all services were up and running at the house. And the room looked nothing like it did when I first saw it.

With the help of local craftspeople, I had all furniture repaired with new varnish and upholstery. Several large rugs, made by a group of mothers from Rocky River school, covered the refinished floors.

Over the past weeks, Monster and I had made the house not only livable but warm and comfortable. We had made it ours. The pretentious extravagance of the previous décor was mostly gone now, replaced by the subtle beauty of local craftsmanship.

Monster insisted on paying for everything, allowing me to keep most of my money in charity programs. With a cheeky smile on his face, he claimed that being able to use his credit cards again—even if through me—made him feel like *a man*.

I stopped in front of the French doors watching the large, fluffy snowflakes falling leisurely outside. The winter hadn't shown any signs of slowing down. Out here it was its realm, with snow covering the ground for six months of the year or more.

Without waiting for the snowfall to stop, Monster was out there clearing the driveway of whatever had fallen down overnight. He assured me it was easier to clear two-three feet of snow at a time than to dig ourselves out from under twice as much of it after waiting for the end of the storm.

The house location was outside an internet service area. I couldn't get a connection no matter how hard I looked into it. But I went to town regularly to check my email account while running other errands, visiting friends, and having weekly phone sessions with my therapist.

There was still no reply from Cecilia, and I kept searching for any woman with that name who'd have any connection to magic. Still, hoping that the Cecilia I had found was the one who could free Monster, I sent a couple of follow-up emails to the organizers of the witchcraft fair in New Orleans and received a response that it had been forwarded to Cecilia but that was all they could do since replying to me would be entirely up to her. As was to be expected, they wouldn't allow me to contact her directly, citing their privacy policy.

All I could do was wait.

My frustration was easier to deal with as I watched Monster's mood improve dramatically. As if the dark shroud surrounding him had been slowly lifting and he gradually allowed himself to enjoy life.

Making improvements around the property gave him a new purpose. I noticed how much he enjoyed working with his hands. Each accomplishment, no matter how small, brought him an obvious satisfaction.

I wished for him to be free but was glad to see him being able to create a fulfilling life for himself, even if within the confines of his prison.

With me here, he was no longer alone. Aside from my visits to town, we spent every day together. And our nights . . . The nights were filled with getting to know each other on a different level.

I wondered if there was a way for Monster and I to try other positions. Something that would allow him to take the lead but wouldn't inadvertently set off another meltdown in me.

We'd learned that his hands were no longer a concern. He didn't need to tie himself up for me anymore. However, the weight of him—the cage of his body surrounding me while I lay under him—still triggered the feeling of helplessness and desperate need to escape, leading to a panic attack.

Holding the coffee mug in both hands, I walked over to the far wall of the room, on the other side of the fireplace, and pressed my back to it.

Closing my eyes, I imagined Monster's large body surrounding me, his arms flanking me. Immediately my breathing turned shallow, my heart jumped high into my throat, and I shoved away from the wall, desperate to escape.

With a frustrated groan, I took a few deep breaths, my gaze sweeping the living room.

Several thick, solid logs supported the upstairs balcony that ran along the perimeter of the open space below. I approached one of them and pressed my back to one of them.

The hardness of it pressed against my spine, but my shoulders were free. If Monster were here with me now, he couldn't cage me with his arms. His hands would have to be high above my head or down under my ass.

I took a step to the side, and the feeling of the post behind my back disappeared—I was free. This was all I had to do to escape.

One step.

The thought of it immediately freed my mind of the impending panic.

Leaning against the log again, I arched my back and closed my eyes, imagining my legs wrapped around him, his hips grinding into mine. His face would be so close to mine, his mane would tickle my skin, and his scent . . .

"Sophie?"

Brought out of my fantasy abruptly, I snapped my eyes open to see Monster by the front door shaking snow out of his mane and brushing it off his shoulders.

"Are you okay, princess? What are you doing?"

"You'll have to come closer to find out." I slid down the post, with my back against it, and sat the coffee mug on the floor. The breathy note in my voice must have been a hint to him. In a moment Monster was next to me, not asking any more questions.

I rose to my feet, my back sliding up along the post.

"Why does that look so fucking hot?" he mused and brushed his knuckles against the side of my neck. The soft tickle of his fur chased a flock of soft tingles down my skin.

"Does it?" I murmured, tilting my head to the side to expose more of my neck to him. "Must be my sexy socks." I smiled, sliding my foot up his calf.

"That's it." He hooked his arm under my knee and lifted it to his waist then dropped his hand down to cup the heel of my socked foot. "The sexiest socks ever." He leaned over me, nuzzling the top of my head. "Let me take you upstairs—I'll blow them off you."

The gruff rumble in his voice vibrated through my chest, sending a shot of liquid heat straight between my legs.

"Take me . . . right here," I breathed out, raking my fingers through the thick fur on his chest and shoulders then sinking them in the mane behind his neck.

He groaned and rocked his hips into me.

Exactly how I've imagined it, and so, so much better.

His other hand cupped my ass, lifting me higher along the support post while I tore at the zipper of his jeans.

Holding me in place, he yanked my long shirt up and ripped it off over my head. The brush of his fur against my nipples made me gasp with the need for more. I dragged his jeans down and over his hard ass with my feet, setting his tail free.

He threw his head back, and a loud roar reverberated through the house in response to my frantic impatience. The scratching noise of claws of his hands embedded in the wood above my head reached my ear. I tightened my arms and legs around him, my lower body wedged between his hips and the log post.

"Let go, Monster," I urged. A hint of trepidation fluttered through the hot wave of excitement rising in me from releasing the beast.

"Sophie," he gritted through his teeth, his arms strained, his biceps flexing on each side of my face.

"It'll be okay," I promised with confidence. "I want it. I can take it." I wiggled my hips, rubbing against his hard erection trapped between us. The desire to have him inside me turned into pure agony. "I promise. I can. Please," I groaned. "Fuck me, Monster."

A dark shroud of lust drew over the hazel of his eyes.

With another deafening roar he drove into me, filling me completely and finally easing the pulsing need between my legs.

I dug my heels into his lower back, bringing him closer to me.

"Don't stop," I begged in a desperate whisper.

"If I stop now—I'll die," he growled, pounding into me in long, powerful thrusts. Each one taking me higher as the pleasure swelled hot inside me.

I clasped my hands behind his neck, riding the rhythm of his thrusts with him.

Don't stop. Just you and me. I don't want this to stop.

The whole world ceased to exist except for the two of us, swept in the wild frenzy with which he was taking me.

Another long roar rumbled from deep inside his chest, and I felt his release pulse hot inside me, taking me over the edge with him.

"My Monster," I panted through the last tremors of our climax. "You're all mine."

His forehead rested against mine, his horns on each side of the pillar behind me. His wide chest heaved, fur stroking my naked breasts with each heavy breath.

"Sophie, that was . . . that was—"

"*Fanfuckingtastic*?" I giggled and buried my face in the side of his neck, basking in his warmth and my afterglow.

He cupped the side of my face.

"Better." His thumb caressed my cheekbone. "Infinitely better."

With my legs still wrapped tightly around his waist, I stroked the top of his tail with my bare foot.

Bare?

I glanced down at my woolen sock lying on the floor near his clawed feet and laughed.

"Well, you did blow my socks off, Monster."

He chuckled and nuzzled the side of my face.

"Did you really like it?" I asked anxiously.

"Mmhmm," he murmured, peeling me from the support post to wrap his arms around me now.

"More than having me on top?"

"Oooh, I like you on top, too."

"You do?" I lifted my head, needing to see his face.

He lifted an eyebrow at my concern.

"Up or down. Over or under. In bed or against a post. Sophie, I'll have you any way I can."

"Unfortunately, there aren't that many *ways* with me . . ." I sighed with a short laugh.

"Sophie." He shifted me higher to bring my face to his eye level. "Sex with you is mind-blowing—in any position—please, believe me. But it's not about that. I mean I love what happens down there." He shot a glance in the direction of his crotch. "But the most amazing feeling is actually somewhere here." Holding me easily with one arm, he grabbed my hand with his and pressed it to his chest. "Somehow, I *feel* what you feel. Your pleasure becomes mine. I want it no less than I crave my own satisfaction. I never knew it could be this way before you." He threaded his fingers through my hair, my messy bun completely destroyed by the action against the post. "For me, being with you is no longer about me *or* you, Sophie. It's about *us*. I've never had that before. But now, I'm afraid I wouldn't want to be without it."

Tenderness, affection, gratitude, along with many other emotions I couldn't name, rose in a warm swell inside me from his words. And I felt them all mold into something much larger, filling my heart to the brim.

I didn't even begin to know how to express this feeling growing in me. Instead, I just wound my arms tightly around his neck again, pressing myself to him as close as I could and wishing I never had to let go.

# Chapter 34

## Sophie

A few weeks later, I returned from Rocky River with a heavy feeling over my heart. Madame Besson, my father's housekeeper, had notified me by email that Henri had a stroke. She noted that my presence in France was not required at this time. His condition was stable. However, it was clear from her email that it was serious.

I sensed that the newest Madame Morel probably wasn't too eager to meet me. But I also wondered if the cool note of my presence not being required had something to do with Henri not wanting to see me.

"Anything new from town?" Monster asked after helping me with groceries, and I noticed him wince when he inclined his head.

"Is the headache bothering you today?"

He grunted softly in reply and moved to the couch.

The regular supply of painkillers kept his headache at a manageable level, allowing Monster to function. But I knew that the pain never went away completely.

"Come here." I sat on the opposite end of the couch, shifting a little to allow for space for his horns, and patted my jean-clad thighs. "Let's see if we can make it better."

Monster claimed my massages helped reduce the pain, and I loved giving them to him as often as he needed.

Placing his head carefully in my lap, he lay down and closed his eyes.

"Tell me about your day, princess. What's new and exciting in Rocky River?"

Through the stories of my town visits, Monster got to know the people who lived there and was now very familiar with the town's life.

"Not much in terms of excitement." I brushed away the long strands of his mane and smoothed the velvet fur of his forehead with my fingers. "You know life is slow around these parts."

"Like molasses," he snorted.

"I kinda like it, actually. The hustle and bustle of a big city gets old over time."

Concern from Madame Besson's news weighed heavily on my chest. Henri was a man full of life and vigor, even as he was cold and indifferent to me personally. I couldn't imagine him being sick or feeble in any way at all.

"I put the mail from your lawyer and the bank on the desk in the observatory, by the way." I drew tight circles at the base of his horns, pressing slightly, and felt his shoulders slowly relax at my thigh. "I also got an email from Henri's housekeeper," I added quietly. "Henri had a stroke." I stilled my fingers over his forehead for a second before continuing with the massage.

I wasn't sure I wanted to tell Monster my news until I blurted it out, feeling the sudden urge to share.

"Will you have to go to France?" Monster's eyes snapped open.

"She said I'm not needed." I stroked his forehead just above the bushy eyebrows, making him close his eyes again. "I'm sure I'd just be in the way of the newest Madame Morel if I went."

"But do you think your father would like to have you there?"

I paused, thinking about the last time I saw Henri. Nothing about the way we parted gave me any hope he'd wish to see me now.

"Honestly, I don't think he would want that. Chances are he'd only get upset again. In the best case scenario, it wouldn't make a difference to him if I was there or not."

Which is the way it has always been anyway.

He lay still for a second.

"Seeing him now may be more for you than him," he offered softly.

"How so? If he doesn't get angry seeing me, he'd be indifferent. He never cared."

"It may be your chance to forgive."

"The last thing Henri ever needed was my forgiveness."

Sad but true. Henri would never admit any failures. As far as he was concerned he was outside of any criticism.

"Sometimes, forgiveness is for the one who grants it more than for the one who receives it," Monster said thoughtfully. "It frees your soul and lets you move ahead, instead of walking around in circles of bitterness and hurt."

I considered the meaning of his words for a second.

"Are you talking from experience? Are you the one forgiving or do you need to ask for forgiveness yourself?"

"Both."

Silence fell around us, allowing me to ponder his reply while I continued to move my fingers over his forehead and through his mane.

Monster didn't talk much about his past. Still, from the little glimpses I got from our conversations, I was able to piece together a picture of his childhood. Born into a privileged family, he grew up with an abusive father and an emotionally absent mother.

"Did you forgive your parents?" I asked.

"I did." He shifted his head under my fingers a little. "For me, their death pretty much settled anything there was to forgive between us. After that, something just got lighter here." He pressed a clenched fist to his chest. "But I still wish I had a chance to say good-bye to my mom."

I remembered him mentioning that she never came up here.

"She didn't see you after your transformation? Would she have accepted you if she knew?"

"God, no!" he scoffed. "One look at me like this, and she'd run for the hills screaming. Appearance was everything for my parents, for my mom just as much as for my dad, if not more. She was incredibly beautiful and vain. Fretting over what people would think sometimes was her only motivation to get out of bed and show her face in public. Otherwise, I believe, she'd have spent her whole life locked up in that room."

I stopped massaging his head and only continued to stroke his mane gently, listening to him talk.

He never told me his name or the name of his family. Because he didn't want to be the man he used to be, he'd explained, and I suspected because he also didn't want to dive too deep into the memories either.

I understood his desire to bury the past as I recognized the need to erase it from one's mind completely. I also knew now that sometimes, the opposite was what brought relief. Talking about the past, released the power it held. So I let him speak, glad that I could be there for him when he needed someone to listen.

"This is one of the regrets I have," he continued. "I wish I could say a proper goodbye to my mom. Lately, I've been wondering how different things could've been if I didn't turn my back on her when she started ignoring me. If instead of distancing myself even further, filled with anger and hurt at her neglect, I'd managed to stay close. Would I've been able to save her?" He paused for a moment, lost in his past then answered his own question, "Most likely not. But now I'll never know for sure because I didn't try."

Monster caught my hand and brought it to the side of his face. He couldn't kiss it. Instead, he gently nuzzled my palm.

"What I'm saying, Sophie, is that I'd love for you to stay here, but if you go to France, I'll understand." His voice had been flowing at a slower pace. Eventually, his breathing grew deeper and his eyelids seemed to be weighted down by exhaustion.

I realized he had a long day working on the grounds. Glad that massage relaxed him enough to help him drift asleep, I didn't want to force him to go upstairs in bed. Instead, I threw a blanket over him and continued to cradle his head in my lap.

Cupping the side of his face with one hand, I gently stroked his head. His chest rose with even, deep breathing as I guarded his sleep.

My heart flooded with tenderness for this huge beast of a man. He had crawled under my skin and into my heart so deep, there was no way for me to ever claw him back out. Horns, tail, and all—he was all mine.

"I love you, my Monster," I whispered, finally recognizing the swell of emotions flooding me.

His eyelids fluttered, and his breathing hitched for a moment, but he didn't open his eyes and didn't reply, leaving me unsure if he'd heard my words. Not that it mattered at the moment whether he heard them or not. Recognizing the feeling myself was overwhelming enough for now.

# Chapter 35

## Sophie

Next time I went to town I sent another email to Madam Besson, asking for updates on Henri's condition. I had a trip to Calgary planned for the beginning of March to visit my mom, and I considered if I should just go to France from there. I decided to wait for the updates first, still worried about upsetting a sick man by showing up at his house uninvited.

The thought of it brought a deep feeling of regret about our failed relationship as father and child between Henri and I—the bond that had never formed and now had no chance of happening.

On the other hand, I was looking forward even more to seeing my mother again when it was time for me to leave for Calgary. I always missed her, but now felt an even stronger need to see her.

"Just one week," I promised Monster when he hugged me good-bye at the end of the driveway. "I'll be back soon. You won't even have a chance to miss me."

It was always hard to leave him behind. The fact that he was tied to this place, literally a prisoner, made it much worse.

"Oh, I will miss you, you can be sure of it," he muttered just above my ear, holding me tight. "I'll start missing you as soon as I release you from my arms."

"One week," I repeated softly, brushing large snowflakes from his mane, then took his head in my hands to look into his eyes. "I will miss you too, more than ever . . . Because I love you."

He stilled for a moment, even his breathing seemed to have stopped completely, long enough for me to worry what *his* feelings for me were.

"Are you happy, Sophie?" He asked unexpectedly.

"I am, Monster." I answered without a hesitation. "There is no place I'd rather be than next to you. You've made me happier than I've ever been, than I ever thought I could be."

The passionate embrace, in which he enclosed me, lifted me off my feet.

"This *has* to make it right then. This is worth everything."

"What is?" His reaction was strong but not exactly what I expected to be in response to my confession.

"This fairy tale. It's everything. As long as it lasts, princess. I want to savor every single moment of it for just a little bit longer."

He sat me down carefully then leaned over a little, searching my eyes.

"I love you too, Sophie. Madly. Your happiness is everything to me, and it's the only thing that matters."

ON MY SECOND DAY IN Calgary, my mom and I had a long talk, during which I told her that I'd met someone in Rocky River and decided to stay there. My lease agreement with Monster was only until the end of the year, but I was more than ready to extend it for longer, much longer. And I had every reason to believe he felt the same way.

I couldn't tell my mom the whole truth about Monster yet. He and I would have to figure out how to go about it later. For now, I was just too happy enjoying this wonderful new feeling we shared for each other.

Mom told me about her plans to move in with Jeff. And I agreed that selling the townhouse would be the best thing to do, excited for her starting a new life with the man she loved.

The next day, I sat on my old bed, sorting through all the things I had collected over my years of living here. I'd figured it'd make it easier for Mom to get the house ready for sale if my stuff was out of her way.

Sorting through some of my old textbooks, I felt the familiar stab of bitterness at my failure. The regret was not over failing to become a doctor but over never becoming anything at all.

I started medical school in the hope of making my indifferent father proud one day. The urge to gain his approval was deep-seated, practically indestructible. Now, I realized that the most appealing part of medicine—what would make me truly happy—was the chance to help people. And there were so many ways to do it. I didn't need to use a scalpel or wear a white coat to make a difference.

Spurred by this idea, I searched for online programs and found several that for the first time in a long time made me excited about my professional future again. Counseling, massage therapy, and even several non-traditional healing courses sounded like something I would love doing. The progress I've been making with my therapist allowed me to hope I could cope with study. In any case, I felt confident enough to try again.

I printed out the information on the ones that really tugged at my heart, with the intention of narrowing it down back at the house, already looking forward to sharing it all with Monster.

Figuring out in my head the best way to manage studying online while, practically, living away from civilization, I went back to sorting through my things when my cell phone rang unexpectedly.

"Is this Sophie Morel?" A female voice inquired on the other end of the line.

"Speaking," I replied, indecisively hovering an old notebook between the two boxes marked with *Keep* and *Throw Away.*

"Well, hi then. I'm Cecilia."

The notebook fell out of my hand, and I sprang up from the bed. "Hi!"

"You've been looking for me."

"Oh yes, I have. Thank you so much for getting back to me. I really need to ask you some questions—"

"Listen, I'm just calling to tell you to stop looking for me and stop bothering the organizing committee. They are busy people, and so am I."

"Please, please don't hang up!" My mind shrunk into a ball of panic, and I clutched the phone so hard it hurt. "A man's future depends on it."

"Sure, it does. But why should I care?"

I hoped against all odds that it wouldn't be the last thing I heard before she hung up on me.

"Please, Cecilia." I was so not above begging. "I need your help to reverse something you did about six years ago, in New York State."

I didn't know for sure if it was the right Cecilia. But if she was, I had mere seconds to catch her attention.

"I'm not sure what you're talking about."

But I sensed the opposite held true—she hadn't hung up on me yet.

"I don't know what it was," I exhaled. "Magic? Voodoo? Some advanced science? But he believes it was you who made him look like an animal and confined him to a lonely life in the woods after an unfortunate one-night stand—" I cut myself off, afraid of sounding judgmental when I wasn't. I didn't search for her to judge, to be angry or jealous. All I wanted was her help. "I meant you spent a night together . . ."

"*Him.*"

"You do remember." I exhaled in relief, feeling a little lightheaded. It was *her* after all. "Can you help? Please?"

The long silence on the other end made me fear again that she'd hung up, and I dreaded hearing a dial tone at any moment.

"Um, Cecilia?" I prompted when she still didn't reply.

"He was an asshole," she bit out sharply. The resentment in her voice dampened my hope.

"He was," I agreed, crestfallen, but unable to argue with her on this. "He admitted he treated you badly, and he is sorry. If you could give him a chance to apologize—"

"I'm not coming up there for that," she cut me off.

"But he can't come to see you. He can't leave—"

"I know. I made sure of it."

Her reply was curt and abrupt. But I sensed some hesitation in her voice and in the long pause she took after.

"Can I come to see you instead?" I offered, hoping it may be easier in person.

"And who are you to him?"

"I . . . I care about him. Very much."

"You do, huh?"

"He's changed." I feverishly searched through my brain for the right words to convince her somehow, but she didn't give me a chance.

"Listen. I'm not supposed to talk about this shit over the phone. If it's that important to you and he's changed as you say, then meet with me at the venue next week. March thirteenth. I'll be having lunch at the restaurant downstairs at noon."

The line went dead.

In a complete stupor, I kept staring at the silent phone in my hand. Then what she'd said began to filter in slowly.

'March thirteenth, venue, lunch at noon.'

With trembling fingers, I opened the browser on my phone and searched for the fair in New Orleans again. It was being held the week of March 13th, and the hotel where it was taking place had a restaurant downstairs.

I dropped the phone in my lap, only to pick it up again almost immediately and open a travel website.

I needed a plane ticket to New Orleans for next week.

# Chapter 36

## Sophie

The snow might still be falling strongly in Rocky River, and the weather in Calgary was still far from spring-like, but in New Orleans it was a beautiful, sunny day.

Feeling the sweat gather under my arms, I took my jacket off, leaving only the thin sweater underneath.

My oversize purse was the only piece of luggage I took on the plane with me. I would've wished for this to be a one-day trip. However, because of the time difference between Calgary and New Orleans, I had to fly overnight to make sure I wasn't late for my meeting with Cecilia at noon.

This was my first time in the city, and normally, I would've loved to explore the French Quarter or go on a paddle steamer cruise. This was not why I came here, though. My sole purpose was to talk to Cecilia. Monster waited for me alone in the woods, and I wanted to be back as soon as possible. Hopefully, with some good news.

I found the venue of the fair convention easily enough. The four-storey historical building, finished in pale-yellow stucco, didn't stand out too much from the rest of the colourful neighbourhood, but there was something just a little sinister in the ornate architecture. I could understand why the organizers of the convention claimed this was one of the most haunted hotels in New Orleans.

The lobby was filled with people, most dressed in an eccentric mix of clothing and headwear. I stopped in the lobby, overwhelmed by all the noise and colour for a moment, suddenly feeling very out of place in my plain sweater, jeans and running shoes.

How will I ever find her here?

Slowly weaving through the crowd, I made my way to the restaurant off the lobby. It was busy here, too. Every wicker table was occupied. I inched along the wall to stay away from the waiters hurrying by and swept the place with my gaze, searching for the woman who matched Cecilia's description.

All I remembered from Monster's story about her was that she had black hair and brown eyes. And neither of these was very helpful—the hair colour was easy enough to change, and the eye colour was hard to spot from a distance.

So, really, I didn't have much to go by at all. I realized she had no idea how I looked either.

I glanced down on the cell phone in my hand—it was ten minutes after noon already.

Had I come all the way here for nothing?

A couple at the table nearest to me paid their bill and left, so I lowered myself in the chair and set my heavy purse down.

"Hi." A tall brunette appeared seemingly from nowhere and plopped in the chair across from me.

"Cecilia?" I exhaled in surprise and relief.

"Who else? Are you here to meet more than one witch?" She leaned across the table and added in a loud whisper. "This is not the right place then. No one here has any real magic whatsoever. You know why I love coming here? Because as different as these people think themselves to be, it makes me feel almost normal in comparison."

She widened her cinnamon-brown eyes at me—gold sparkles glistened inside her irises in the bright sunlight from the floor-to-ceiling windows of the restaurant—then gave me a lopsided grin.

"I'm glad you found me." I smiled back. "I was worried, with all these people—"

"It wasn't that difficult to spot you, Sophie. Anyone can see you came from way up there." She waved her hand high over her head, but I understood she referred to the North. "You must be the palest person in the city. And by *pale*, I don't mean just your tan-less skin. You stick out like a sore thumb. No offence."

"None taken," I smoothed the sleeve of my beige sweater, glancing at the bright attire on people around us. Some wore all black, like Cecilia. It didn't make them appear any less colourful as characters, though.

Cecilia waved one of the passing waiters over to take our lunch orders, and I used the moment to study her.

Glossy, ink-black hair reached past her waist, bangs over her perfectly shaped eyebrows. A number of chains and beads circled her neck and wrists, and there was at least one ring on each of her fingers. She was tall, slender, and very attractive. And she did not appear evil to me.

"Where did you get your magic, Cecilia? How do you turn a man into a beast?"

It came out a little more accusatory than I intended, but I didn't apologize for it.

"My magic?" Her fingers traced one of the leather cords around her neck, sliding down to the amulet on it—a cloudy piece of dark amber, carved in the shape of a flat disk with a round hole in the middle. "It's hereditary. We're not allowed to talk about it to strangers. Let's just say, I come from a peculiar family." She inserted the point of one finger in the hole in the centre of the disk and twisted it around with another. "Just to make it clear, though, even my magic—as strong as it is—can't turn a good man into a beast."

"But you did—"

"Nope. He already was a beast on the inside—a mean, heartless animal. All I did was make him look like one on the outside."

The waiter brought our lunch salads, but I barely glanced at mine, instead watching Cecilia quickly spear the green leaves with her fork.

"Can you change him back?"

"Why?" She asked between the mouthfuls, regarding me with curiosity. "He deserved what he got. Why would you even bother asking for him? Do you have a thing for assholes?"

"He's not—" I cut myself short to draw more oxygen in my lungs and to figure out a better way to explain myself. "I'm not defending him. He told me all about the night you spent together . . . I mean, the morning after. His behaviour towards you was appalling, to say the least—"

"He basically called me a whore." Cecilia emphasized her point by stabbing her fork through the air.

"And he is very sorry about it, believe me. He would give a lot for the chance to apologize to you. If the purpose of your punishment was to make him realize his mistakes and come to regret them . . . Well, he's certainly done that. Cecilia . . ." I shook my head, willing to convey through my words everything I was feeling. "He's had a long time to think about who he was and what he's done. He's lost everyone and spent years completely alone with only his remorse. There is a man inside him now, not a beast. There is so much more to him as a person. He is caring, thoughtful, and attentive. And he is striving to be a better man every day. Really, Cecilia. If you wanted to punish him for that night, it happened. If you wanted him to change, he did. Now, please, let him be free again. Let him have a full life."

I clasped my hands in front of me, willing the lump in my throat to dissolve.

"Well." She cleared her throat. Her fingers fidgeted with the pendant again. "He's made you care for him."

"He's made me love him," I corrected.

Her expressive brown gaze shot to my face.

"Do you? Do you really love him?"

I nodded without any hesitation.

She leaned back in her seat.

"Like, really?" Her eyes narrowed at me. The scrutiny in her stare was almost offensive, as if she didn't believe me at all. "His appearance doesn't put you off at all? You know—the horns, the fur, the tail? None of it repulses you, nothing creeps you out?"

"It used to. There was a time his looks terrified me. But not anymore. To me, they're just a part of him now. The horns and the tail don't matter. I, um . . ." I focused on the untouched salad on my plate. "I actually like his tail," I confessed. "It's prehensile and . . . um, dexterous."

I felt a hot blush slowly creep up my face.

Cecilia's loud laugh made me lift my gaze to her face again. From the corner of my eye, I noticed other people in the restaurant were staring our way too.

"You are kinkier than you look, girl." She shook her head, still laughing. To my relief, the atmosphere between us seemed to get lighter. The initial tension had eased significantly if not disappeared completely.

The blush on my face burned hot, though, and I steered the conversation back to where I needed it to go, more hopeful now that she seemed to be in a better mood.

"I don't care about his appearance, but he needs to be free. He can't lead a normal life, looking the way he does. He is a prisoner of the estate in more ways than one."

"Sophie." Her voice turned serious again. "You seem to think I can do something about the curse, but I can't."

"You can't?" Everything inside me dropped.

"Nope." She shook her head. "That's the way this curse works. You place it on someone then let it work its course. Nothing can be done after it has been laid."

"Nothing?"

"Listen." She fisted the amber disk in her hand. "I was young and a little impulsive back then. And he really pissed me off. Here I was thinking I'd just had the best lay of my life—he could fuck like nobody's business, you know—but what we had meant absolutely nothing to him."

"I'm sorry, Cecilia."

"Don't be." She waved her hand at me. "I'm glad he is less of an asshole now as you said. He must have changed enough for you to love him." She propped her chin with her fist, considering something for a moment. "Maybe, I shouldn't have used that curse, or at least I should've defined the time of its power. Like when I made Peyton's face break out just before prom night. I had set the curse for two days. So the bitch had to go to the prom with a pound of makeup on her face to cover the ugly pimples for stealing Mason from me. But at least two days later she was fine, looking all pretty again and back to her whoring ways."

"What you're saying is that Monster's curse is forever?" I clarified. "You can't undo it?"

"No, I can't." She shook her head. "Once it's been laid, there is nothing anyone can do. That's why my aunt, Ingeborg, doesn't like it when I use irreversible curses. She says I'm too hot-headed to realize the consequences of my own powers. I never told her about me using this one—she'd be furious. The woman's almost two hundred years old. Trust me, you don't want to make her angry."

"Who?" My mind was still reeling from her statement that she couldn't rescind what she'd done to Monster to closely follow her ramblings.

"My aunt. We call her Inge in the family, for obvious reasons. Her full name is a bit of a mouthful, but it must've been fine when her parents named her in Finland, two centuries ago."

"Cecilia." I blinked, shaking my head. I'd lost the thread of what she was talking about, struggling to keep the conversation on track. "So, there is absolutely nothing you can do to reverse your own curse? Shouldn't there be some counter spell, like anti-venom?"

"Listen, I laid the curse, but it's not mine. It's as old as time. You know The Beast, the rose bushes, the Beauty—the usual." She eyed me critically. "Well, beauty is in the eye of the beholder, they say. Don't get me wrong, you are cute. In that ordinary kinda way. Anyway, like most curses, this one has a provision built in that reverses it once a condition is met."

"A condition?"

She rolled her eyes up to the ceiling.

"Well, you know how it goes. *Until a woman falls in love with the beast—all of him—even despite his hideous appearance . . .* Or something along those lines. You said you love him." She narrowed her eyes at me again.

"I do," I whispered.

My heart sank. If love was all that was needed, why hadn't it worked then? Did I not love Monster strongly enough? Were my feelings for him too weak to reverse the curse? I searched deep inside for them. Friendship, affection, trust, and love—warm, caring, and so strong it hurt.

"I love him," I confirmed with absolute certainty. "I love him with everything I have. I'll do anything to make him free again. Please tell me there is something I can do."

She leaned back in her seat.

"I'm afraid that's all there is, Sophie." Her voice softened with genuine sympathy, compelling me to believe her. "I was really angry that morning. Maybe, I fucked up some words while laying the curse in the first place?"

Tears burned my eyes, but I blinked them away, refusing to acknowledge my disappointment in public.

"For what it's worth, I am sorry." Cecilia covered my hand with hers. "Please tell him I accept his apology. And I'm truly sorry that I can't help him."

I exhaled a shuddered breath and nodded.

"Thank you. I'll tell him that. It'll mean a lot to him."

She squeezed my hand lightly.

"I've gotta go now, hon. My lunch break is over. I have to do another speaking engagement soon."

She tossed a few bills on the table and headed for the entrance of the lobby.

"Cecilia," I called out to her.

She glanced at me over her shoulder, lifting an eyebrow in question.

"What was his name?" I asked. "Do you remember?"

"You don't know his name?"

"He refuses to tell me. He says that name is not important anymore. But I need to know." I sighed. "His name is all he has left from his past."

She nodded.

"Hunter."

"What?" Despite the heat, chill slithered along my spine and spread through to my heart.

"I don't know his last name." Cecilia shrugged but added with confidence, "However, I never forgot his first. It's Hunter."

# Chapter 37

## Sophie

I headed up the driveway, expecting to catch the familiar flash of Monster's brown fur between the tree trunks any minute.

It wasn't the usual feeling of warm excitement that reigned over me as I approached the house this time. Heavy dread and trepidation sat deep, weighing on my heart.

I spent close to two days travelling back to him from New Orleans—two flights with a layover to get to Calgary, then two more flights to Rocky River, each airplane smaller in size than the previous the closer to town I got.

It was late afternoon. I was tired, but I didn't want to spend the night in Rocky River. I needed to see Monster. I needed him to tell me that his name was just some insane coincidence, even as deep in my mind I knew it was not.

Hunter Reed, the man of my nightmares, may not be the only one with that first name. However, there were simply too many other things to ignore. Like Hunter, Monster came from a prominent family, with both parents passed away. Just like him, he went to university in New York State. The timeline of the events also added up.

Everything simply could not be coincidental.

While waiting at one of the airports on my way here, I looked up his name for the first time ever. Hunter Reed, the heir to a vast fortune after his parents' untimely death, had not been seen in public for years.

According to some accounts, he remained on the East Coast of The United States after dropping out of university for non-attendance. Others claimed he was spending his days in the wilderness of northern Canada, disillusioned with the world and living completely off the grid. Yet some reported having seen him in countries like Taiwan and Cambodia, doing humanitarian work under a number of fake names, living the legacy of his benevolent parents.

The last pictures of him were from his first year of university, over six years ago. I stared at the painfully familiar face—breathtakingly handsome, if it wasn't for the arrogant smirk and cold, detached expression in his eyes—and saw nothing of my Monster there.

How could it be the same person?

Monster would never lie to me.

Yet he never shared his name.

I stopped the truck in front of the entrance, not bothering to park it in the garage.

Monster was still nowhere to be seen, and I assumed that he must've gone to another part of the property, maybe to the river for a swim. In any case, he would have sensed me by now, and he'd be here soon.

Anxious to do something, anything, about the dark suspicion gnawing at me from the inside, I went straight into the kitchen and grabbed a heavy meat cleaver out of the knife block then ran up the stairs to the octagonal glass observatory on top of the roof.

Here, an antique writing desk stood next to one of the floor-to-ceiling windows. I knew that Monster stored all correspondence I brought for him in the ornate hatch of the desk. He always locked it, and as expected the key was nowhere to be seen.

I would have never done this before, invaded his privacy. His mail arrived at Bob's Place in envelopes with my name on them, and I always delivered them unopened to him, not once considering looking at the contents.

Now I *had* to know.

I inserted the meat cleaver between the desktop and the cover of the hatch and wrenched it up with all the force I had. The lock broke, letting me roll the cover open.

The papers were organized in neat stacks. With shaking fingers, I shuffled through them, uncertain what exactly I was looking for. I needed indisputable proof—in black and white—to believe the unbelievable.

The heavy front door downstairs slammed shut, and I heard Monster's steps in the living room.

"Sophie?" he called, his voice cheerful. My heart clenched for a moment with the desire to run to him, to let his arms wrap around me, to pretend none of this was happening right now, but then my gaze landed on the piece of paper in my hand.

Our lease agreement, the last page was signed by *Hunter Reed.*

Everything inside me went numb at seeing his name, the proof I searched for.

Clutching the paper in my hand, I moved to the winding staircase that led from the observatory down to the second floor.

"There you are." Monster lifted his head at the noise of my footsteps. "What are you doing up there—" His voice cut off, as his gaze flicked from my face down to the piece of paper crumpled in my hand. "Sophie?"

Walking down the stairs from the second floor, I took all of him in. His fur spiked with frost—the waistband of his jeans dark from icy water. He must've been swimming, then ran all the way from the river when he'd sensed my arrival.

My Monster.

Not anymore. He only looked like him.

"It's you," I croaked, reaching the main floor. Speaking suddenly proved extremely difficult. "And all this time . . . you've said nothing."

"Sophie," he exhaled, his shoulders slumped.

He took a step to me, and I scurried backwards until my back hit the wall, letting the paper in my hand fall to the floor.

I couldn't let him touch me. Monster's touch had the power to make me weak in the knees. It had the magic to deprive me of sanity, driving me mad with desire. Now more than ever I needed strength and a clear mind.

No, this man's touch causes nightmares that last for years.

I shuddered.

"Sophie." He shook his head slowly. "Please, don't be afraid of me."

I splayed my hands on the cool timber of the wall behind me to stop them from trembling.

"How could I not be afraid of you? You have been the main cause of my fear for the past eight years. You made me scared of the dark, terrified of the night and my own shadow. And I . . . I've been alone with you here. I've trusted you . . . I've . . ."

Hurt burnt in my throat.

"Sophie, it's still me—"

"Who is *me*?" I interrupted him. "As far as I know you are a fake and everything you told me about yourself is a lie."

"All my feelings for you are real. Every single one of them."

"They *can't* be true. How could you deceive me if you truly cared?"

"How long would you have stayed anywhere near me had you known my real name?" He raised his voice, making me flinch. "What would be the chances of you spending even a minute under the same roof with Hunter Reed, not to mention a whole night? You would've run the moment you learned who I was, fuck the twisted ankle!"

"So, you lied to me. You made me believe you were someone else. Why? Because you were bored and lonely, and you thought I'd be easy to trick into keeping you company here? Because you needed a connection to the world, someone to improve your life in here, and you figured I was weak enough to be manipulated into doing things for you?"

"No, Sophie. No. Your kindness is your strength, not your weakness." He paced agitatedly in front of me, fingers deep in his mane. "When I asked you to bring things for me, I simply devised excuses to see you again. The first time I saw you that night—really saw you—I didn't think you were weak." He stopped in his tracks, fixing me with his stare. "Years ago, I took your confidence, your faith in yourself. And I'm sorry, I'm so very sorry, Sophie. But what I did to you, it didn't change who you are. The monster I was could not take your strength. You are smart, kind, and strong. Even faced with certain death from exposure in the woods that night, you kept fighting, determined to survive. That was the person I saw."

His words echoed in my head but hardly registered. I couldn't allow myself to believe him anymore.

"And you did improve my life. Infinitely," he continued. "But you did so, so much more. Sophie, I love you—"

"Don't." I shook my head vehemently. "Don't even say that word right now. It's wrong . . . Cruel."

Despite what he'd said, I didn't feel strong at the moment. Not at all. I felt like a trembling pile of nerves, ready to collapse any minute.

He lowered his head and stepped closer to me. I pressed my back into the wall behind me, with no way of getting away from him now.

"You think it's wrong for me to love you?" His voice was grave.

The familiar smell of him hit my senses, and I struggled to remember *who* really was in front of me. His physical proximity overwhelmed me.

It was all a lie.

"The man I love doesn't exist," I said firmly. "Hunter Reed has always been a selfish, entitled monster. And you are a liar and manipulator. You've never changed. Do you understand what you've done? You've pretended to be someone I could love, but it was all a lie. It's as if you stole the love of my life from me!"

The air in the house got scarce, and I gasped for oxygen. The sound came out more like a sob.

My hand to my chest, I exhaled, "I need to go."

A low snarl, deep inside his throat alerted me, an icy jolt of adrenaline shooting through my system.

His expression grew dark. His features hardened.

I inched towards the front door along the wall.

He lunged for me, closing the distance between us. With a loud thud, his claws sank into the wood of the wall on each side of my head, making me jump.

"No!" he growled, hulking over me, his brilliant hazel eyes dark, a storm brewing inside.

"I—I have to get out of here." I swallowed hard, fighting for my next breath. The dense, heavy cloud of his presence suffocated me. Everything that I had worked so hard to overcome during the past weeks threatened to come crashing down.

"You can't leave!" He thundered, shoving with force against the wall as if trying to break through it. "You took from me whatever life I had, and became my entire world instead. If you leave now, I'll have nothing."

I froze in the face of his rage and fought the impulse to squeeze my eyes shut and block the view of his bared teeth and of the fire in his eyes. My whole body shook with nerves and emotions, but I stood straight, holding my head high.

"I need to go," I said, low but firm. "I can't stay here."

I heard his horns hit the wall above me as his forehead touched mine. The soft tendrils of his mane caressed my face.

"A bigger man, a better man, would let you go." His voice grew much deeper with a growl rolling through each word. "But I'm not a man, am I? I'm a monster. And you're *mine*."

I stopped being afraid of Monster long ago. However, *this* was not him in front of me now.

Hunter Reed never earned my trust.

All I felt was betrayal and fear. Thick, sticky, nauseating fear that urged me to the front door to escape my tormentor.

"You are mine." The firm conviction in the hollow rumble of his voice slithered cold along my spine. "And you're staying." The side of his face rubbed against mine, and his hips rocked into me.

My breathing turned shallow, and my head swam at the tsunami of feelings I no longer knew how to handle—an unexpected wisp of arousal from his familiar scent and closeness laced through the rising panic and fear.

My mind knew to run away, but my body still recognized him as mine.

Hurt at the loss of what I thought I had speared my heart.

Afraid I would either faint or explode into a million little pieces if I stayed another moment longer, I squeezed through my teeth, "Let. Me. Go."

He leaned away from me a little, and I felt the soft caress of the calloused pads of his fingers against my cheek.

"I could *make* you stay with me." His words were still alarming, but infinite sadness drowned the threat in his voice. "But your mind, your soul, and your heart would be forever lost to me. And I want everything. I need all of you, princess."

"Let me go," I repeated, this time louder.

He still didn't appear to hear me. He sounded as if he was talking to himself now.

"Small and fragile. And so incredibly strong." He yanked his claws out of the wall behind me suddenly then slammed them hard in again. "You bring me to my knees." With a loud noise of his claws cutting deep grooves through the wood, he slowly sank to his knees at my feet. "Every. Single. Time."

His head bent, he groaned out one word, "Stay."

I didn't know what was harder to resist for me—the plea in his submissive pose or the dominant command of that one word.

Trembling like a leaf, my throat painfully tight, I no longer trusted myself to speak. Silently, I made a move along the wall in the direction of the front door. My hip bumped into his arm blocking my escape with claws deep in the wall.

Without looking up, he dropped his arm to his side, setting me free.

"Go," he rasped. "Run before I stop you."

I rushed to the door.

But I couldn't resist one last glance back at him before going outside. He remained seated on his haunches, facing the wall, both arms at his sides, his head down.

He was not my Monster anymore—he was the monster of my nightmares—I felt betrayed, afraid and confused, but no matter what, I still couldn't leave him like that.

"Mon—" I stopped myself in time. I couldn't call him that anymore, could I? He had a name, a real name. I sighed, getting ready to say it out loud once again.

"Hunter."

His shoulders stiffened.

"Cecilia wanted me to tell you she is sorry about what she did to you." My voice rang hollow, empty even to my own ears. "She accepted your apology."

Unless the apology was a lie, just like everything else.

The thought twisted my insides.

He lifted his head. The pain and devastation on his face made my heart bleed with a memory of the one I thought I loved—the one who was never real.

It was the last straw. With a sob, I ran out into the cold.

As I drove away, whatever little control I had over my emotions finally snapped, letting hot tears run down my face.

How could I mourn someone who never existed? How could I accept that the biggest—the only—love of my life was nothing but a lie, a trap?

Through the haze of my tears in the receding light of the early evening, I looked straight ahead. I didn't search the woods for a large, furry shape running through the trees, but I felt his eyes on me and knew he followed the truck.

The feeling stayed with me as I turned from the driveway onto the road and continued along the chain-link fence. And when the fence ended at the south-west corner of the property, I felt the string that attached me to the place stretch impossibly thin the further I drove away, threatening to break for good.

Then a long, blood-curdling howl of a beast reached me. As deafening and terrifying as ever, it was full of sorrow and eternal longing.

# Chapter 38

## Monster

She was gone.

His love. His light. His life.

And he had no one to blame but himself.

Whatever true happiness he ever had in his life was with her and because of her. And he cowardly stole every little bit of it, hiding behind his curse as if it could shield him from his past forever.

The desperate longing reaped another howling roar from his chest as he watched the truck disappear behind the trees, knowing that this time there was little hope of her ever coming back. This time, she was leaving without a promise to return.

The thought that it might be all he'd ever see of her filled him with chilling fear. Then the old rage slammed into him, and he let it reign, surrendering his control to the familiar anger because *she* was no longer here to sooth it.

And without her what was the point in fighting it?

Without her, there was no longer a point to anything. She'd given a purpose to his life, and now there was none.

"Sophie!" A pained cry tore through his insides and he threw himself against the hated fence. The impact sent him flying back, flinging him against the frozen ground with force.

The crushing pain came as a relief from the agony of loss stabbing him from the inside. Physical pain was so much easier to handle. The internal one was unbearable.

He sprang to his feet immediately and lunged back at the fence again, with renewed force. Propelled in the air, he landed flat on his back this time. The blow knocked all air out of his lungs. His muscles screamed with pain, but his soul demanded more.

More.

His body could take it. It was his heart that couldn't. It was torn and shredded in a million little pieces. Destroyed.

His own scorching need for destruction burnt through him.

With another roar he attacked the nearby tree, punching it with his fist, then shoved at it with both hands . . .

No, not hands.

Paws.

What came into his vision were two ugly, furry animal paws, complete with a full set of black claws. Only *she* could ever think of them as a man's hands.

Another spear of raw pain shot through him, sending him into a mad run. Sprinting through the trees, he ran faster and faster, until the woods around him smudged into a blur dashing by in his peripherals.

Hardly slowing down, he darted through the open door into the house.

Her scent greeted him. Everything inside was filled with her spirit.

But *she* was gone.

A heavy armchair fell into his line of sight, and he sent it flying across the room with a swing of his arm, new upholstery torn to shreds by his claws.

Next was the bar stool in the kitchen, thrown through the air it slammed into the opposite wall. Its loud crash against the timber made the beast pause.

She wasn't here.

The house remained. The furniture, her things upstairs were still here. But she was gone. And taking his madness out on the lifeless objects would not ease the excruciating emptiness she left behind.

He leaned with his back against one of the support posts and slid to the floor, suddenly drained.

She was not coming back. Because he hurt her. Again.

His actions eight years ago defined him in her eyes, stripping him from any chance of redemption.

He dared to believe that he could make her happy. He hoped he could help her, rescue her. But he was never meant to be her knight in shining armour. In her life, he was doomed to remain the dragon to be slayed.

Even in his own story, he turned out to be not the hero but the villain. Someone who hurt people. And the more he loved, the stronger he wanted to protect, the more pain he ended up inflicting.

The villain never got the girl at the end—his redemption was only through death and oblivion.

# Chapter 39

## Sophie

I had no idea where I was going. The intense need to get away drove me out without any clear destination in mind.

I made it to Rocky River after nightfall and would have kept driving if I hadn't felt like I'd collapse with exhaustion after days of travelling and hardly any sleep.

Instead, I crashed on the couch in Jo's apartment in town, intending to take the first flight out I could.

Lying in the dark, listening to Jo's soft snoring from her bedroom, I couldn't sleep despite being bone tired.

The turmoil of emotion inside me twisted and writhed, keeping me awake.

I thought I'd never see him again. After he graduated high school and left the city, I hoped I'd never have to hear about Hunter Reed. I carefully avoided anyone who might know of his whereabouts. And until yesterday, I was extremely cautious when using social media, steering away from any mention of him.

Meanwhile, I had let him come so close to me that I often felt we were one. Crashing through all my defences, he climbed deep into my very heart. Now that his lies had exploded, they left nothing behind but utter devastation. Everything, my heart, my very soul, had been annihilated.

I could feel the darkness rising from the house in the woods, reaching out for me, threatening to suffocate me with panic all over again. Huddling under the covers, I curled into a ball, counting my breaths again, waiting for the sun to come up.

I wished I could crawl under a rock somewhere on an undiscovered planet or at least on an uninhabited island—somewhere where no one would look at me or care to speak to me, where I could be invisible until I could regain the ability to face life.

A ping from a new email came sometime after five in the morning, and I opened a message from Madam Besson.

Henri had another stroke, which left him fully paralyzed and unable to speak. Doctors feared that due to complications, he didn't have much time left.

The phrase *'your presence here is not required'* was not there this time, but it didn't matter even if it were. I realized I didn't want the yelling in the heat of the argument to be the last words my father heard from me in his life.

France. I'm going to France.

# Chapter 40

## Sophie

"Bonjour, Mademoiselle Morel. I'm really glad to see you again. Your room is ready." Madame Besson stepped to the side, opening the front door of the chateau wider to let me in with my suitcase. She motioned at it. "I'll have someone to bring your luggage upstairs for you."

Like always, she looked poised and professional in her uniform. Her raven dark hair had much more silver in it since I saw her last, but her eyes shone with the familiar smile.

"It's very nice to see you too, Madame Besson." I fought the desire to enclose her in a hug, knowing all too well it would not be welcomed. Madame Besson had lasted as long as she did in the Morel household and survived working under the numerous Madames Morels in part because she maintained her distance and professionalism at all times.

"Monsieur Morel is in his room," she informed me. "I'll ask Mademoiselle Perrin, his day nurse, when would be the best time for you to see him."

"Um . . ." I came with the intention to see Henri. However, now that I was about to do it, nervous anxiety filled me

She spun on her heel to face me again, raising an enquiring eyebrow.

"How is he?" I asked. "I mean. Are you sure he wants to see me? I wouldn't want to upset him."

"Mademoiselle, if you want to say goodbye to him, do it for your sake, not for his. He will be gone soon. Make sure you're not left with regrets. Besides." She pursed her lips for a moment. Her eyes narrowed in thought then met mine with more warmth than before. "Give him a chance, too, because he is not in a position to take action himself now."

AS SOON AS I SETTLED in the room I had always stayed in when visiting my father, I sent a quick email to my mom, letting her know I had arrived at the chateau safely.

I didn't get to see her in Calgary where I only had a brief stop at the townhouse to pack a suitcase with some clothes from the boxes I had filled ready to be shipped to Rocky River before I'd left for New Orleans.

I told her about Henri's condition and that I was going to France to see him but didn't mention anything about what happened between me and the person I'd been sharing the roof with. The pain was still too raw to touch that subject with anyone.

After unpacking the few things I brought with me, I had dinner in the kitchen with Madame Besson. The current Madame Morel was away in Paris for a few days, and there was no reason to serve dinner in the dining room just for me.

Afterwards, I sat on the bed in my old room, staring at the wall without actually seeing it. Plagued by more than I could process, my mind must have blown open and every single thought had floated away, leaving complete emptiness inside.

Emptiness was good. It meant there was no pain and no darkness. And I let myself sink into it, grateful for the absence of any feelings.

I seemed to have outrun the darkness after all.

A knock on the door broke me out of the empty cage.

"Monsieur Morel can see you now," Mademoiselle Perrin announced when I opened the door.

She was young and attractive, with thick chestnut hair brushed back into a neat bun. In fact, she was far too pretty for any of the Madames Morels to let her come anywhere near Henri under normal circumstances. He must truly be on his deathbed for that to happen.

"I'll take you to his room."

I'd spent months in Henri's house over the years of my childhood, and I had never entered the bedroom behind the high double doors.

Until now.

The usual position of the large four-poster bed must have been right in the centre, between the two tall arched windows, but it had been moved to the side, making room for the white hospital bed and several tables and rolling carts with medical equipment.

"Henri?" I took a few steps into the semi-darkness of the room, the sterile smell of medicine and impending death filled the air.

"Monsieur Morel can hear, Mademoiselle, but he does not acknowledge anyone," replied Mademoiselle Perrin in a subdued voice. "He is fully paralyzed and can no longer speak."

I came closer to the pale figure on the hospital bed, barely recognizing my own father.

His smooth, always perfectly tanned skin had paled to the point that it almost blended with the white sheets on the bed. The rich, walnut colour had been entirely bleached out of his hair by time and sickness.

"He is asleep?" I whispered.

"He often has his eyes closed and seems to doze off at times. Take a seat, Mademoiselle." She maneuvered a high-backed armchair between the roller carts closer to the bed and removed the textbook she must've been reading from it. "Talk to him if you wish. You can hold his hand, too. I'll leave you for a few minutes. Ring the bell when you're done." She pointed at the button on the frame of the bed before exiting the room and leaving me alone with Henri.

I stopped short of touching his hand and lowered myself into the armchair.

How does one say goodbye to someone when you never had anything to say to each other even when both of you could speak?

My last conversation with Henri ended with me slamming the door and running away in tears, cut by his bitter disappointment in me. And I still had nothing to tell him that he'd want to hear.

My gaze fell on the stack of books in the bottom tray of the nearest roller cart.

"Do the nurses read to you?" I wondered out loud, my voice invading the somber peace of the bedroom. I picked up one of the books. *Jane Eyre* by Charlotte Bronte. The others that I could see were also classics, *Anna Karenina, Madame Bovary, Lady Chatterley's Lover.*

I'd never seen Henri reading a book and had no idea what his reading tastes were. Still I guessed these must have been left here by the nurses for their own use, possibly to kill the time by reading during their long shifts at his bed.

I opened *Jane Eyre.*

*"There was no possibility of taking a walk that day* "I started reading just to break the heavy silence in the room.

I lifted my gaze back to the bed after finishing the first paragraph, and almost dropped the book—Henri's eyes were open. Unable to turn his head, he stared straight ahead, but his eyes flickered my way when the reading stopped.

"Hi, Henri," I said quietly. "I hope you don't mind my being here." A feeling of unease slithered inside me. The nurse claimed he didn't respond, but there was a clear awareness in his eyes. The gaze itself was a response.

He glanced my way again then down, to the book in my hand.

It occurred to me that he might be just as burdened as I was by the complete silence around him interrupted only by a faint buzzing of the machines keeping him alive.

I nodded and continued.

"I was glad of it: I never liked long walks . . ."

# Chapter 41

## Sophie

Over the next two weeks I read daily to my father. We finished *Jane Eyre*. Then I brought *La Reine Margot* by Alexandre Dumas from the library of the chateau, guessing that Henri might prefer historical adventure to romance.

Not that he ever let me know either way. The only communication we had was through his eyes, and even that was extremely limited.

He didn't always open them at my greeting when I entered the room, and would mostly keep them closed while I read. The only thing that remained consistent was that he opened his eyes whenever the reading stopped and glanced at the book, urging me to continue. I would keep going until eventually his eyes remained closed when I stopped, signaling to me that he must have drifted asleep to the sound of my voice.

This was by far the most time I had ever spent one on one with my father.

I began looking forward to going to his gloomy, way-too-quiet room every day to re-read old classics. I wanted to believe I was doing something useful and hoped he enjoyed these hours as well, or that it at least distracted him from reality, even if for a short while.

Reading to Henri freed my mind, too. Day after day, I followed the flow of the familiar language of the old masters, losing myself in the story. But at night . . .

At night, the thoughts of *him* returned. I couldn't think of him as Monster any more. That name belonged to someone who, apparently, existed only in my imagination. I couldn't bring myself to refer to him as Hunter either, for reasons I hadn't figured out yet myself.

I just thought about him as *him*.

And I thought about him every moment I had to myself.

Every night I would lay in bed for hours, waiting for sleep to come. Darkness lurked on the edge of my awareness, but it didn't scare me as much as it once did.

At first, I thought it was because I had run halfway around the world to get away from it. But then I remembered that no physical distance used to ease fear in me before.

I had fought the darkness and fear and won.

'The monster I was could not take your strength.'

He was right, he hadn't. My strength was all mine, and it was still within me. I just needed this long to find it again. I'd allowed the assault to gain power over me. Now, I'd been working hard, taking that power back, little by little, and regaining control over my own body and emotions.

Ironically, the man in the woods, no matter what I'd call him, played a huge part in the process of my recovery.

And this was where my thoughts and emotions tangled into a Gordian knot.

He was the assailant, the perpetrator, someone I vowed to stay away from. Yet, would I have taken those first steps on the way to healing without him?

He was the one who made me open up about my issues, leading me patiently and helping me cope.

On the other hand, I wouldn't have these issues to deal with in the first place if it wasn't for his actions eight years ago, would I?

This was where my mind came full circle, leaving me unable to decide if I was supposed to feel gratitude or resentment. Hate or love?

Which one of the many conflicting emotions should I even allow myself to feel for him?

Was it up to me to choose at all? I was afraid I had very little control over my feelings for him.

Every night, in bed, at that moment when commonsense had drifted asleep already but the longing was still awake, the pillow in my arms turned into his back, and the fabric under my cheek into his thick, familiar fur. I could almost hear the soothing rhythm of his heartbeat, falling asleep with the memories of feeling calm and safe at his side.

My dreams in France were not nightmares. Yet all of them were about him.

A FEW DAYS AFTER MY arrival to the chateau, I finally met Henri's current wife.

"Gabrielle Marceaux," she corrected me curtly when I greeted her as Madame Morel. "I've built a successful career in modeling under my name and have no intentions of changing it." Her gaze, the colour of dark chocolate, swept me head to toe. "Well, you can call me Gabrielle. Since we are a family."

Over the years while Henri aged, his wives had become increasingly younger. Gabrielle was no older than I, making it even more difficult for me to see her as my stepmother.

In any case, I never got a chance to figure out the relationship between us because Gabrielle didn't stay long enough or often enough at the chateau for us to build any relationship at all. She preferred to stay in the city, mostly because of her work there as she explained, but she didn't make a big secret that '*the hospital smell upstairs made her nauseous.*'

She did inform me on one of her brief visits to the chateau that Henri had a legal will.

"It will be read a week after his funeral, to give an appropriate time for grieving for the deceased first," Gabrielle explained when she ran into me on my way to Henri's room with yet another book under my arm and warned, "If you intend to contest his will, I won't make it easy."

"I have no plans of contesting anything, Gabrielle," I snapped, truly infuriated now with my father's taste in women. "My only intention is to spend as much time as possible with Henri. Before he is *deceased.*"

That evening I started *La Dame de Monsoreau*. I had made it through a couple of chapters when I saw that Henri must have dozed off as his eyes failed to open during a pause in my reading.

I closed the book and noiselessly got up from the chair. The rolling cart, where I usually left my book overnight, had been moved to the other side of the bed, so I opened the top drawer of Henri's nightstand, with the intention of leaving the book there this time.

On the bottom of the otherwise empty drawer, an envelope with familiar handwriting caught my attention. It was an unopened letter from my mother addressed to my father.

"She wrote to you."

Using traditional mail was the only way for my mother to reach my father directly. Over the past two decades, my parents had been communicating mostly through each other's lawyers. She had no other contact information for him but this address since the chateau had been in the Morel family for generations.

I looked up to see my father's eyes directed at me.

"Did you know that Mom wrote to you?"

Whether or not he knew, he couldn't open the letter himself. And whoever brought it here—either the nurse or Gabrielle—didn't bother to do it for him.

I sat back in the chair, holding the letter in my hand.

"Would you like me to read it to you?"

Henri continued staring at me.

Despite his severe limitations, we could have developed a more sophisticated system of signs, using whatever movement of his eyes he still had left to communicate. Except that Henri wouldn't go for it. Whenever I tried to build a better understanding between us by asking him to blink once for *yes* and twice for *no*, he didn't cooperate. Gabrielle questioned his cognitive abilities, wondering if they had been impaired due to his strokes. But I was convinced it was either his rebellious stubbornness or innate laziness that prevented him from even trying to cooperate.

In my opinion, the intelligence in the clear grey eyes staring at me now did not allow for any doubts in his cognitive abilities.

I tore the envelope open and took out the folded piece of printing paper, tightly filled with my mom's girly handwriting.

"Dear Henri," I started reading after clearing my voice. "I can't believe I'm actually writing to you after all these years. But life circumstances change. Sadly, it took hearing from Sophie about your condition for me to finally reach out to you. I honestly wish I'd done it sooner.

You and I would have never worked as a married couple. I know it now—we weren't right for each other. Even as lovers, we couldn't stay together for long.

It took me years to get over you. And only now that I've finally met my soulmate, I realize how wrong you and I were. There was no one to blame for things not working out between us, and I'm sorry I blamed you all this time.

My biggest regret is that we didn't work harder on remaining friends. If not for our own sake than for the sake of our daughter. I regret Sophie's growing up with parents unable to stand each other long enough to even have a civil phone conversation.

I loved you too much in the first place to even consider a friendship after we parted our ways. I'm sorry. I let my broken heart reign over my feelings for you for too long.

After all these years of hurt and bruised egos between us, I just want you to know that I have no ill feelings towards you. I hope you have no regrets with the life you've lived. And if you do, I hope you make amends and let them go, because above all I wish you peace."

It wasn't signed. It didn't need to be.

I lowered the letter to my lap and lifted my gaze to my father's face. His eyes were closed, but a single tear rolled down the papery white cheek.

I wondered if he felt any regrets at the moment, and suddenly I didn't want to be one of them, not anymore. I knew all his life he regretted having me, but I was in this world because of him. Whatever his motives for showing any interest in my life were, it was because of him that I was able to have the life I had.

I took a tissue from the nightstand and dried the lone tear off his face.

"Thank you, Henri. Thank you for being the only father I ever had."

I covered his thin, frail hand with mine and squeezed it gently. For the first time in my life, I held my father's hand.

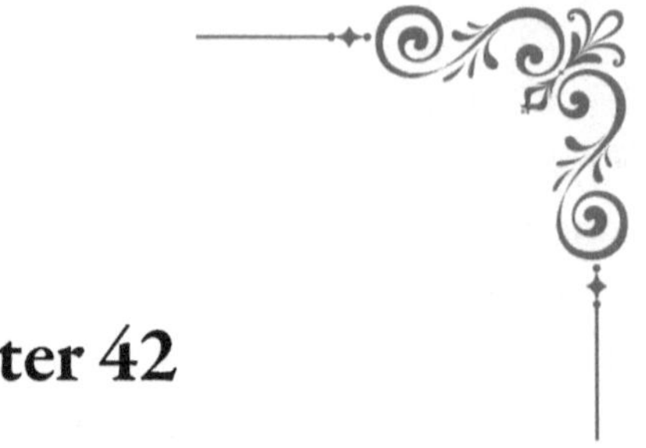

# Chapter 42

## Sophie

Four days later, Henri was gone. He passed away while I read the final pages of *La Dame de Monsoreau* to him.

I looked up after finishing the chapter. His eyes were open, but unseeing, as if he was afraid to close them to the very end, lest I stop reading and he would be left in the silence alone.

My father spent his life surrounded by people. That was how he preferred to live—among the noise and bustle of an endless party with a multitude of colourful characters, none of whom stayed in his life for too long.

It gave me comfort to know that he didn't die in complete silence at the end, even if my voice was his only companion during his final hour.

I watched the dirt hit the lid of the coffin at his funeral, feeling sadness for the man who had passed, but filled with light instead of regret, grateful that I was there to share the past weeks of his life. I hoped I managed to make those weeks a little brighter for him, too.

I hugged myself, rubbing the mid-morning chill of the cemetery out of my upper arms, and desperately wished for someone else's arms around me. The weeks spent in the cool, distant household of my father made me miss human contact that much more.

What wouldn't I give for a simple warm hug right now?

To feel big, furry arms wrap around me again.

His hug.

The thoughts of *him* came back once again, bringing along anger and disappointment, as well as confusion and longing.

During the weeks spent away from him, these emotions had a chance to settle to the point that I was able to think back to our last conversation more calmly.

He had lied to me. There was no excuse for a lie.

Still, it could be understood, couldn't it? I believed I understood the reasons for him keeping silent about who he was.

'How long would you have stayed anywhere near me had you known my real name?'

The answer was, *I would not*. Had I known who the monster in the woods was from the beginning, I would not have come back. Ever.

The right thing would have been for him to tell me the truth right away and let me go.

But then the past few months would have never happened.

Longing swelled tight around my heart at the memories of those months, the happiest time of my life. I was not ready to give those memories up, even if they were a lie.

Were they?

'My feelings for you are real.'

I closed my eyes and for the first time since I left him, I allowed myself to remember everything. The tenderness, even reverence, in his touch when he made love to me, as if he tried to exorcise the dark memories of our past from my mind by replacing them with loving caresses. The warmth and yearning I always found in his eyes for me. The passion in his words. I fell in love with him, feeling the sincerity of it all.

He didn't tell me his name, but did he try to pretend to be someone else?

He didn't embellish the kind of person he was when he spoke of his past. Could he have truly changed? I could not reconcile the arrogant teenager I knew years ago with the loving, caring, passionate man who told me he loved me. Could anyone pretend this well to fake it all?

The person in the woods might not be my Monster the way I thought of him, but he also couldn't be the Hunter Reed I remembered. How could the pain and remorse I felt in him be faked?

I begged Cecilia to give him a chance to say sorry. The least I could do was to give him the same chance myself.

Besides, regardless of how I felt about him, I couldn't turn off my worrying about him. There was no way for him to get help if he needed it. He was alone, a prisoner of the estate, and I was the only one in the world who knew about his existence. No matter what, I felt responsible. And if something happened to him while I was away, I'd never forgive myself.

Here, at the cemetery, the permanence of death felt more acute. And all the misunderstandings of the living—including the ones between myself and the man in the woods—seemed fleeting and insignificant in the face of the final infinity we all ultimately faced.

Without even knowing it, my mother helped me in my decision.

'I hope you have no regrets with the life you've lived.'

If I didn't at least try to find my way back to the man I'd fallen in love with, I knew it would become the biggest regret in my life.

# Chapter 43

## Sophie

My heart beat frantically in my chest as I drove up to the house. I'd told myself I needed to check on him, to make sure he was doing well being here on his own, but I wasn't sure what to expect. Neither was I clear what exactly it was that I hoped for, coming back here.

My memories kept alternating between the loving, caring Monster I lived with for months and the cold-blooded monster who hurt me years ago.

Thinking back, I'd caught the glimpses of the angry beast inside him many times. I'd witnessed the battle that raged in him, bubbling up to the surface every now and then. I knew of the struggle he led.

I wasn't sure whether there was any hope for us to put our past behind us or if there even still could be an *us*.

What I did know was that I had run from him in hurt and disappointment. Too much passion and too many emotions were coursing between us when I confronted him—he never got a chance to explain or apologize.

If the pain I'd glimpsed in him was real, he had his own demons to exorcise, and I was coming back ready to listen this time.

I KNEW SOMETHING WAS wrong the moment I entered the house through the garage.

It was cold inside. Freezing cold. I knew that the power was still on—the garage opener worked for me without a problem. Then I noticed that the front entrance door had been left wide open. The biting wind blew in, leaving white drifts of snow all through the main floor.

A large armchair had been thrown across the room and was now lying on its side, the new upholstery slashed with the foam underneath sticking through. One of the heavy barstools was also upturned.

Something happened here. Something bad enough to drive Monster away from the house? The few paw prints in the snow on the floor were all too small to be his and weren't that fresh.

I'd heard people at the airport talk about the weather—it hadn't snowed here for at least a week. He hadn't been inside since then. Where was he?

Was he okay?

My heart dropped and icy fingers of fear gripped my throat.

I did a quick search through the house, calling his name—Monster's name—then ran back in the garage.

A list of possible reasons for his absence ran through my brain. None of them were comforting.

Did the cougar attack him again? Had a pack of wolves come into his territory while I was gone, looking for a meal? A bear?

Or, worst of all—people?

It was April. The busy part of the hunting season had long ended. The next one wouldn't start until August. So, if people found out about Monster's existence, they most likely wouldn't be hunters trespassing in their pursuit of prey, but someone with possibly more sinister motives.

Worry had sent my mind into a tailspin, coming up with horrible scenarios. And I stopped in my tracks for a moment, my fist pressed to my chest, counting my breaths. With no real evidence of anything terrible happening to him, I needed to think more rationally.

I'll search for him outside.

I hesitated at the door.

The cougar.

The thought prompted me to grab an axe. Then my gaze fell on the locked rifle cabinet standing next to the tool bench.

Quickly, I found the key from the drawer in the tool chest—where I remembered Monster put it when he showed me how to shoot the rifle a few times—and a cardboard box of ammunition.

With the loaded gun in my hands, I ran outside.

I couldn't distinguish the paw prints in the packed snow around the porch and didn't know for sure if any of them were his.

Taking his most frequently travelled route, I walked through the passage between the rose bushes east of the house then along the path to the river.

Holding the rifle in front of me, I searched the surrounding forest for his shape, hoping I'd see him running through the woods to me at any moment.

The powerful blow to my shoulder from behind was so sudden it shocked a gasp from me and threw me to the ground, knocking the rifle out of my hands.

My face pressed into the packed snow, I couldn't see, breathe or scream. The impact with the frozen path knocked the air out of my lungs.

A heavy weight settled on my back and pressure pinned my neck through my thick scarf. Something sharp tore through my jacket, with a loud ripping noise.

Then a wild, thunderous roar shook through the woods.

The crushing weight on top of me was gone the very next moment. Coughing and spitting dirt out of my mouth, I sat up and blindly patted the ground in search of my rifle.

Blinking the snow out of my eyes, I twisted around, taking stock of the situation.

Two large shapes tangled into a mass of russet and orange fur, fighting each other. Monster and cougar. They rolled on the ground between the trees just a few feet away from me, leaving a bright red trail of blood behind them.

I spotted my rifle about ten feet away in the other direction, jumped to my feet, and dashed for it.

Pointing the gun at the beasts in front of me, I realized it was impossible to shoot one without risk of hitting the other—their bodies were so tightly intertwined.

Monster rolled on the ground, his claws deep in the cougar's shoulder. Its fangs dug into Monster's neck, sinking deeper and deeper in search of the vital artery with every motion. The feline's hind paws shredded the fur, skin and muscle on Monster's side, almost in the same place where the scars of its last attack had just healed a few months earlier.

It seemed the cougar got lucky this time by getting a better hold of Monster's neck. The thick mane filled its mouth, preventing the cougar from tearing Monster's artery out at once, but it was Monster's blood painting the snow red around them.

The sight of so much blood filled me with fear for his life. A new kind of fear. Not the one that used to paralyze me with terror, but the one that ignited me with anger instead, spurring me into action.

"Get off him!" I yelled on the top of my lungs—wild with rage—and stormed through the snow over to the beasts locked in a deadly embrace.

Monster sank to his side with the cougar on his shoulder, its teeth locked in his neck. His clawed feet plowed deep trenches through the snow, ice, and frozen dirt, as his strength slowly flowed in crimson streams out of him through the long slashes on his side and back.

Still concerned about firing the rifle when the two were so close together, I grabbed the heavy gun by the barrel with both hands instead and swung it, aiming for the cougar's head.

With a thud, the wooden stock of the rifle slammed into its skull. Its body went limp, and Monster shoved it off him.

Not taking any chances, I flipped the rifle in my hands and fired a single shot in the cougar's head. Point-blank.

"I told you, get off!" I yelled at the dead body, vibrating with adrenaline, before flinging the rifle aside.

Hands shaking, I sank to my knees at Monster's side. The nauseating smell of blood hit my nostrils. I swallowed hard, closing my eyes for a second to regain my composure.

"You're here."

My eyes flew open at his voice.

"I am." I leaned over him.

"Did he hurt you?" His gaze searched my face.

I evaded it, forcing myself to focus on his wounds.

"No. I'm fine. You got here in time." I needed to confirm where all this blood was coming from. "Now, be quiet, I need to assess your injuries."

Parting his mane with my fingers, I inspected his neck carefully. The puncture wounds there were small but deep. Blood filled them, but it didn't gush out in a spray.

"He didn't get any major arteries," I muttered under my breath, silently sending thanks to every deity out there.

Still, Monster's shoulder, his side, and his back—everything that came in contact with the cougar's sharp teeth and claws—were one big bloody mess of mangled fur, muscle, and skin. He was losing a distressing amount of blood, and I had to stop it as soon as possible.

"I'll need to clean these and stitch what I can," I mumbled to myself, going through the details in my head while trying to recall whatever I could from my medical studies. "First, we need to get you back to the house."

Seemingly unconcerned about his condition, he lifted his hand to my face. His eyes on me, he gently traced a line from my temple to the edge of my jaw then stroked my hair carefully.

His touch was so light—barely there—as if he was afraid I'd disappear on contact.

"You're back." Disbelief coloured his voice.

"I am." I heaved a sigh then grabbed his hand with both of mine and buried my face in it.

The coppery smell of blood tainted his usual scent, and I felt my throat tighten.

"I'll take care of you," I promised.

# Chapter 44

## Sophie

The loss of blood was too much for him—he fainted as soon as he sat up. Quickly, I ran back to the house and drove the ATV up the path to the spot where he lay.

"Come on." I patted his cheek gently. "Please, help me get you back home."

He stirred, and I threw his arm over my shoulders to support him on his good side.

"Slowly this time." My legs shaking with strain, I helped him to his feet and took a large part of his weight on me as we made the few steps to the ATV.

Back at the house, I led him to the couch where he collapsed with a low moan. Then I kicked the snow away from the front door to close it. With the heat on, the temperature inside would rise soon enough.

I filled a large, metal bowl with warm water then ran to the main bathroom and fetched my oversized first-aid kit, grateful that I had stocked it with additional items bought through Jo.

Always paranoid about Monster's lack of access to proper medical care, I had made sure to have as many supplies and equipment on hand as possible for a worst case scenario.

Monster lay on his side now as I stood over him with the first-aid kit in my hands, staring at his gruesome wounds.

Where does one even begin to treat something like this?

I sat the kit on the floor next to the bowl with water and carefully unbuttoned his jeans. The waistband was slashed in several places, and I needed a better access to those cuts on his skin. Gently, I rolled the top of his jeans down as far as I could without disturbing him too much, still he groaned. The adrenaline must have been wearing off.

"How many pills have you taken today already?"

He lifted his hand with four fingers up.

I gave him a large glass of water with a couple of more painkillers then set to work.

Fighting the sickening feeling of worry swimming in my stomach, I washed the blood off his wounds then trimmed and shaved the fur around them the best I could.

The bleeding had slowed, but the cuts were deep, the skin jagged around the edges on some and hanging in loose ribbons in places.

He definitely needed stitches.

I got the surgical needle and thread ready and inhaled deeply.

"I'll have to sew you up." I tried to keep my voice light, pretending I was encouraging him, not both of us, but he knew me too well.

"You can do it, Sophie," he rasped, managing a smile. "Haven't you just bashed in the head of my arch-nemesis?"

Holding the needle at his skin, I paused, trying to calm my racing heart and still my shaking hands.

"I should give you something to bite into," I croaked.

"To shut me up?"

How could he still be joking?

"No, so that you don't bite your tongue or break your teeth." I glanced up at him in the silent question.

"Nope. Chances are I'd break anything you give me. Go ahead."

Still, I hesitated. His wounds were gruesome and—I was afraid—well above my level of expertise as a medical school dropout. I was sick with worry that I'd cause more harm than good.

But he has no one else here to help him!

"Remember how angry you were with me?" Monster misunderstood the reasons for my hesitation.

"Still am," I bit out.

"Hold on to that thought. It should help you stab me with the needle."

I shook my head with a sigh as more worries rushed my mind. What else would he need? Was there a chance the cougar had rabies? How about other possible diseases?

"When was your last tetanus shot?"

"Do you think I remember?"

What if there was an infection? He'd need antibiotics.

I dropped the hand holding the needle in my lap.

"I'll need to get you professional help," I resigned. "Someone who is more qualified to deal with this."

"Like a vet?" He gave me a crooked smile, but I caught him flinching in pain on an inhale.

"Don't try to be funny," I chided. "You need your energy for other things."

"I always have the energy for *other things*," he rasped, cupping my knee.

I twitched from the unexpected gesture.

"You're incorrigible," I whispered, the warmth of his palm through the fabric of my jeans made my voice breathy. When he touched me like this, he was my Monster once again, no one else. And his touch held power over me.

"Fuck, I missed you," he groaned. "So much it hurts."

I removed his hand gently.

"You've been mauled by a two-hundred-and-fifty-pound cougar. That's what hurts."

"Wrong. He was barely two twenty." His tone was flat.

I rolled my shoulder, remembering the heavy weight pinning me to the icy forest floor. I still couldn't believe I shot and killed an animal, even if in self-defence. The most incredible part was—I didn't regret it. The cougar threatened Monster's life. It had to die.

"I'll have to drive to town quickly." I started bandaging his wounds.

I could make it to Rocky River in time to Jo's shift end. Provided no emergency required her attention at the nursing station after hours, I could bring her here tonight. "I'll cover all of it here for now, but you'll need a lot more than I can do—"

"Sophie." He halted my hand in the air, his expression pensive. "What were you doing walking in the woods alone?"

Obviously, it wasn't possible infection and rabies shots that occupied his mind right now.

"I had a gun," I replied.

"Where were you going with that gun, princess?"

His nickname for me, spoken softly like that, caressed my ear.

"To rescue you," I confessed with a sigh then rushed to explain. "The house was cold and empty, the door open, snow on the floor . . . I had no idea where you were."

"In the river. Swimming. It didn't take me that long to get here after I'd sensed you."

"It felt like forever. I was worried something had happened. The house seemed deserted, and the front door looked like it had been left open for a while—"

"Since you left," he confirmed. "You left it open. Somehow in my madness after you were gone, I believed that if I closed it, it would mean you'd never come back. And I couldn't stay at the house, either. There is so much of you in here. I could feel you in everything around me, but I couldn't touch you. It was pure torture."

His hand found mine and squeezed it as if needing the affirmation that I was physically here.

"I followed you all the way to the end of the fence." He said softly. "It was like you had tied a rope around my neck, and I started to suffocate the further away you drove. And then . . ." He frowned. "Then it was just blind fury."

He spoke with visible difficulty, breathing around the physical pain that must be tearing at his side with every inhale. Yet I didn't stop him. It seemed the pain that urged him to speak was deeper and had been torturing him much longer.

"You see, my appearance has only changed once, but inside the man and the beast are always at war. When you left, I had no idea what to do with myself. The beast took over, and I let him. Once again I was mad at the world. I was angry at you, too—for waking the man in me, for letting me feel human pain again, for making me love you and then leaving me, knowing I couldn't follow you. I couldn't go and bring you back. I wanted to crush everything inside the house, annihilate whatever you'd touched to exorcise your presence from here. But you weren't in the house or in those things. You're so deep inside me—I'd have to rip my own heart out to get rid of you. The hurt of having lost you burned like hot iron through me, no matter what I did. You have become my entire world, my reason for living. I had no idea how to go on without you."

He shifted, adjusting his injured shoulder, and slowly drew in a breath through his clenched teeth.

"The real agony came from knowing that the only person responsible for all of this was me. I had no one but myself to blame for your leaving. You didn't owe anything to Hunter Reed, the monster and the liar. But you've done something to me. You made me want to be the best man I could be. And I didn't want to let go of that man, even after you left. No matter how I look on the outside, Sophie, I don't want to go back to being a monster *inside*.

"I knew it was wrong to continue hiding from you, but I had no idea how to come clean without losing you. Ever. I convinced myself that as long as you were happy, everything was justified. Still, I should've found a way to tell you who I am. I'm sorry I didn't."

"Thank you, Mon—" I started and cut myself short. "Hunter?" I winced with a nervous smile. "I'm not sure what to call you now."

"My name is Hunter," he said in the tone of a formal introduction. "But the woman I love used to call me Monster." A lighter note slipped into his tone. "When said by her, it sounded like an endearing nickname."

I smiled in response but couldn't bring myself to address him either way—none of the names rang true at the moment.

"Both are me, Sophie," he urged.

I patted his hand and said gently, without addressing him in any way at all, "Thank you for apologizing. I'm sorry, too. For running away without giving us a chance to talk." I covered his legs with a blanket and moved the side table closer to the couch, intending to leave some food and water for him. "I promise we'll talk more as soon as you get better. I'll have to go now to make it back today," I said and warned, to make it clear, "I'll need to bring Jo to help you. Can I tell her about you? I'll ask her to keep your secret. And I trust she will."

"Sure, I don't care," he brushed it off, seemingly unconcerned. His worries must have lain elsewhere as he took my hand.

"Just answer one question before you go. Why did you come back, Sophie?"

My chest heaved as I met his eyes and told him the truth, "Because I can tell myself I hate you, but I can't make myself stop thinking of you or caring about you. No matter what I do."

# Chapter 45

## Sophie

"What, on Earth, is this?"

Jo's eyes opened wide, big and round, like two saucers of baby-blue.

I had told her that a man had been attacked by a cougar near the house in the woods. Jo had access to the drugs needed in case of a wild animal attack. As a nurse working in a remote community, she also had the authority to prescribe antibiotics in a doctor's absence.

She followed me in her car because I didn't want to leave Monster alone again to drive her back to town tomorrow.

"I told you, he is a man with a condition." I'd tried to warn her about Monster's appearance. However, I knew nothing I said would have prepared her for what she saw in front of her now.

"It's not a man," she whispered, shaking her head quickly and not moving from her spot about ten feet away from the couch where Monster appeared to be asleep.

"Jo, he's very sick. He needs stitches, shots, antibiotics. God knows what else." I got down on my knees at his side and touched his hand. He didn't open his eyes, and a new burst of worry shot through me. His breathing was heavy and his hand felt hot to the touch. I left him hours ago. Infection might have been setting in already. "He needs help, Jo. Quickly."

Hesitantly, she took a couple of steps towards the couch.

"Maybe, you should call a vet? There are different treatments for people and animals, you know. Are you sure he's not dangerous?"

"Jo!" I glared over my shoulder at her. "He is not an animal."

"Do you see him, Sophie? He doesn't look human. His biology—"

"His biology is very compatible with human. Trust me," I bit out, getting rather offended for Monster at this point, even as I understood that seeing him for the first time would be a shock for anyone.

"And how can you be so sure about that?" Jo tilted her head to the side.

"I just am," I asserted, not ready to divulge any details of just how intimately I had become familiar with Monster's biology. "Human medicine seems to work on him. Antibiotics should too. Let's just increase the dosage to account for his above average size."

Not that we had a choice here.

She sighed.

"Fine. For you. I'll do what I can. No guarantees, though," she warned, opening her medicine case. "This is the first time in my life I'm treating someone like this."

I nodded with relief, noting that at least she referred to him as "someone", not "something" this time.

Jo immediately started an I.V. for Monster then cleaned and expertly stitched the gaping wounds. I assisted her as best I could.

He opened his eyes once during the process and even managed a greeting for Jo—which almost sent her to the floor on her butt. He seemed lethargic when he spoke or attempted to move, and I hoped it was for the best when his eyelids dropped and he appeared to doze off again.

"It must've hurt like a bitch, without the meds," Jo noted as we were dressing Monster's wounds with fresh bandages.

"I gave him some over-the-counter pain medication before I left. Not much, though, as he already took some this morning. He takes it for chronic headaches. The horns." I waved my hand over my head. "They bother him."

When we were done, I made us some tea.

"How long have you known him?" Jo asked.

"Since last fall." I sat on a bar stool at the island next to her. "He attacked me then helped me through the night when the others left."

"He attacked you?" Jo's eyes flew wide. "So, *he* was your infamous bear?"

I nodded, not taking my eyes off the tea in my cup.

"Why didn't you tell anyone then?"

"*Why*? Jason was out for blood to cover up his own cowardice. All he needed was confirmation about a beast in the woods to have people out with pitchforks, starting a hunt. Besides, I promised *him*," I tipped my head towards the living room, "not to tell anyone."

"This . . . um . . . *man* attacked you. Sophie, I treated the scratches on your legs and back." She shot a cautious glance towards the couch where Monster was still passed out.

"He did," I replied slowly, afraid to sound like a woman justifying abuse, even as I knew that was not our case. "He was hardly a human at that point, more like a feral animal. He stopped when I said no, though. And he helped me to survive that night."

"*What* is he, Sophie?"

"He is a man." I shrugged. "A man who happens to look like a beast."

"Okay." Jo stared inside her cup for a few seconds too then met my eyes again. "This is a personal question, Sophie, but I need to ask. How . . . closely are you involved with this *man*? I mean, I can see how you look at him, how you touch him. You worry about him."

"I do. I care about him." Now that I had almost lost him, I realized I had no intention of letting him out of my sight, ever again. "And I was . . . um, involved." I inhaled before confessing. "All the way."

Jo just gaped at me wide-eyed for a moment.

"Like . . . really?" She turned towards the living room, staring at one of the long horns spiraling over the back of the couch. "Sophie, I'm sorry. But, this is just crazy. How is it even possible?" She leaned a little closer to me and lowered her voice. "And *how* was it?"

How?

I thought back to our nights together when Monster loved me and I believed that I loved him too—when his hands touched me, healing me from the inside. I smiled with confidence.

"How? Fanfuckingtastic, Jo."

She giggled unexpectedly.

"Well, to each their own. Whatever makes you happy. I mean *whoever* that is. Are you happy, Sophie?"

I couldn't talk about the present yet, but the past . . .

"He did make me happy. Yes. Very much."

She shook her head, but a wide smile quickly chased the expression of disbelief off her face.

"Well, then I'm happy for you, too." She jumped off her barstool and gave me a big hug.

"So, are you going to just keep hiding him here forever?" she asked more seriously, taking her seat again.

"He has no choice but to stay here." I sighed. "And I'm afraid it's not safe to tell the rest of the world about him. I can't predict everything bad that could happen to him if people knew. Unwanted attention from the media and tourists would be bad enough. But what if there were a scientific interest from someone who could hurt him? Or some idiots decided to hunt him?"

"Well, if he is a person, he has rights like anyone else."

"That might require some time and effort to prove to the world."

Jo was right, though, Monster had a name and an identity. He had the right to live and a right to privacy, just like anyone else. And he should be able to live his life openly, like everyone else.

Sooner or later, coming out of the woods—figuratively speaking—might become necessary for him. His official identity documents must have expired by now or would be expiring soon. Without them it was as if he didn't exist, which could even mean potentially risking losing ownership of the house in the future. And that would be a real disaster in his situation.

New worries clouded my mind.

First of all, he needs to get better.

I hopped off the stool and walked to the couch. His breathing was heavy, but his expression remained peacefully relaxed.

"Thank God for you and your drugs, Jo," I whispered as she came behind me and watched him over my shoulder.

"Don't worry," she replied softly. "He'll be okay now. No vital organ damage. The muscle tissue and skin will heal in time. But I have to warn you—the scars will be extensive. Honestly, he would need a plastic surgeon if you want to minimize the scarring. Well," she continued, as if thinking out loud. "The fur will grow between the scars, hopefully long enough to hide them because the scar tissue won't allow for new fur growth." Her brow wrinkled in visible concentration. "I have no idea what is better, aesthetically, in this case. Which would you prefer? More fur or less fur?"

She looked at me, completely serious.

For some reason Jo's genuine concern on this matter seemed way too funny to me, and I burst out laughing, covering my mouth to avoid waking up Monster.

It must be the stress of the past several days and the finally receding adrenaline that made me so lightheaded, but it felt good to laugh.

"No, really." Jo smiled back at me. "Is there an optimal amount of fur that makes him sexy for you?"

"It's not the fur, Jo." I grinned wide. "It's what underneath it that counts."

"I bet it is!" She giggled.

"Honestly." I elbowed her side. "It's what he does to show how he feels about me that makes him sexy to me."

# Chapter 46

## Sophie

Jo left the following morning, promising to come check on Monster again.

I was relieved to hear that she had decided to extend her contract in Rocky River for another year after all. And I was delighted when she told me why she changed her mind. A young and, according to Jo, impossibly hot pilot just started a job at the airport. He flew Jo in after her last visit home, and they'd even been on a date already.

"Sophie, trust me, this is the guy I'm going to marry one day. I never believed in love at first sight, but this is it," she told me with confidence, making me smile.

I hugged her as tight as I could when we parted.

After she left, I set a pot of broth on the stove to warm it up for Monster then went back to the living room to check on him.

He appeared to be asleep. Jo had removed his I.V. but left a bunch of pills for him to take for the next little while.

I was no longer the only person in his life. Now, Jo knew of him too. Maybe, instead of despairing over his isolation, we could see about bringing more people into his life? Just because he couldn't leave here didn't mean he couldn't have friends who'd visit him.

My mom had been asking when she could come over. Maybe instead of coming up with more excuses to keep her away from Monster, I should arrange for them to meet? With his permission of course. Would he want to do it?

As long as he is well and healthy.

I knelt by the couch and touched his forehead, feeling for signs of fever. It was hard to tell through the layer of fur if his temperature was elevated, and I touched his nose instead.

He snickered and opened his eyes.

"Is it cold and wet, like a good dog's nose should be? Or is it a cat's nose that's supposed to be that way?"

His voice sounded normal, I noted with relief, just a little raspy from sleep.

"Both. Healthy pets usually have wet, cold noses," I replied, a little concerned myself—his nose was dry and rather warm.

"So what kind of a pet does my nose make me?"

"You? A pet?" Brought out of my worries by his words, I studied his face.

His eyes twinkled with humour—he was teasing me again.

"You'd make a horrible pet." I shook my head, hiding a smile. "I doubt you'd ever make it through an obedience school with your temper." I patted his arm, getting up. "I'll need to get a thermometer to check your fever."

"I'm fine," he growled as I walked to the hallway on my way to the bathroom.

"Just in case," I said in a pacifying tone, returning with a thermometer.

Propped on his arm, he heaved himself up into a sitting position.

"Careful," I warned, rushing to him. "You shouldn't be moving yet or you risk damaging Jo's handiwork."

I stuffed a few pillows under his back, and he leaned on them a little sideways, avoiding putting pressure on his freshly bandaged injuries.

"How are you feeling?" I leaned over him, contemplating if it would make any sense to put the thermometer under his arm—the layer of fur would undoubtedly skew the reading.

"I'm fine," he repeated, then solved my dilemma by grabbing the thermometer out of my hand and sticking it into his mouth.

"That works too, I guess," I muttered and went to the kitchen for a bowl of broth for him.

The thermometer beeped when I returned, and he gave it back to me without looking.

"It's not bad." I sat the bowl on the side table and lowered myself on the couch next to him. "Your temperature is a little elevated, but it doesn't look like you have an infection. Let's hope it'll stay away."

"Thank you."

"For what?"

"For everything. For looking after me. For getting Jo. For coming back." His brow furrowed for a moment. "Where have you been? Where did you go when you left? What did you do?"

"I went to France. Henri passed away."

"I'm sorry, Sophie." His hand covered mine.

"Thank you. I'm glad I went. I got the chance to say goodbye. We both did." I squeezed his fingers gently. "You were right, it's better to forgive. Hurt and regret would be a heavy load to carry for the rest of my life."

"Sophie." His thumb stroked my hand. "I'm not saying I deserve your forgiveness." He shifted on the couch, wincing from the pain it caused him. "But I'll ask for it anyway. That night in Calgary has been the greatest regret of my life. I'm not sure an apology can ever make it right. But I am sorry. I'm sorry I attacked you. I'm sorry I ruined your life. I'm sorry I hurt you again the first day I saw you here. God, Sophie," he groaned and pressed my hand to his forehead, "I would kill and die for you, yet I keep hurting you over and over again."

"Why did you do it?" I asked quietly. "Why did you attack me?"

"When?" he exhaled with a sad smile "Which time?"

"Well, the last time you were more of an animal than yourself, still you stopped when I asked you. Why did you attack me *then*, eight years ago?"

With a deep inhale, he turned his face to mine.

"Sophie. You happened to cross my path at the worst of times. I was stupid, drunk, and angry."

"Why? Why were you angry?" I asked and urged when he hesitated, "Tell me. Trust me, it'll be easier once it's out."

"I had a fight." He dropped my hand and broke our eye contact, staring somewhere in the distance now. "My father, he … Well, I have his temper. I hate it and I try to fight it, but he didn't even try. He attacked me instead. Ever since I can remember, all of his *lessons* were taught with his fists. Even when I did what felt like the right thing to do, I often got punished for it because my father's rules vastly differed from common morals and ethics."

A steel band of sorrow for him tightened painfully around my heart. But I had come back to him ready to listen. So, I clasped my hands in my lap and stilled my breath, hanging on his every word.

"That day, I thought for once I could fight him back, but he brought a baseball bat to the fist fight. Defeated, hurt, and pissed off, I tried to drown myself in whiskey, which only made it worse. I was angry at my father, at myself for being so weak I couldn't fight back. I was mad at the world and everyone in it. That's when you happened to be there …"

He leaned in, his eyes on me again. Dark shadows of pain clouded his expression, surfacing from wherever he had been carrying it inside him all this time.

"Innocent, oblivious of all that shit in my life, completely blameless, you ended up being hurt the most. I'm so sorry, Sophie. Nothing that happened that night was fair. Especially to you."

"Was it revenge?" I wanted to understand.

"Revenge." He inclined his head. "Irrational one. But most of all—power. My father made me feel small and weak. Attacking someone, defeating them, was supposed to make me feel stronger. It didn't. It made me feel like shit when I realized I turned into my own father, hurting people to get high on power over them. I let you go—"

"You did?"

I never paused to think about the reasons why I was suddenly able to get away that night. Too consumed by the panic, I simply ran the moment I could.

"I let you go then waited for you to report me and for the police to come for me to dish out a well-deserved punishment."

"I didn't want to report it."

"I know it now. Anyway, the police would've been way too easy. Instead, my punishment was supposed to take years and come from within, in the most torturous ways. I had to feel it every moment of my life until I fully comprehended the gravity of every wrong I've ever done. Then the pain of regret was supposed to end me."

I realized I had been sliding my hand up and down his forearm for some time, in a comforting gesture.

"Never would I have dreamed to find salvation in the one I had hurt the most. Sophie, you were like a ray of sunshine and a breath of fresh air for me in this dungeon."

His eyes on mine, he reached for my face, but didn't touch it. Instead, he pulled back at the last moment and balled his hand into a fist.

"You know," I said, wanting to share this, to make him feel better and because it was the truth. "You might be the one who caused the darkness, but you have been helping me fight it, too."

"Will you ever forgive me?"

"I already did. It's easier to forgive than to carry the weight, remember?" I smiled and leaned closer to him, unable to stay away.

He wound his arm around my waist, drawing me into him.

"Come here, where you belong." He leaned back on the pillows taking me with him.

"There is not enough space here." I giggled, burrowing myself into his chest.

"I'll make space. I need you close." He lay on his uninjured side, holding me firmly with one arm. My legs tangled with his. I inhaled a lungful of his familiar scent and closed my eyes, feeling completely at peace.

It was nice to be home again.

# Chapter 47

## Sophie

Even without the infection, it still took Monster weeks to recover. Jo came to visit him regularly during this time.

The first few nights, afraid to be too far away in case he needed me, I slept on blankets and pillows on the floor in the living room. But by the end of the first week, Monster felt well enough to walk up the stairs to bed with me.

He insisted we sleep in the same bed. However, I made sure to keep cuddling to a minimum, afraid his wounds might re-open. I even got us separate covers to minimize the contact between us through the night.

It felt strange and at times simply torturous to lie in the same bed with him, actively enforcing a limit on touching, when what I really wanted was to hug him to pieces. I knew that popping his stitches would delay the healing and demanded we reduce any intimacy to holding hands for now.

As his wounds healed, Monster started slowly regaining his strength. Jo instructed him to avoid any heavy work around the property for a while, but he was allowed to take short walks outside.

We sat on the back porch one sunny day in May. The snow had mostly melted by now. But the true signs of spring were in the bright sunlight flooding the air. Monster sat in a deep Adirondack chair, and I perched on the wide armrest at his side, his arm around my waist for support.

"Your horns look kinda dull, not as shiny as they used to be," I noted lightly, gliding my hand up to the very tip of the spiral closer to me.

"Must be because I haven't speared a deer for a while," he smirked. "They've dulled from not being used."

"Well, maybe we'll find a little less violent way to give them some shine."

"Like what? Horn polish?" He chuckled, making me smile.

"Is there such a thing?"

"Apparently one can find anything and anyone if they look hard enough nowadays," he said slowly. "You never told me how you found Cecilia, by the way."

Right. I hadn't mentioned her since I came back, avoiding the same feeling of disappointment I felt after my conversation with her in New Orleans.

"I found her through the internet and went to see her. She was the one who told me your name. And I'm sorry I broke your desk," I added somberly.

His forehead furrowed into a deep line.

"You shouldn't have done it, Sophie. Fuck the desk. I mean you shouldn't have met with her. I'm not denying she had reasons to be mad at me, but the woman is dangerous. God. It makes me wild just thinking about all the things she could've done to you." He slid me along the armrest, bringing me a little closer to him.

"I don't believe Cecilia is evil," I replied. "And it was not about me anyway. She said she couldn't turn you back to a human again."

His chest heaved with a sigh, but he said nothing.

"She admitted she'd laid a curse on you," I continued. "One that turns a man into a beast until a woman falls in love with him. Cecilia said it cannot be reversed, but it would be broken once the condition of falling in love is met." I went quiet.

The love I felt for him was still there. The trust I used to have had been slowly returning too. However, now every one of my emotions had to encompass more of him.

There was not just our cozy present, there was also our troubled past. I forgave him wholly in my mind and my soul. But my heart seemed to still be working on reconciling the past and the present in order for us to have a future.

"Do you think you could ever love me again?" His voice was pensive.

I threaded my fingers through the strands of his mane.

"I believe I never stopped."

"Is it true?" He swept me off the armrest and into his lap, making me gasp in surprise. "Do you still love me, Sophie?"

"I couldn't ever stop," I said with a smile. "Trust me, I tried."

A great sigh left his wide chest, and he crushed me to him.

"But it doesn't matter, darling," I said quietly. "Don't you see? It didn't work. The curse is not broken. And you're not free."

"I don't care, Sophie," he whispered in my neck. "I can deal with all of it as long as I know you love me."

"I do." I raked my fingers through his mane. "I love you."

"And you will stay with me?"

"I will. I'll stay and take care of you." This was where I belonged. Right here with him. There was no place for me to go, nowhere I'd rather be.

"Take care? But I need more, princess."

"You do?"

"Mhm." He lifted his head to see my face. "I want a lover and a partner. I want it all." His expression was serious when he tightened his arms around me. "I want a wife."

I stared at him, startled. "That wasn't a question."

"Because I'm not asking." He held my gaze. "I want you to be my wife. I want to wake up next to you every morning. I want to spend the rest of my life loving you and striving to be the man worthy of your love."

For better or for worse, I already knew my life was tied with his to the end.

"Will you marry me, Sophie?" His voice softened.

Being his wife would be in the name only—we could never make it legal in front of an official, without disclosing his secret. Legal or not, though, the commitment between us would have to be real.

"That *was* a question," he prompted impatiently. "And I need an answer."

Essentially, I'll be marrying Hunter Reed. I'll be Mrs. Reed . . .

Anxiety hampered my happiness.

"How much time do I have to give you the answer?"

"I'd love to say take as much time as you need, but I can't wait too long. Especially if it's a *no*."

"It's not a *no*," I shook my head. "It's a very strong *maybe*. More like a delayed *yes*."

A relieved smile spread on his face, erasing the stern expression.

"Well, I guess I could *try* to wait a little then."

# Chapter 48

## Sophie

Two nights later I woke up feeling hot. Monster seemed to have kicked his covers off then rolled to my side of the bed, his leg draped over my hips, his arm pressing me to his chest. His injuries were healing well. The pain didn't stop him from rolling all over the bed any more.

Enjoying his scent, I nuzzled the fur on his chest discreetly, so as not to wake him up, then wiggled my way out from under his big, furry body. I needed to get some cold water. Sleeping with him was like having a wooly mammoth in bed—I was hot and thirsty.

I tiptoed out of the bedroom and down the stairs then padded to the fridge in the kitchen.

The cool water felt wonderful to my parched throat. I put the half empty water bottle back in the fridge and stilled, my hand on the door.

No sound alerted me. It was all quiet in the darkness of the night. Still I couldn't help the feeling of being watched by a pair of hungry eyes from the shadows.

I closed the fridge, and stole into the living room, stepping softly with my socked feet.

Faint silver moonlight filtered into the room through the many glass doors to the back patio. Still, I couldn't see anyone, but the feeling of someone stalking me in the semi-darkness intensified.

The fine hairs on my arms rose, my skin prickled with excitement when I heard a low sound, something like a deep purr, from the shadows by the far wall. The familiar rumble in it sent flutters of anticipation inside my stomach.

"So, I'm hunted by a beast at night," I whispered, facing the sound, while slowly creeping towards the stairs, sideways. "Well, catch me if you can!" I challenged, sprinting for the stairs.

The purring behind me grew into a loud growl, vibrating through the open space of the house.

I hooked my arm around the nearest support post, intending to swing around it on my way to escape, but stopped in my tracks at that growl.

The deep, velvety undertones of its vibration reverberated through my body, reaching my very core. With my knees suddenly growing weak, I hugged the log post with both arms and pressed my forehead to the cool surface of the polished wood.

The growling rumble trapped me like a fly in a net.

In France, I missed Monster's arms around me, his mere presence in my life. I missed him as a person. Right now, I fiercely wanted him as a man.

My breath grew heavy, as the desire for him assaulted all my senses at once, and with a soft whimper I pressed my aching body into the support post in my arms.

Suddenly, he was behind me, his large form flush with mine.

"Fuck, Sophie," he groaned, the soft vibrating ribbon still woven through his voice. "You know I can smell when you're turned on. The scent drives me wild."

I could only moan in reply as the thick, heavy need for him kept spreading through my body in waves. I arched my back, pressing my ass into his crotch. He cursed under his breath and lifted me up, sliding me along the smooth wood of the pillar. Moving his hands up along my sides, he hiked up my nightshirt to my waist and rocked his hips into me, pinning me to the post.

Nuzzling my neck, he cupped my breast under my shirt. His thumb brushed my nipple, sending another electrifying charge through my core. I arched my back like a bow when he slid the other hand between me and the post and found me slick and hot with need.

"How did you get so wet so fast, princess?" His whisper hit the side of my face. "Have you been missing me too, my sweet?"

"Yes," I panted. "I missed this. I want you."

He slipped his finger inside me, massaging me in circles, stretching, getting me ready for him and driving me mad with lust.

With a moan, I writhed against his hand, aching for more.

"God knows, I missed you too, Sophie," he rasped.

Stepping back from the post, he slid his finger out of me then angled my hips a little and entered me in one powerful thrust, driving me up the wooden post.

I closed my eyes for a moment, savoring the feeling of being filled by him again, the feeling of being complete.

"I love you," he groaned above my ear. "So much, my princess."

A wave of pure happiness came over me at his words. Yet I could only moan in response.

Impaled and pinned to the timber post by him, I squirmed impatiently, and he sucked air in through his teeth with another groan. His arms shook with strain, as he struggled for control before letting it all go.

With deep growls, he took me in frantic thrusts. His hand cupped me between my legs to protect me from being hurt by the hard surface of the post as he pounded into me.

The blissful ache of pressure built inside me as I rode the tsunami of his desperate passion, wave after wave, until he made me shudder against his hand. My inner muscles rippled in sweet tremors around him.

With a loud roar to the high ceiling of the house, he followed me, the frantic rhythm of his thrusts broken.

Then he leaned over me, covering me completely.

Warm. Safe. Mine.

With a happy sigh, I melted into him, catching my breath.

"This is like coming home, my love," he exhaled.

Home.

Everything was just the way it was supposed to be. And all felt right.

The angry teenager, the self-loathing monster, and the wonderful man I had discovered underneath—they all merged into one.

One person.

My man.

"Hunter," I whispered, because that was his true name.

His hands at my waist, he turned me around to face him.

"What did you call me?"

I slid my palms up his chest to his shoulders, raking my fingers through his fur.

"I love you, Hunter. All of you."

His sins, his darkness, and his light—I accepted it all. Unconditionally.

He hugged me to his chest, lifting me up, and I wrapped my legs around his middle. Tight.

"Is it a *yes* then?" His eyes glistened with hope in the moonlight. "Will you marry me?"

"Yes." I smiled, giddy with happiness.

"The way I am?" he asked, holding me close.

"I love you, Hunter. All of you. Just the way you are."

# Chapter 49

## Sophie

It was a beautiful spring morning the next day. I woke up to the sounds of birds singing greetings to the arriving spring. Sunshine warmed my face.

His large body was under me, my cheek on his hard chest, my hand flat on his abs. But even before I opened my eyes I felt that something was different.

Shifting slightly, I slid my hand up his stomach to his chest, expecting the usual ticklish sensation of the silky undercoat between my fingers. Instead, the hair felt crisp and springy. There was also considerably less of it, with the smoothness of skin underneath.

Understanding struck like lightning through my initial confusion as I jerked my head up, opening my eyes.

Covers off, he stretched under me, streaked by the bright light bursting through the glass doors.

Shock made my heart race at a neck-breaking speed as I stared at Hunter Reed sleeping in my bed.

My hand to my mouth, I muffled a startled scream and scurried to the other side of the bed.

The teenager of my past had grown up. His appearance had matured—his forehead had more lines and face more angles. But there was no mistake, it was the same person.

The longer I stared at him, the more similarities I found with his beastly appearance, too.

His hair, the brown colour of fallen leaves, had the same russet undertone with golden highlights. It was long, past his shoulders, fanned over the pillow in disarray.

The thick full beard, a shade darker than his hair, concealed the lower part of his face from me. However, I could still see his peaceful expression as he slept.

Used to a long snout, I had to blink a few times at the sight of his human nose—straight, skin-coloured, and completely hairless.

He didn't seem to have lost much of his bulk. Strong torso, thick muscles in his arms and thighs appeared to remain the same or close enough to what they had been. Even in his human form, lying on his back, his body still looked large and imposing.

His wide shoulders spread halfway across the bed, the expanse of his chest just as broad. I also noted with an odd sense of relief the fair amount of dark, curly hair on his chest and forearms. The shade of it also reminded me of Monster's fur.

The top sheet, draped over his thigh, tented over his crotch. One long, muscular leg lay on top of the covers, ending with a normal human foot. No claws, paw or hock.

Hunter was all man, in soul *and* body.

But his physical similarities with the beast I loved slowly calmed my racing heart, as I sat at his side waiting for him to wake up and taking all his features in.

No matter his looks, he was still *him.*

And he was all mine.

Hunter stirred, stretching to the side, and patted my pillow in search of me. Squinting in the morning light, he opened one eye. The brilliant hazel was absolutely the same, as was the adoration with which he looked at me warmly.

"There you are." A smile parted his beard when his gaze found me. "Good morning, princess. My bride." He winked at me, smiling wide. "You know, I'm going to order you a ring. The biggest there is.

One that will drive you nuts, catching on your clothes. It would make you curse my name when you're getting dressed or folding laundry. Because I love hearing you say my name over and over again."

He sounded definitely human now, but the deep rumble in his voice was so familiar, I would recognize it anywhere. And his words, his gestures didn't change at all.

"Oh, Hunter." I shook my head in disbelief at how much yet how little this transformation was.

"*Hunter* or *Monster*. Doesn't matter to me, as long as you say it." He stretched, arching his back. The sheet fell off, and his hard-on bobbed free. "Now, come here, my sweet princess," he murmured, reaching for me. "I'll make you scream it—"

His gaze fell on his hand and he stopped abruptly, curling his fingers slowly, then straightened them, spreading wide.

"Sophie?" His eyes shot to mine, searching for confirmation.

"It happened, Hunter." I nodded. "It worked."

"When I stopped caring whether it happened at all," he whispered, still inspecting his hand.

"There was no mistake in the curse after all." I shifted a little closer to him. "A woman had to love you. *All of you*. Past and present. The beast and the man. Inside and out."

He lowered his hand to his lap, his gaze sweeping down his body.

"What do you think, Sophie?" He turned to me. "How do you feel about seeing this?" He gestured at his face.

"Me?"

He nodded, staring at me expectantly.

"It's not about *me*, Hunter. You're now free. No need to hide anymore. And you don't have to worry about me." I raised my hand and stroked a strand of his hair draped over his shoulder. It felt soft, silky, and very much like the mane he used to have. I slid my hand up to his beard. Thick and a little springy, more like the fur that used to cover the rest of his body. "I can see *you* beyond your looks." I smiled. "No matter what your appearance is, I love *you*."

He grabbed my hand, leaning into my touch.

"How do you feel, darling?" I asked.

"I don't know." He smiled against my palm. "Weird." He touched his forehead, raking his fingers through the hair above it. "Without the horns, it feels like a ton of weight is gone."

"No headache?"

"None at all." He lowered his feet to the floor. "I need to move."

I hurried to his side, ready to help him if needed.

"No." He laughed, shaking his head. "You better stay back, Sophie. If I fall, I'll take you down with me."

Holding the bedpost, he got up carefully—shifting his weight from foot to foot—then took a couple of tentative steps forward, leaving his hand on the bedpost.

"Yep. It *is* weird," he sighed then laughed again. "I'll need to get used to walking on human feet."

"Do you feel like getting down on all fours at all?"

"The urge is definitely there. I just don't think it'd work any more." He tipped his chin at the bathroom door. "I need a mirror."

I nodded and took his hand. He didn't protest this time.

Hunter used my hand for guidance, but his confidence visibly grew with each step he took. By the time he approached the counter in the bathroom, the reason for his still squeezing my hand could've been for emotional support only.

"So, this is me." He leaned into the mirror over the sink, studying his reflection, then touched his nose, his forehead, his beard. "Not exactly what I remember."

"Of course not. And it's not just you getting older, Hunter." I glanced along the intricate web of raised scars criss-crossing his back and shoulder. With no fur to hide them now, the scars were an open reminder of everything that had happened to him. "You've changed in so many ways."

"True." He gazed at me in the mirror then pushed off the counter, taking a step back. "It feels rather chilly now." He exhaled another laugh, gliding the palm of his hand along his chest and down his flat stomach. "Without all that fur."

I followed the movement of his hand down his torso then along the hard curve of his ass, as he twisted his hips a little.

"No more tail," I whispered. The tiny pang of something like regret made me smile.

"Are you going to miss it?" He lifted an eyebrow at me, which gave his face a very familiar expression. "Did you like my tail, princess?" he teased, his eyes twinkling with amusement.

"I did," I confessed. "Your tail had quite a personality and a mind of its own. A dirty mind, I might add." I stroked his buttocks with my gaze, enjoying the sight of the toned, rounded muscles, and added under my breath, "I'm sure I'll get used to having the unobstructed view of that ass, though."

His erection twitched at my words, catching my attention again.

"Not all has changed it seems," I noted and took a step closer.

He intercepted my gaze and closed the distance between us, his expression turning more serious. His brilliant eyes darkened, eyelids at half-mast.

I stared at his face, hungrily taking in every detail. Hands flat on his chest, I slid them up to his shoulders then down to his hard pecs again, learning the new sensations of touching him.

His chest vibrated with the familiar growl under my palms.

"The beast is still in there," I whispered as a hot wave of pleasure at this discovery washed over me.

"Should we let him out?"

With a nod, I gave him my silent permission.

He walked me backwards then lifted me on the counter. Hands on my knees, he parted my legs to step between them, bringing us flush against each other. His gaze slid along my face then glided to my lips.

"You know what has changed?" He asked, his eyes dark with lust, his hands sliding up my sides. I inhaled sharply when he cupped my breasts, kneading them through my nightshirt. "Now, I can kiss you."

He covered my mouth with his, and my breathing accelerated along with my heartbeat. His lips, at once firm and soft. His tongue, urgent and persistent. I savored his taste and the softness of his beard against my skin.

All the new sensations mixed with the old, loved and familiar ones. The firmness of his embrace. The passion of his touch. His wild scent of winter forest and my man.

I slid my hands up his back, feeling the hard muscles rolling under his skin. Smooth, human skin marred by thick ropes of scars.

Without breaking the kiss, he moved his hands higher, tracing my collarbones with his thumbs, then cupped my neck with both hands, before he finally let me come up for air.

"This is even better than I've imagined," he exhaled, leaving a trail of kisses along my jawline and down the side of my neck, nibbling, kissing every inch of my skin there, the soft prickle of his beard enveloping my body in a web of tiny shivers.

I hooked my legs around his waist and slid my foot down the hard curve of his ass. The ridge of his erection hit just the right spot, sending a hot charge of desire through me.

He slid his hands down my shoulders, hooking his thumbs in the neckline of my shirt, and tugged it down impatiently. When the neckline proved too tight to move past my breasts, he easily ripped the shirt down the middle, setting them free.

Eagerly, he sucked in my nipple the way he never could before, but the sensation of his tongue swirling around it was tantalizingly familiar, sending another maddening wave of desire through my body.

I whimpered, gripping the hair on the back of his head, as I arched my back, pushing my breast into his mouth, unable to get enough of the sweet torture of his lips, teeth, and tongue.

He let go of my breasts, his hands replacing his mouth, as his fingers gently plucked and twisted my nipples. I moaned and rocked against him with increasing urgency, wanting more of him, all of him.

"Hunter."

He knew me well to know exactly what I needed. For a moment, his hand left my breast, as he aligned himself with me, then I felt the blissful sensation of him sliding inside me.

My breath hitched, and I buried my face in his hair, the silky feel of it new, yet so very familiar. His arms enclosed me in a tight circle as he began to move, long and slow at first, drawing out the pleasure for both of us.

I tangled my fingers in his hair, losing myself to the wonderful sensations building up inside me under his ever-increasing rhythm.

The roar that started low and deep inside his chest tore through his clenched teeth, its vibrations stoking the fire inside me—higher, hotter, brighter—as the speed of his thrusts increased to frantic, and my need spiraled out of control.

The beast came undone, his head thrown back, his chest flush with mine, our hips fused. His roar rolled through the walls of the house, reaching the woods outside.

I closed my eyes, riding every last wave of my own orgasm, before collapsing into him, boneless. My nose buried into his neck under his beard, I inhaled the beloved scent, savoring the feeling of his body around me.

I stroked his back, my fingers tracing the ridges of his scars.

"One thing will never change, princess," he whispered. "No matter what—man, beast, or both—I swear I'll always love you."

# Epilogue

## Hunter

A Year Later.

He watched the rapids churn through the rocks in the river then swirl lazily in the dark pools of open water in between. Lost in his thoughts, he stroked Sophie's head on his shoulder, raking his fingers through the strands of her ponytail.

He sat on one of the half a dozen Adirondack chairs placed around the new fire pit in his favourite spot on the riverbank. Sophie was in his lap, the best place for her to be as far as he was concerned.

A seven-month old yellow lab mix stretched by the fire, tired after fetching sticks from the river earlier. His paws jerked occasionally as he whimpered in fitful puppy sleep. They got him from one of the animal shelters that Sophie had on her list of charities, and Hunter fell in love with him immediately.

It was early spring again. His second spring as himself, whole and complete. Sophie was right when she noted that his human form on its own was not that much of a change. The biggest changes happened while he was still a beast. Physically being a human again, however, wasn't as simple as slipping into the old pair of shoes.

It took him a while to get used to the odd feeling of being exposed without his fur. Sophie had to order a number of wool sweaters to keep him warm through those early weeks. The first few days, he wore a pair of knitted gloves, even at night, because the air felt unusually chilly against his bare knuckles.

He was glad she loved his beard too much to let him shave it off. The beard and longer hair felt somehow more natural to him. Warm and familiar.

He still dreamed at night about being a beast, about running wild through the forest, taking a plunge in the icy river, or stalking prey in the woods.

The same things that brought him satisfaction when he was an animal, he discovered, still brought him joy as a man.

The first time he ran through the forest in the early morning chill, wearing nothing but sweatpants and a pair of runners, excitement pumped hot through his veins. The invigorating sensation of feeling alive was so wild and familiar, he had to stop for a moment to make sure he still had his human body and didn't revert back to the beast somehow.

He sprinted all the way to the river, stripped naked, and jumped into the cold waters, just like he used to. There was no more ice on the river. Still, the chilly water knocked the air out of him when he dove in.

He climbed out onto the riverbank afterwards, shaking the water out of his hair and beard. The chill prickled his skin, but the fire inside him burst through with a loud, hearty laugh that bounced through the trees, sending small animals scurrying through the woods, not unlike his roars used to do.

The joy of being alive coursed through him along with the incredible feeling of finally being whole.

She did it. He drew Sophie closer in his lap. She was the glue that held all his pieces together, making him complete. His beacon if he ever felt lost.

Whenever anger, bitterness or unexplained sadness threatened to lead him astray, she was his light to guide him back to joy.

He could swim all the way across the river now or cross the fence to the road to go anywhere in the world. Free. But the place he really wanted to be, where he truly felt at home, was right here. With Sophie.

"There were times when I loathed this forest, hated it with a passion," he said, nuzzling her hair.

"It was your prison, Hunter." She stirred in his lap, snuggling closer under the checkered wool blanket thrown over her shoulders. "Do you love being here now?"

He was sure she knew the answer but said it anyway.

"I do. It's home." He twirled a strand of her ponytail between his fingers, admiring its honey-coloured highlights brought out by the setting sun, and smiled. "Home is where I have my wife."

They got married last summer, right here on the riverbank. Sophie's mom and Jeff came to stay for the wedding, as well as most of the folks from Rocky River.

They decided not to tell the details of his story to everyone. Jo was the only one who knew everything, even though she confessed she still had a hard time believing it herself.

Shortly after their wedding, the old hunting lodge by the airport went out of business before the busy time of the season started. He and Sophie offered to house the hunters at their house through the fall.

They got the bedrooms upstairs ready. And for the first time ever, the house that his father built under the pretense of a hunting cabin actually hosted a real hunting party.

He loved going out with the guys early in the morning, helping to track the game for them.

The peace of the woods right before the sunrise, the thrill of tracking and pursuing prey, the satisfaction of providing for his family—the experience of hunting as a human was new, but it resonated with the memories of the beast in him. Just like the feelings he had during his daily running and swimming.

Halfway through the season, watching how much Sophie enjoyed taking care of guests, Hunter had the idea of running a permanent hunting lodge right here, on their property. This was how they became not just a husband and wife, but also business partners.

A few times a week, Sophie travelled to Rocky River, to visit friends and to take courses online. She chose to study youth and family counseling, a program that would allow her to work in Rocky River upon completion. The subject was close to her heart and she enjoyed her studies, filling Hunter's heart with pride at her success.

He leaned in and found her lips now. Soft and sweet, they welcomed his kiss. And he felt her melting into him, the way she always did when he kissed her.

"My Monster," she exhaled dreamily when he let her come up for air. Kissing her was something that never got old, and he couldn't get enough of it.

"Warm me up," Sophie murmured, sliding her cold hand under his sweater then between the buttons on his shirt, and settled it against his warm chest. The huge diamond of her ring felt even colder on his skin.

It must be the Reeds' inherent love for extravagance that made Hunter keep his promise and buy her the biggest diamond he could find.

She laughed and shook her head when she first saw it. Still, she never took it off after he put it on her finger on their wedding day, vowing to love and cherish her for as long as they both should live.

"I'm so looking forward to the beach and sunshine in Barbados next week." She rubbed his chest under the shirt, warming up her hand.

"Whatever makes you happy. And warm." He took her other hand in his and tucked it under his sweater too.

She exhaled a small contented laugh.

"*You* make me happy." She placed a small kiss in his beard. "You keep me warm too. Inside and out." She pressed herself even closer to him. "Vacations are just for fun. And if you don't like it, we can always come back."

"I'll like it," he promised. It would be his first trip anywhere in many years. He felt nervous, excited, not a little apprehensive. His head still swam from knowing he was free to travel the globe now.

No walls, no fences were there to keep him in place any more.

Sophie wanted to show him the world, and as far as Hunter was concerned with her he would go anywhere.

He would go to the end of the Earth and back without batting an eye.

As long as Sophie was by his side.

# DEMON MINE

# Chapter 1

Source

I heard them coming. Their footsteps echoed in the hallways and reverberated through the concrete floors. I'd been here long enough to know that they could be extremely stealthy, but they didn't care about being quiet right now.

With a whimper, I scurried to the opposite side of the ratty mattress on the floor until my back hit the wall, and I curled into a ball. Not that it mattered—they'd take me with them anyway. I couldn't fight them. I'd tried. Their unnatural, inhuman strength was no match to my own weakened body.

I wasn't sure how long I'd been here. At one point, I made marks on the wall of my cell with a spoon, one for each day. However, I didn't start until I'd been here for a few days. Or was it a few weeks? Things had been blurry in my mind for a while now.

Sometimes, in rare moments of clarity, I wondered if this was how it felt to lose your mind. Days and weeks would disappear, un-accounted for, until all of what made *you* would vanish into a thick fog, never to be found again.

The door to my cell slid open, and *they* walked in. Calm, cold, and silent.

After all my time here, I still had no idea who they were. By now, I doubted they were even alive. I simply thought of them as ma-chines, automated armour suits.

At night, there were always three of them. All dressed the same, in grey uniforms made of thick fabric covered with hard plates on their chests, shoulders, forearms, and legs. Matching grey helmets concealed their heads, including faces, with just two slits for the eyes. Leather gloves and heavy boots of the same charcoal grey completed their uniforms.

One stepped forward while the other two stood on each side of the door. They expected me to get up and walk out of the cell. I knew that's what they wanted, but I wasn't moving. Willing them to disappear, I curled more into myself and shut my eyes. Shouldn't all nightmares disappear eventually?

Then I heard the first of the three take a few more determined steps towards me, and I lost it.

"No!" I shrieked. "Don't touch me. Keep your disgusting gloves off me!"

I jumped as he reached out, and I ducked under his arm, surprising myself with the agility of my movements.

I knew they were incredibly strong. As far as I could tell, though, they moved with normal speed. A crazy idea sprung into my troubled brain.

I can outrun them! I just need to run very, very fast . . .

I made it all the way to the door before the others grabbed me. With those two there, I never had a chance in the first place and deep inside I knew it. It's not like it was a solid plan on my part anyway, more like an act of desperation spurred by insanity.

Panic exploded hot inside me. They each held one of my arms with ease, and I kicked the air between them, twisted in their grip and screamed until my lungs burned and my voice came out in a raspy croak no longer resembling anything human.

Through the black fog of terror, I barely registered another pair of arms coming across my midsection. The hard chest plates of the first one pressed into my back as he grabbed me from behind.

I finally got a target for my feet now, furiously kicking him in the shins and stomping my heels into his boots. The men holding my arms let go of me, and I immediately smashed my fists against his forearms at my front.

Unsurprisingly, he remained unfazed by all of it. If I had a sliver of sanity left, I would realize that I was just hurting myself on the hard bracers of his armour without causing him any harm whatsoever.

As it was, though, I had no common sense left. After having been locked up alone with not a single word spoken to me by anyone, I finally lost it. Who could blame me? It was a miracle that I'd lasted as long as I had.

Blinded by panic, I didn't even care if they killed me at that moment. At least it would be the end of this and they wouldn't be able to force me to do anything for them anymore.

Then, the desperate rage—the hopeless terror—stopped abruptly. The feverish panic that consumed me from inside out cooled. The sensation of calm numbness was so sudden that I looked around, half expecting to see a discarded syringe with some kind of a fast-acting drug somewhere, although I was positive I didn't feel a needle sting for this explanation to be valid.

The side effect of my newly found calmness was that I no longer worried about anything, not even about why and how it had happened. I stopped thrashing, and the arms holding me released me a moment later.

## Handler

HE SCANNED THE SOURCE for emotions as he entered the cell. She was curled on the mattress with her back pressed into the wall, as if she wanted to push herself into it and disappear.

Her hair was matted, tangled, and of the same dirty-grey as the surrounding walls. She glanced up, her eyes wild and unhinged. He couldn't tell what colour her irises were because of how wide her pupils had dilated. Her eyes appeared black, empty, with a wild, glossy shine.

He reached inside her mind, and the powerful hurricane of her emotions assaulted him. The impact felt almost physical, forcing him to brace himself by digging the heels of his boots into the concrete floor, as if to avoid being knocked over.

Horror, anger, and hate raged in a black pool of panic.

The realization came to him with unusual clarity—she couldn't go through a Feeding in this state. She shouldn't even be presented to the Council like this or she'd be drained immediately.

Unless . . .

If he were to take her negative emotions, she might be able to function long enough to survive the Feeding. Except that if the Council ever found out about what he did, he'd be punished severely—taking from Sources directly was strictly forbidden to anyone outside of the Council.

She was his very first Source. He had spent three months in training to become her Handler, and he was about to lose her on his first day on the job.

He knew everything he was allowed to know about her from her file.

She was taken just over a year ago and had been used for Feedings almost daily. During the past several weeks, she had become increasingly more aggressive.

He also knew something that was not in the file. The average length of useful time for a Source was about a year at best, and it appeared her time was up. The Council gave her to him in one final attempt to extend her useful life. However, nobody would blame him if it didn't happen.

He stared at her again.

Her body was shaking, she was too thin and filthy. Sources were provided with highly nutritious food and with water to bathe. However, whether or not she actually ate and bathed was entirely up to her. By the looks of her, she hadn't done either in a while.

Well familiar with pangs of hunger, he wondered why anyone would decline food when it was readily available.

He searched for the light of her life force and found it enclosed in the dark shell of her current emotions. Deep in the churning mud of them, it was still burning bright and pure—just a tiny sliver of beauty.

It seemed so painfully fragile.

A long-forgotten urge to protect rose inside him—a single emotion of his own. It had been a long time since he felt anything other than pain and hunger, and he frowned behind the mask of his helmet at the foreign invasion of *a feeling* in his chest.

He stepped forward and reached for her. The gesture was not intended to intimidate. Neither was he trying to comfort her in any way. He just wanted to get a reaction, any reaction, out of her.

Was she still lucid?

Suddenly, she shrieked and dashed past him with a speed and purpose he did not expect from her. Startled but not worried, he knew the Janitors by the door would stop her.

He heard a loud growl and turned around to see that they had indeed caught her and now held her by the arms as she struggled in their grip like a trapped animal. The frustrated growl was coming out of her throat, turning into a deafening screech a second later, mixed with incoherent yelling and cursing.

He didn't need to scan her feelings to see that she was suffering. His concern about the Council melted into the background, as an overwhelming feeling of pity joined the protective instinct inside him.

Even if temporarily, he had to stop her sufferings and ease her emotional pain. He wanted to help her to survive the night.

Stepping forward, he folded his arms around her middle, pressing her back to his chest, then motioned to the Janitors to let her go.

Her kicks and punches landed on his legs and arms immediately, but he did not care. She had no strength to hurt him.

To help her, he needed to touch her skin-to-skin. Unfortunately, his clothes were designed specifically to prevent any direct contact between a Handler and a Source, as touching skin-to-skin was strictly forbidden.

Trying to concentrate through the thick fog of hunger clouding his mind, he moved one of his hands under her arm, simultaneously turning her away from the Janitors' view, lest they guessed what he was up to and reported him.

He dragged his hand out of the glove a little, exposing a narrow strip of his skin, and pressed the outside of his wrist directly to the bare skin of her underarm while she continued to thrash desperately.

For a moment, he was afraid he had forgotten how to do it. It had been so long since he'd touched anyone like that. So long that he wasn't even sure if it had ever happened at all. He closed his eyes, reached into the toxic pit of her dark emotions, and drank . . .

His starving demonic essence opened up hungrily, ready to swallow any nourishment, even if it was poison. He drank greedily, reeling from the false sense of fullness, knowing it would not truly sate him that it would only hurt him in the end.

Yet he took everything. The acrid hate, the foul anger, and the putrid-tasting fear. He stopped only when he reached the sweet fragrance of her life essence, without touching it.

The toxic cocktail of her emotions filled his mind, clamped his brain in a vise, and twisted his insides. Bile hit the back of his throat instantly, and he was glad it had been days since he last consumed any human food. Otherwise, he would have vomited it onto the concrete floor of the cell.

His arms around her, he bent over in pain, hoping he could pretend that he was still restraining her while he struggled to remain upright. He needed just a second to let the poison settle a little in order for him to get his bearings. However, he would have to deal with the consequences later and pay the full price for foolishly consuming toxic negative emotions from a human.

She no longer fought in his arms, he noticed belatedly then straightened and released his grip on her.

She stood upright with her back turned to him, her shoulders relaxed. Slowly, she took a long breath in, as if waking from a long sleep then raised her head.

He scanned her emotions carefully, trying to focus through the pounding ache in his head.

Nothing. There was nothing there, just a blank empty space.

Was it enough to go ahead with the Feeding? Would she survive it now?

She didn't give him much time to consider, as she calmly walked towards the door. He signed to the Janitors to let her pass and followed the required three steps behind her. His stomach twisting in knots, he tried not to stumble and keep his pace steady.

He knew the pain would gradually get worse, reaching unbearable levels by morning before it would finally decrease and dissipate. He just needed to make it through the Feeding.

AVAILABLE NOW

# More by Marina Simcoe

Demons (Completed Series Series)
Demon Mine
The Forgotten
Grand Master
The Last Unforgiven - Cursed
The Last Unforgiven - Freed

———— ❧ ————

Stand Alone Novels Set in Demons World
The Real Thing
To Love A Monster

———— ❧ ————

Midnight Coven Author Group
Wicked Warlock (Cursed Coven)

# THE WORLD OF THE RIVER of Mists
### Cursed in Glass (Duet)

---

Joyless Kingdom (Trilogy)
Somber Prince
Joy Guardian
Pleasure Trader

---

Wingless Crow (Duet)
Wingless Crow – Part 1
Crownless King – Part 2

---

Fire in Stone (Duet)
Fire in Stone – Part 1
Hearts on Fire – Part 2

---

Serpent's Touch (Duet)
Serpent's Touch – Part 1
Serpent's Claim – Part 2

---

Madame Tan's Freakshow (Trilogy)
Call of Water
Madness of the Moon
Power of Rage

# Fantasy Romance

*Seven Horny Sins*
Let Me Claim You
Let Me Win You
Let Me Feed You (coming soon)
*Dark Orcs of Helfallow*
Agor
Grat

# ALIEN ROMANCE

*My Holiday Tails*
Married To Krampus
My Tiny Giant
My Birthday Getaway
New Year, New Planet
Mail Order Mom
My Pumpkin
What Makes an Alien a Dad?
My Family Day

---

*Dark Anomaly Trilogy*
Gravity
Power
Explosion

---

*Standalone Novels*
Experiment
Enduring (Valos Of Sonhadra)

# ABOUT THE AUTHOR

Marina Simcoe likes to write romance stories with regular human heroines and non-human heroes who just can't live without them. She firmly believes that our contemporary world could always use a little bit of the extraordinary.

She has lots of fun exploring how her out-of-this-world characters with their own beliefs, values, and aspirations fit into our everyday life.

She lives in Canada with her very own sexy beast, their three little cubs, and a cat who is forever wild at heart.

For more illustrations of all of her books please visit Marina Simcoe Author page on Facebook or www.marinasimcoe.com.

# Please Stay in Touch

If you enjoy my work, please consider joining my Patreon for early access to my WIP, custom art (including NSFW art), ebooks, and signed paperbacks:

Newsletter signup on www.marinasimcoe.com
Facebook Readers' Group:
Marina's Reading Cave
www.instagram.com/marinasimcoeauthor
www.marinasimcoe.com
www.facebook.com/MarinaSimcoeAuthor/
www.bookbub.com/profile/marina-simcoe
www.goodreads.com/MarinaSimcoe